"Yuck.'

Pretty much covered the whole freakin' day.

A blinding red-white, red-white strobe, reflected in my brand new Wrangler's rearview mirror, seized my attention. The police. I tossed my hands skyward, ready to surrender. I shouldn't have been too surprised. Like I'd commented this a.m. to my roommate, Jenny, "Today, anything's possible."

My Bad Day checklist included:

- Crappy job interview, one which might have provided desperately needed income.

- Wore gut-busting panty hose on a hot day which had now worked past my waist and strangled my diaphragm.

- A barely blowing air conditioner indicated something had malfunctioned in my new, fun car.

I stole another glance in the mirror, and with great reluctance, flipped the right turn indicator. My vehicle coasted to a stop on the shoulder of Boston Avenue in my hometown of Sommerville, a nice suburb located between two large cities. Four lanes of cars and trucks zipped by as I sat there where every single one of my family, friends, friends' friends, and their friends—including Rat Fink Suzanne—would see a police vehicle positioned right behind mine. Gleefully, drivers would chant the "Ha-ha, got you, not me" ditty.

How embarrassing.

Praise for Vicki Batman

"*TEMPORARILY EMPLOYED* is one of those books that will keep you turning the pages while you're giggling. I've read just about everything this author has written, and she never fails to disappoint with her witty dialogue and fast-paced narrative."

~Liz Lipperman, national best selling author

~*~

"Nobody blends humor and great characters like Ms. Batman."

~Harlie's Books

~*~

"Vicki Batman never fails to entertain. This novel is a perfect showcase for her humor and spunk. I've eagerly awaited its debut."

~Kathleen Baldwin, award-winning, bestselling author

~*~

TEMPORARILY EMPLOYED is Jennifer Cruise on steroids. I only stopped reading to laugh. Readers will love Hattie Cooks and Officer Whatshisname!

~Donnell Ann Bell, bestselling romantic suspense author

~*~

TEMPORARILY EMPLOYED
placed Third in the Single Title Category
of the 2007 Lone Star Contest.

Temporarily Employed

by

Vicki Batman

Temporarily Employed

Cover Art by *Debbie Taylor*

The Wild Rose Press, Inc.
PO Box 708
Adams Basin, NY 14410-0708
Visit us at www.thewildrosepress.com

Publishing History
First Crimson Rose Edition, 2014
Print ISBN 978-1-62830-497-8
Digital ISBN 978-1-62830-498-5

Published in the United States of America

Dedication

To Handsome
To Susan Ard—thanks for the push
To sissies, the PP girls, Guilty Girls, & funsisters—
thanks

Chapter One

"Yuck."

Pretty much covered the whole freakin' day.

A blinding red-white, red-white strobe, reflected in my brand new Wrangler's rearview mirror, seized my attention. The police. I tossed my hands skyward, ready to surrender. I shouldn't have been too surprised. Like I'd commented this a.m. to my roommate, Jenny, "Today, anything's possible."

My Bad Day checklist included:
- Crappy job interview, one which might have provided desperately needed income.
- Wore gut-busting panty hose on a hot day which had now worked past my waist and strangled my diaphragm.
- A barely blowing air conditioner indicated something had malfunctioned in my new, fun car.

I stole another glance in the mirror, and with great reluctance, flipped the right turn indicator. My vehicle coasted to a stop on the shoulder of Boston Avenue in my hometown of Sommerville, a nice suburb located between two large cities. Four lanes of cars and trucks zipped by as I sat there where every single one of my family, friends, friends' friends, and their friends—including Rat Fink Suzanne—would see a police vehicle positioned right behind mine. Gleefully, drivers would chant the "Ha-ha, got you, not me" ditty.

How embarrassing.

After killing the engine, I flopped back in the seat. Shooting the morons the finger was an idea. *Nah. I'm too exhausted to care.*

A litany of: "No, not hiring." "Just filled the position." "You're over qualified." "You're under qualified…" tornadoed through my head. Coupled with the intense job search through various outlets like the internet and completing numerous online employment applications, no wonder my body had been depleted of all life force.

Not even a breeze blew to take the edge off the unbearable summertime heat. Tangled wild trees and dry scrubby bushes banked the roadside. The grass had taken on a scorched look. Rolling down the driver's window, I surveyed my surroundings. Nothing great. Nothing new.

I stole a glance in the side mirror at the policeman who strode purposefully along the shoulder. The gravel crunched under his boots. He looked huge, probably because his uniform, which appeared to be bulked with a bullet-proof vest, made him resemble a buffed-up superhero in size. Exceedingly intimidating.

Sigh. When things went wrong, they were really wrong.

As I viewed him drawing closer, my heart pounded harder. Awkward circumstances usually brought out the worst in me like shyness, ineptness, and uh…more shyness, hang-ups I carried from childhood. Back in the dark ages, I'd deliberately steered clear of embarrassing situations by developing the best self-protection—avoidance. Over time, I'd adapted to embarrassment, but every now and then, some unusual situation would spring out, and like a stealthy cat, those old prickly feelings crept back inside me.

The policeman stopped by the driver's side, his head slanted to better peer inside.

Up close and exceptionally personal, I saw his sunglasses with dark lenses which shielded his eyes.

"Ma'am, I'm Officer Wellborn. I need to see your driver's license and proof of insurance—"

Something unknown possessed me. I bulldozed in and snapped in an overly loud voice, "What do you want? Why did you pull me over?"

His body stiffened like a package of frozen chocolate chip cookie dough.

Oops. My brows shot skyward as my hand quickly smothered my mouth. Had I really done that? Had I really hollered at a policeman, a very big no-no? *Now, he'll surely ticket me.*

"Shouting at me could result in disorderly conduct charges," he said.

Golly. His stern tone intimidated me. *Maybe babbling and apologizing profusely will make amends.* "I'm so sorry. I'm not normally rude. Mom would give me her little talk on Being Polite to Other People if she'd heard me. I'm really, really sorry."

A quick glance told me he'd tilted his head in an attentive manner which indicated he appeared to be listening to my explanation with professional interest. "I've had an appalling, hideous, horribly dreadful day."

"I know."

His flat statement struck me momentarily dumb. How the hell would he know? He didn't know me. He hadn't followed me around all freakin' day and seen what I'd gone through. Perhaps, everyone said these things when they were pulled over, and his "I know" reply was the stock answer.

Maybe a so-so explanation would cover my ass. A duck of my chin rendered my meek and mild look. "Let's say absolutely nothing has gone right today. Can we start over?"

His affirming nod indicated receptiveness. Thank God his patience training had paid off.

Closing my eyes, I meditated on a mythical Zen place, inhaling several deep cleansing breaths. Innn... And out. Innn... And out. As I released the last huff, my shoulders softened, my heart rate returned to nearly normal. I opened my eyes. "Is something wrong, Officer?"

"I need to see your driver's license and proof of insurance, ma'am."

While batting my eyelashes, I drawled with—albeit a feeble attempt and completely out of character—my most gracious Scarlett O'Hara voice. "Why, officer? Was I speedin'?"

"No, ma'am, not speedin'."

He mocked me. The more I considered how he'd answered, the more I believed he did so. *That seems...impolite.*

Pen in hand, he began to scribble in a little book. His gaze returned. "Could I see your driver's license and proof of insurance?"

"Were you following me?"

"No, ma'am."

"I didn't see you." I shook my head in disbelief. "You appeared out of nowhere."

"I was parked on the shoulder of the road." A lift

of his chin indicated where. "Waiting."

Waiting? How odd. *Why would a cop be waiting?* "Uh, okay, but why?"

"Waiting for someone like you."

Why would he say "waiting for someone like me?" Regrettably, my life's experience was pea green in police matters. My best guess was Officer—*oh, Whatshisname?? I can't remember*—parked in a covert spot to nab speeding drivers and ticket them. That was what they usually did.

"Ma'am? I still need your driver's license and proof of insurance."

Fine. He'd already started writing the citation. Getting one appeared inevitable. Blowing a huff, I burrowed through my red tote and found my cellphone. *Not that* and pitched it to the passenger seat. I located my driver's license in my wallet. To my dismay, the required-to-carry insurance slips had multiplied like rabbits. My frustration intensified as I fumbled with each piece of paper, chasing them all over my lap— *nope, not that one*—and floor board, wasting *our* time.

Eureka! A flush of relief passed over me as I handed him the requested items. "Here you go."

"Thanks." He inspected my license with a thorough gaze. "Is this correct? Your name is Harriette Lee Cooks?"

Mom's Manners 101: Be polite. "Yes, sir."

"This is your current address?"

"Yes, sir."

"You're the owner of this vehicle?"

"Yes, sir."

"Ma'am, I'll be bahhck."

Is Officer—oh, what's his name?—trying to be

funny? Possessing all the power, he sat in his vehicle and took his sweet time while checking for outstanding arrest warrants, violations, or...whatever, while I sat cornered. Waiting. Squirming.

I crossed my arms. The lights on top of his vehicle continued to flash. Pretty soon, my eyeballs would be imprinted by the exceedingly annoying lights. If only I could evaporate or get the hell out of Dodge.

Hell, just escape from everything.

At the toot-toot tap of a horn, I narrowed my eyes while following a way-too familiar, red compact car with the top down zooming past. Exactly as I had predicted, Rat Fink Suzanne waved with a gay flip of her hand, the wind blowing her hair in a perfectly tossed fashion. *Great.* She would be deliriously happy to spread gossip about where and what had transpired. Soon, I'd be explaining everything to everyone.

Wait a minute. Wait a freakin' minute. I pressed my finger to my cheek. *Explain exactly what?*

Had I run a red light? Or was it yellow? I felt pretty sure the light had just changed to yellow. According to the officer, I wasn't speeding. So what, what in the wide world had I done?

Inspection and license tags up-to-date? My glance went to the stickers stuck inside the corner of the windshield. I thumped my palm against my forehead. Since my vehicle had been purchased new, I was up to speed on the plates and the inspection sticker stuff. Anyway, would it really matter? It was your word against the establishment—That sounded like sixties radical jargon.

Baffled, I scrunched my brow. *Can this be about the naughty things I'd done in a former life?* They'd finally caught up with me. I shook my head. *Impossible.* With a mom like mine, I never, ever did them.

During our formative years, Mom had given her daughters "little talks" on doing naughty stuff with embarrassment as a consequence. Mom wanted her *little darlings* to mature into perfect *little ladies*. As a result, I hesitated to do anything which would cause humiliation, mortification, or shame.

I'd tried. Truth told, even as an adult, I still tried. I ticked off these items from Hattie's Lifetime List of Bad:

1) Toilet papered a friend's house in eighth grade.

Not so terrible considering the girls with me had lied to the police about not doing it.

2) Stole gum from the grocery store when I was six.

Guilt caused me to throw away the pack when the wad had stuck in my throat, making me hack up something resembling a fur ball.

3) Upped my age to eighteen to gain entry into a trendy dance club.

Honestly, I'd enjoyed every disgraceful minute.

Without a doubt, Mom would have made me pay for these indiscretions—had she known about them.

These few things were nothing compared to what my wild and crazy girlfriends had done. I was a Very Good Girl with a Very Perfect Life. My mouth curved downwards. *Until lately.* My perfect job, my perfect life had detoured and crashed.

And I wanted it back—now.

I tapped my right foot. This guy seemed to be taking a long time, while I was melting, meelllttting in this summer heat like the scary green gal from The

Wizard of Oz. My scalp grew sweaty and oily. My carefully applied makeup trickled in a stream down my cheeks. I wiggled, feeling my underwear squishy with sweat, a puddle spreading across my back. Definitely scary.

I reached to turn the car key to activate the inadequate air conditioner while hoping-praying-hoping not to deplete the battery. Should the car die, I supposed I could phone Dad for Daughter Rescue.

Or would Officer Whatshisname? think I was fleeing the scene of the crime? Would he chase me down and shoot me? *Nah, better not.* I released the key and let my head flop to one side. Mom wouldn't like the shooting part.

Hold on... I lengthened my spine. *Exactly what crime?*

I shouted out the window, "What's taking so long?" The problem must be my ugly driver's license picture. I'd always hoped for something resembling a Glamour Shot and what I really got was glamour snot. Hopefully, this guy saw a tall, pleasant-to-look-at young woman. I checked the rearview mirror to verify him laughing, only to find him talking on his radio.

I viewed my reflection in the clip-on visor mirror and tucked an errant hair strand behind my ear. Everyone said I was a teensy weensy bit obsessed with my hair vanity. *So what?* "I was Meant to Have Curly Hair" according to my sister, Tracey. She believed in "When Shopping, Buy One in Every Color," a pro-shopper guideline, one which saved beaucoup de time and dinero.

"Don't Bury me in Panty Hose," said another friend. Every girl knew tight hosiery caused gas.

I propped my elbow in the open window, my cheek resting on my palm to study cloud formations. Briefly, the idea of easing off my hose while waiting for Officer Whatshisname? crossed my thoughts. I shook my head, confirming what I already knew—he'd catch me with an exposed derriere, and I'd suffer more embarrassment.

"Ma'am."

Startled, I jerked my head aside and smacked the small SUV's doorframe. He'd returned like the creepy character that popped up in all horror movies. *Has he uncovered awful news? And what's up with the "Ma'am" stuff anyway? Doesn't that apply to my mom's generation? I'm not over the hill—yet.* I rubbed the owie at my temple.

"Good news," he said.

His words surprised me. I paid close attention when he returned my driver's license and insurance slip. His hand brushed mine, shooting warmth through my veins. *Gee. How...unexpected.*

"You have no outstanding warrants, and your license picture isn't a turn-off."

I expected him to say he'd found no warrants based on being a Very Good Girl. But to comment on my photo—*Is he being funny?* I didn't think cops were known for their humor, unless it was weird cop humor.

"Ms. Cooks," he asked, "could I ask you to step out and let me escort you to the rear of your car?"

Seemed he wasn't finished with me after all. Since being a Very Good Girl made me inexperienced with the police, I hesitated and with good reason. Routinely on television dramas, two officers dragged Mr. Bad Man to the back of their vehicle where they shoved him into a spread-eagle frisking position. After being cuffed, the cops stuffed him in the squad car to haul him off to jail.

Nasty, gross, perverted things occurred in jail. I didn't want terrible things to happen to me. No way.

With the cops and robbers programs forefront in my mind, I angled my gaze with a skeptical glint, but all I caught was powerful sun rays which blocked my examination. I lifted my hand to shade my eyes visor-like. Better. "Why? What kind of citation are you writing anyway? Are you going to frisk me?"

A little smile quirked at the corners of his mouth. "No, ma'am, I hadn't planned on frisking you. You haven't been arrested." His head turned away.

I caught him saying in a barely audible voice, which for certain I shouldn't have heard, "I could if you want me to."

This guy sounded like every other man wishing to get their hands on a woman. And politically incorrect. My eyes rolled heavenward at the smart aleck comment. "I don't think so. I don't know you."

Oops, too late. My brainless musings popped out like they were self-propelled.

"Maybe you do," he said without an expression on his face.

Which meant what? Not recalling being personally acquainted with any policemen, my gaze surveyed him carefully. He'd flashed a bit of a smile, but I couldn't really tell if I knew him because his sunglasses half-obscured his face, and the sun still messed with my eyesight.

Exasperated out the wazoo, I sighed. "Why are you writing me a citation?"

"Because your taillight is out."

A huge revelation, one which captured my undivided attention. "Taillight? Out? Really?"

Like he'd suggested, I opened the car door and exited. The loud bang of the door, which I'd slammed unintentionally, caused me to jolt. Wasn't a warning standard procedure for a taillight out? How did that happen on a new car? I needed to ask him for clarification later.

I trailed Officer Whatshisname? to the Jeep's rear, stumbling and bumbling along the shoulder in my black business pumps. I was known with great—but mostly laughing—notoriety for tripping while wearing high heels. Turning my ankle would be the grand finale to an appalling day. Amend to month. Year. Lifetime.

I pulled the shirttail from the waistband of my tailored black skirt and flapped the ends. Good ol' Sommerville had clocked in a record-setting temperature.

He stopped suddenly and I collided with his back. I sniffed. *Ooh, he smells great, piney like a household cleanser.* "Sorry." Rolling to tippy toes, I peeked over his shoulder, following his finger which pointed to the car's backside.

"Whaatt?!" I cried in unladylike shock.

The problem wasn't a case of taillights out. There was a *big* lack of taillights. To be specific, the car had *no* taillights and *no* bumper. All of the rear end equipment was gone! Vanished! Poof!

I circled, clutching my hair and searching for an answer. Something. Anything.

His jaw tightened, yet he didn't volunteer a comment.

I sidestepped around him, my hands reaching out to stroke the vandalized area.

"No, don't. Fingerprints." His hand snagged my shirtsleeve and yanked me to his side.

So close to his body, I could feel his man-heat penetrate my skin and warm my blood. An overwhelming compulsion had me wanting to fan my face, but I squashed it instead.

"Technicians are on their way."

Fingerprints? Technicians? My chin dropped, and I sensed my eyes widen in disbelief as the facts sank in. With my golden highlights, I might be a pseudo-blonde. But I was no dummy. No taillights and no bumper meant one thing: Someone had stolen parts off my car. My Jeep. My baby.

This was so unfair.

The combination of heat, not-so good interview, bunched panty hose, and now, stolen car parts caused my emotional bank to tip. Very angry, terribly unhappy, tears formed in the corners of my eyes and leaked out one by one. "Why t-technicians?"

"Now, Ms. Cooks, don't cry. Everything will be all right."

With a glance, I found he looked conflicted, like guys usually do over a few girly tears. Head inclined. Hands resting at his waist. *Right. Like I planned for this to happen.*

"It's just a bumper and some taillights. Do you have something for..." He touched his nose.

Had he hoped a tissue was the be-all, end-all solution? I smudged away the droplets. My hands went to my skirt's pockets and fingered.

He patted his pockets and also came up empty

handed.

As a last resort, I smashed the inside elbow of my white shirt sleeve to my nose in the fashion kiddies had been taught in school nowadays.

Head tipped and wallowing in which seemed best described as continually escalating misery, I wobbled to the side of the road and plopped my butt on the concrete curb. My arms dropped on bent knees. My forehead rested on my forearms. As I mulled over my Jeep's mishap and took control of my sniffles, I heard the occasional car whiz by like a zippy bee.

Probably my underwear showed.

Why does everything happen at once? Who knew the trials and tribulations of everyday life can be so tremendously stressful at times?

With a soggy inhale, I said, "My brand new car has been destroyed by some part-stealing pig. I scrimped and saved for it, and now, it's ruined. Ruined." My words were semi-muffled by my body cave.

At the sound of an approaching vehicle, I looked up. Some uniformed guys—indisputably the technicians—exited and swapped a secret manly hand exchange with Officer Whatshisname? They went to work, whirled gray powder over my vehicle's rear end, and lifted prints just like on crime scene investigative television shows. Another snapped photos and scribbled notes.

Following me to the curb, Officer Whatshisname? stood in front of my pointy-toed heels. "Ms. Cooks, we need to determine what happened. Any ideas?"

His body towered over mine. "No."

"When was the last time you saw the entire Jeep?"

How many times a day do I—or anyone for that

matter—scrutinize the rear end of their car? I gulped a sob. "I don't know."

I usually paid particular attention to my Wrangler, painted a gleaming white with dark gray cloth seats, a paler shade of gray vinyl interior, and topped with a black hardtop and matching rubber bumpers. However, lately, my mind had been occupied with other significant matters, items like the necessities of life: Finding employment, paying overdue bills, and, more importantly, procuring much-coveted peanut M&Ms. Now, I was sure to get a stupid-stupid-stupid citation and missing taillights and bumper to add to the equation. At the rate things were headed, I'd have to ditch the chocolate and move in with Mom and Dad. My body shuddered.

Certain the mascara smears streaking my face didn't look pretty, I stared at my sleeve soiled with greasy black blobs and rubbed nose gunk. A thought clicked. "At my parents' on Sunday, Dad and I changed the oil. I washed the Jeep. The taillights and bumper were on the car then."

"Done," a technician said.

"Check you later." Officer Whatshisname? saluted.

We watched the van drive away. He swiveled his head back to me.

Noticing his intense look, I said, "I'm upset because I've had a really bad day. My whole life seemed picture perfect and... Well, nothing seems to be going my way lately, including these damn panty hose I'm wearing which are now screwed around my boobs."

He curved to one side and cupped his hand around his mouth to stifle a laugh.

Me and my honest mouth. I felt positive my face

turned redder than crimson red. Now, he knew everything about me. Perhaps, too much.

Funny, I didn't know anything about him.

His finger rubbed his chin. "Today's Tuesday. So, sometime between Sunday night and now, someone lifted the taillight assembly and bumper from your car..." he said. "Most likely when parked in your apartment lot."

His logic made sense, and I nodded. Hey, I'd take any small effort right now. My head wound around what he'd said about my bumper, the taillights being lifted, and calling technicians. All of a sudden, an understanding piqued my sixth sense, informing me he possessed lots of information on stolen car parts. Creasing my brow, I aimed a studious stare his way and wondered how much more he knew than what he'd said.

He adjusted the Ray Ban's earpiece. "Ms. Cooks, I suggest you go home, call the police, and your insurance company to file a report. The insurance company will help get your car fixed. Shouldn't be a huge chunk of change if you have a low deductible."

Insurance? Deductible? My hands felt heavy with the national debt I now carried.

From my curbside seat, I crooked up my head, a long way up. Drawing my body upright, I blinked away the remaining scum clouding my contact lenses. Officer Whatshisname? stood around six feet, one hundred-eighty pounds. He looked not too old, like thirty-ish. A well-pressed, navy regulation uniform covered his body. Uniforms make a man.

My assessment continued past the utility belt and the holstered gun, resting my gaze on his face. His nose appeared long, but slightly crooked, and his chin cut square. Trimmed short, his chocolate brown hair had been combed away from his face. *Probably used gel.* I still couldn't see his eyes because of the Ray Bans. I squinted harder with the perplexing thought something about him seemed familiar. However, the sun still shone in my eyes, and I couldn't recollect anyway.

"Okay. Hold on." I frowned. "Aren't you the police?" God, how awful, I sounded nasally like...Elmer Fudd. I pinched my nose. My other arm waved toward the Jeep while my gooked-up finger pressed the shirt tail. "Can't I report the stolen taillights and bumper to you?"

"No, ma'am. Today, I'm only writing tickets."

"Only writing tickets?" Un-be-lieve-able. I'd never heard of a policeman "only writing tickets." He appeared to be a by-the-book kind of officer, not one who ignored extenuating circumstances to help a poor distressed young woman. Just when I needed a lawman, I got bureaucracy crap. *How mean.*

"Can't you please help?" I begged one last time. *Call me shameless.* "Pulleeaasse?"

While his feet shifted, he looked like he considered my request. "No. Can't. Wish I could. You'll have to call it in. They'll take a report over the phone. Sorry."

Officer Whatshisname? wouldn't budge one bit. So not helpful. Looking at the hand extended my way, I placed mine in his and found a strong grip. He would want to use hand sanitizer after all my nose-wiping issues. He hauled me to my feet so hard, our bellies bumped, which made an awkward twinge grab something unknown inside me.

"Thanks." My body—and ego—felt bruised and

battered. I followed him at my own slow pace, my heels scrubbing along the asphalt. At the car door, I paused a bit, eventually opened it, and flopped in the seat. After closing the door, I shifted my gaze his way.

He ripped a page from a small book, a pen clenched in his teeth.

I took the paper he passed me. "What's this?"

"This,"—with his mouth shaped in a smirk, he tapped the paper with the capped pen—"is the citation for the taillight—"

"But I don't have—"

"—out. Don't forget to file your report and call your insurance company. And have a nice day." With hard firm steps, he strode with confidence back to his squad car.

Nice day? I gritted my teeth. *I'd kill for a really nice day.*

I caught his reflection in the mirror, and for a sec, his fitted pants emphasized a well-shaped behind, distracting me and my anger.

After a while, he pulled his cruiser alongside my car, nodded, and drove away.

With a shake, I cleared the clouds cluttering my mind. *What about me? What about my predicament? What about the fingerprints? What about the photos?* I wanted to ball the citation and lob it out the window.

What. An. Asshole.

I compressed my lips in a firm line and searched for a solution. Suddenly, my mission became crystal clear—go to court and fight the citation. No way would I pay anything as I didn't deserve a ticket for something I didn't do. And in doing so, I would save myself much-needed cash.

Yeah. I smacked my right fist into my left palm.

I would call the insurance company and report the theft. Something weird could be going on out there in good ol' Sommerville. With a wicked thought, I lifted my brow. And I could show the judge that Officer Whatshisname? was a rude, crude jerk who needed reprimanding.

Chapter Two

As the apartment door crashed behind me, a mirror hung next to the door frame rocked back and forth. Jenny had placed it there for a final beauty check before heading out. Above the sofa, the cartoonish paintings of squiggly people and boxy cars, newly purchased at the library art show for mere pennies, tilted. I dropped my bag on the khaki club chair, sending a less-than-heartfelt prayer nothing had broken.

Thank God, my apartment seemed a tad more tolerable temp-wise than the great outdoors. I'd turned my car's air to full blast for the ride home, but the indicator on the gauge hadn't budged. I still felt sweaty, sticky, and stinky—I took a whiff. Amend to extremely smelly.

With a little kick, the black pumps flew in the air and landed near the kitchen. I removed the despicable panty hose and popped the skirt's hook. My hips shimmied and wiggled as the garment dropped to the floor. I massaged my waist, hoping in the near future my breathing would return to normal.

Lead me to chocolate.

I stomped through the living area to the thermostat. Punching a button over and over, I lowered the setting to a more comfortable level. From the fridge, I grabbed an ice-cold bottle of water and returned to the sofa grouping, snagging my cell phone on the way. With a sloppy plop, I landed sideways on the club chair, knocked off my bag and stuff, and dangled my legs across the armrest.

I sat lackadaisically. Just sat with no purpose, no agenda. Looked around, but didn't care. Rubbing the bottle across my throat and forehead refreshed me. I snapped the bottle top and swallowed a gulp as the day's events replayed in my head. However, the more I thought about what had transpired, the more my foot began to jerk in an agitated rhythm.

"Have a Nice Day," Officer Whatshisname? had said.

Wonderful.

How about you have a nice day, buster, right after I finish poking needles in your eye. See how that feels.

The not-so-white shirt sleeve caught my eye. My favorite top sported a new label—TRASHED. Even when pretreated with stain remover, the black spots and green slimy splotches wouldn't wash out easily. *Crud.*

I unfastened the top three buttons and took another swallow. An unrefined burp spouted out. Nope, not a red-letter, A-plus kind of day. Rather an F-minus, never-forget-me kind of one.

The sooner I got this reporting stuff over with, the better. Then my life could return to picture perfect, everything back to normal.

Well… Almost. I still needed to find a job.

I reached for my totebag and pulled the citation from inside. Before taking the time to review the document, I used it to fan my face. I suspended waving to give the slip a once-over. On the backside of the citation, I found the "For Help" number and punched the phone's buttons with hard stabs.

"Oh, you'll need to leave your information with Detective Wellborn," a woman answered and fielded my question.

Detective Wellborn? Who the heck is that? I narrowed my brow into wrinkle-making-folds while I consulted the slip. "Ma'am, don't you mean, uh…" I glanced again, "officer?"

"No, detective."

And without giving me an opportunity to ask any further questions, she switched me over. Surely, she meant somebody else. I knew for a fact he said officer, not detective. My fingers undulated in an edgy rhythm on the club chair's arm while I waited for him to pick up. Pick up. PICK UP! Perhaps he still manned the streets, searching for other drivers "just like me." *Lucky them.*

Eventually, his voice mail came on, saying he would return my call.

I heard the beep and said, "This is Hattie Cooks. You pulled me over earlier and gave me a citation. I'm calling to file a stolen parts report." Then I rattled off my phone number. Hanging up, I sat some more. Niggles of dissatisfaction took over my brainwaves.

I hit redial. After three rings, the same efficient woman came back on. I explained how the detective hadn't answered. "Since he's unavailable, I want to leave a report with someone else."

"Oh, ma'am…"

Called ma'am twice in one day? That one word brought images of my back curving into a "C" like a little hunchbacked grandmotherly type. I was in no hurry to hit the old lady milestone.

"I'm sorry," she continued in her brisk, efficient

tone. "Let me transfer you."

And with a beep, she shifted my call to a different police person. He took my statement, saying he would pass it on.

Fantastic. I disconnected.

Staring at the citation, I found Officer Whatshisname? had scrawled the date, my name, and address details in the designated spots, all of which looked accurate. Sometimes, the police made errors when filling in these sections which helped when fighting the citation in court—so I'd been told. Obviously, Officer Whatshisname? didn't make mistakes. *Taillight Out* had been checked in the appropriate box. *Go figure*. I also found in the lower right hand corner of the citation his name—A. Wellborn—and his badge number...

Wait a minute. Wait a freakin' minute. A. Wellborn—as in Allan Wellborn? *Officer Whatshisname? is Allan Wellborn?* The same Allan Charles Wellborn who had gone to the same high school two grades ahead of me? My best friend's brother?

Is it possible? Oh golly, it could be. Funny squiggles seized my gut. I hadn't seen the guy in at least four plus years. My finger pulled my lower lip while I counted back, and *yeah*, now I knew why he'd looked vaguely familiar.

I'd seen Allan Wellborn at my graduation from Sommerville High. With diploma in hand, I'd wrapped my arms around Sarah Anne, his younger sister and my best friend, as our parents snapped the traditional cap-and-gown photos. He'd stood off to one side, studying me in his curious way, which had always unnerved me.

I'd been surprised when he'd pushed through family and thrust a card in my hand. To this day, I remembered the cartoon cap tossed in the air and the bits of glitter decorating it.

Inside, he'd written in tiny man-scribble:

>*Good luck in college.*
>*Love, Allan.*

Weird.

Six years later, he'd been a groomsman at his sister's wedding, but hadn't participated in the wedding party activities because-because... My finger screwed into my cheek. I hadn't a clue. I couldn't recall. At the time, my contact with him had been minimal, just the processional pairing. I did recollect his fingers gliding over mine, and for a tiny beat, my pulse had heightened when we'd briefly glanced at each other.

Weird.

I needed confirmation. If this really was him, his picture would be in my high school annual. And I knew just where to find it.

I schlepped to my bedroom to rummage for the box of childhood memorabilia stored on the top shelf in my closet. After a dinner visit with my parents for meat-for-the-week, I shoved a box of mementos on the front seat of my car. Mom had insisted I take the container home, saying, "You might need it."

Sure, Ma. Only if I intend to play dollies. The real truth—she wanted to store her winter clothes in my old bedroom closet.

This time, however, the stuff might come in handy.

Rising en pointe, I pulled the bulky box off the shelf inch-by-inch, careful not to dump the contents. I carried it to the kitchen table, removed the dusty lid, and blasted loose a loud *ah 'choo!* My fingers hit my pockets. Still no tissues on my person. *Oh, what the hell* and rubbed my nose across the dirty shirtsleeve, adding more stains.

I uncovered the annual buried under a French II workbook. Returning to my comfy chair, I passed my hand across the black-and-yellow cover, pausing to smooth over the embossed letters which spelled Sommerville High. A few years had passed since graduation—fortunately.

I ran my fingers down the index page and *voila!* located Sarah Anne Wellborn, my most cherished girlfriend. As the warmth of friendship overtook me, I poked her name looped in raspberry ink and smiled. *Miss her.*

I checked one notch up and located Allan Charles Wellborn, Senior. A frownie face had been drawn next to his name in black ink. Beside that was a column of page numbers indicating where he could be located. I flipped to the traditional senior portrait on page fifty and my lips split into a wide grin.

Good ol' dependable, always Mr. Perfect, never, ever did-anything-wrong Allan Wellborn. His black-framed glasses looked similar to Buddy Holly's. And like other kids, multiple zits polka-dotted his face. His brown hair had been parted down the middle, bangs laid over his forehead. He looked totally geeky.

Recorded under his name was a list of his club activities—Treasurer in the Future Accountants Club. First trombone in the Sommerville Marching Tiger Band where he served—this was not a stretch—as Treasurer. Math Competition listed as his favorite hobby.

I wasn't surprised. No wonder everyone had thought him nerdy; yet, we all knew the universal idiom: Geeks Rule.

Paging to the Accounting Club photo, I giggled. A pocket protector, a bane to every mother and repellant to every potential girlfriend, had been stuck in the breast pocket of a button-down, white shirt. A mechanical pencil, a fat yellow highlighter, and what resembled a pocket level were tucked inside, too. I rolled my eyes to the ceiling. "If only."

Most people would love to exploit the excellent blackmail material I'd uncovered. I reached back to Officer-slash-Detective Wellborn and contrasted him with this picture. My suspicions were confirmed, definitely the same guy. Only he'd improved for the better. Officer Wellborn's face had looked kind, and his hair appeared better styled. He didn't wear glasses any more, except for the sunglasses which looked mysteriously sexy. And instead of a vinyl protector in his shirt pocket, he packed a gun on his hip.

Then, a replay of this afternoon's events hit. The citation and my stolen car parts surfaced. My brain obsessed over how he'd treated me. Fury fired from the pit of my belly. It devoured me, threatening to erupt like Mount Vesuvius. I wanted to smack him. Smack him. Smack him. Smack him.

I jumped up and stalked to my roommate's boudoir where I slapped the yearbook page on the scanner. With a press of a few buttons, I produced an eight-by-ten copy. Returning to the kitchen, I dug in the junk drawer for packaging tape. I stuck the photo on the kitchen wall right above the trash can.

Back at the drawer, I unearthed three small stress

balls—one red, two blue—the squeezy kind used for anger management given away by a vendor at a health fair. Each of my friends had picked up one and given them to me because I was going through a stressful period. I banged the drawer shut and stomped to a place in front of my creation. Just as I eyeballed the distance, I heard my roommate open the apartment door and saw me planted there.

Jenny's brown-eyed gaze flicked from the wall and back to me. "What's goin' on?" she asked in her Louisiana drawl. "And where's the rest of your clothes?"

"This guy…" I ground out the word, "wrote me a ticket."

Her gaze went back to the photo. "He looks kinda young to be writin' tickets."

"Aren't you funny?" Determining I stood too close, I took two steps back. "I knew him a long time ago."

She pressed her hand over her mouth. "You know the cop who wrote you a ticket?"

"Sorta."

With a drawn-out sigh, she dropped her handbag on the couch. "Explain sorta."

My arm rose and reached behind, my front leg lifted in a baseball windup. The first squishy ball landed on his left temple. "He's Sarah Anne Wellborn's brother, and he wrote me a citation today."

"And throwin' things..."

I took a step to my right and eyeballed again. "Stress balls."

"'cuse me. Throwin' stress balls will make you feel what…happy?"

The second ball hit his mouth smack dab in the

middle. I blinked. "All the time he knew who I was. Why didn't he say something? He didn't have to write me a ticket. He was being a smart ass. The creep. The asshole. The..." The third ball smashed the bridge of his glasses. The paper split. "The geek!"

Jenny glanced at the squishy balls which now lay on the floor. "Better?"

"Nope." I picked them up, returned to my spot, and let the red one rip.

"How much longer you gonna be? I'm starvin'." She plopped in the club chair I'd vacated and watched as the third ball flew by. "Tell me something about him."

I stared, wondering where in the heck to begin. The Wellborn and Cooks families lived in the same neighborhood in Sommerville, a picturesque suburb made up of highways and byways, a wide variety of restaurants, and most importantly for me, excellent shopping. Historic municipal buildings and old warehouses restored into lofts were located downtown. Compared to other places, Sommerville enjoyed an excellent reputation.

Many college graduates wanted to transfer to high-energy cities with all their economic and cultural opportunities. Sommerville was large enough that I'd wanted to return after college upon obtaining the job I'd desired. Clearly, A. Wellborn had come home as well.

I set my hands on my hips. I knew the Wellborn family had discussed my visits ad nauseam over the dinner table. The same thing had taken place at my house with my parents employing the Cooks' Spanish Inquisition. These examinations were interspersed with table manners and Mom's *little talks*, more Cooks' trademark tortures.

I picked up the instruments of anger management. "When Sarah Anne, his sister, and I were younger and had play-dates, I saw him then."

Jenny tapped her lips with her fingers to suppress her yawn. "I'm well acquainted with Sarah Anne."

"In my teen years, he gave me long glances—very disturbing. Mostly, I avoided him like the plague. After all, something nasty could have rubbed off and contaminated me for life."

"Okay," she said. "We've determined he was a geek. What else?"

I shifted the spongy balls from one hand to the other. "Our mothers are good friends and wholly devoted members of The Mothers Always Know Network, the one which would inevitably bust you for the most minor infraction, like trading clothing. Or eating candy instead of lunch. Or… Well, you get the idea."

Years passed before I'd determined they weren't lying about the connection—they really had known everything.

To my everlasting embarrassment, the network operated much too well on numerous occasions. Yelling my whole name was a sure sign of trouble and not music to anyone's ears. Even now, I could hear the dreaded words, "Harriette Lee Cooks! Come down here this instant!"

I knew better than to dawdle.

Front and center, Mom had curled her fingers into my shoulders. "Hold it right there, missy."

Cringing in holy terror, I'd prayed for a distraction. Her right index finger had nearly poked my nose. Inch-by-inch, my feet shuffled in the opposite direction.

"At the grocery store today," she began with her probing technique, "Shirley Wellborn found out Sarah Anne and you are hosting a boy-girl party on Saturday night. I thought you had planned a sleepover. What exactly is going on? Give me details. Now."

I'd cave. I'd always wondered how Mom had known exactly what we'd done.

"Mothers always know," she'd replied with a smug smile.

I bet Mr. Perfect Allan Wellborn had tattled.

When Jenny swung her feet, her designer sandals went flying. "So what, Hattie? He wrote you a ticket. Deal with it."

Jenny's comment rubbed me raw. She should be more supportive. I put the evil eye on her. "As you well know, I am currently unemployed and am down to counting pennies and nickels and dimes. Now, I have a ticket to pay and no extra cash to do so."

"You know your parents would help."

Which was something I wanted to avoid.

"Tell me more."

My nose scrunched. "After graduation from Southern U, Sarah Anne married, moved to Colorado Springs, and last year, birthed a baby girl. When she comes to town—which has not been in a while, now that I think about it—I've never seen A. Wellborn. We never talk about him."

The admission sounded self-absorbed. My mouth curved downwards, quite unlike me. I must be getting all whiny from the job-hunting thingy.

Jenny pointed to the poster. "So… Allan Wellborn is a cop."

"I thought he was an accountant like his dad. His mother had told my mother who told me he'd studied accounting and finance in college."

She tilted her head. "Why isn't he practicing as a CPA now?"

"Good question, Sherlock. I don't know." I shrugged and squeezed the blue balls. Life with Mom and Dad had been perfect back then. We lived in a two-story brick home, the yard landscaped with oak trees and a pool in the back. Dad was employed as a mechanical engineer at an architecture firm. Mom sewed, cooked, and cleaned like a maniac. She volunteered at our schools and community service organizations.

My sisters and I had shared bedrooms and one bathroom. Because of the limited mirror space and the high demand, elbows were in the face and jabs elsewhere. Sisters were annoying until a miraculous breakthrough occurred after college when we'd developed a tight bond no one could sever.

After picking up the annual, Jenny paged over to the sophomore class. "Look what I found...Cooks, Harriette Lee." She flipped the book in my direction so I could see too.

For me, an unusually good day for photo taking. Long straight hair, parted in the middle, fell to my bra clasp. Rectangular tortoiseshell glasses stuck out from my face. A large pimple distorted my chin, and sure-to-repel dandruff had decided to not make an appearance.

My parents had pinned on me an old-fashioned name, Harriette, which wasn't French, nor trendy like the girls named Heather or Taylor or Katie. Mine came from my grandmother. In fifth grade, I'd discovered the nickname "Hattie," which sounded more acceptable, even sassy, but not dorky.

I liked sassy.

"This is so funny." Jenny waltzed around the room with the book and sang, "You two geeks…were meant…to be together."

I snatched the book from her hands to flip nonchalantly through the rest of the pages, and an odd thing caught my eye. All the sophomore girls had long straight hair parted down the middle. So did the juniors. And seniors. We looked like clones. Or clowns.

With a slap, I closed the volume and set it on the counter. I sipped more water. "You know, it's a small world."

"So they say." Jenny tossed me my cell phone. "Why don't you ask your mom what he's been doing?"

I caught the phone and bounced the device in my palm. I could find out from Mom where A. Wellborn had been since high school. Over bananas, cantaloupes, or whatever produce was on special in our neighborhood grocery store, The Mothers Always Know Network continued to trade information about their kids.

On second thought, this could be a really crazy idea with Mom assuming my asking concealed something, and—surprise, surprise—she would interrogate me to death. After my reluctant confession, she would pontificate on "What a Nice Boy Allan Wellborn Is," her favorite little talk I'd heard way too many times in the past.

And she would ask me about today's bloody interview and I wasn't ready to discuss it. I rubbed a circle on my throbbing temple and set the phone on the dining table. *Yeah, I should revisit this plan some more.*

After graduation from Sommerville High, I'd attended State Tech and received a Bachelor of Science in Human Sciences, majoring in Fashion Merchandising. I loved clothing. Being a self-proclaimed pro-shopper, I wanted to dress the world in beautiful clothes at bargain prices.

Mom had said, "Look where it got you."

Her tone had intimated my education was worthless. She would have been overwhelmingly ecstatic if I had majored in accounting like my sister and A. Wellborn. To this day, I felt the need to justify my degree by explaining I'd taken lots of business courses. I'd nearly failed accounting, the most boring class ever. Even with a calculator, adding long columns of numbers became tedious.

Still was. And on top of that, rarely did I get the same answer twice.

Emphatically, I'd disagreed with her opinion. Being unemployed right now didn't count. I'd studied other courses—Art Appreciation, Food & Nutrition, History of Costume, Archery, and Geology. But no basket weaving.

What is Mom thinking? If A. Wellborn's Accounting Club photo was an example of what accounting professionals were perceived, weren't they geeky? Geeky could never be an option. What's more, I didn't wear shirts with pockets on the chest—a huge fashion no-no—for the pocket protector. Large pockets made a girl's bosom resemble an inflated life preserver, the only exception being a specialty shirt worn for fishing or on an African safari.

Sommerville's premiere department store, Tuckers,

had recruited me for the job I'd truly desired. Steadily, I'd fishtailed my way up the food chain to become the menswear assistant buyer. The bonus of being the only woman in the men's division meant I received an enormous portion of flattering male attention, too.

I'd loved my job. I'd held the everlasting wish to continue my retail career with Tuckers. I'd visited our sister stores in nearby smaller towns to arrange merchandise and consult with the staff. At the Men's Wear Show, I'd purchased new inventory. Did relevant paperwork. Pride and accomplishment consumed me when an order went from paper to merchandise to display.

However, when I'd fallen victim to department reorganization during a slight economic downturn, my bubble had burst. Translated—I was let go.

Today, I'd taken the initiative and implemented Plan A—interviewing with Tuckers' closest competitor on the off-chance *something* was available. I'd borne sky-high hopes for the meeting, only to find they weren't hiring either. My heart broke with disappointment. I didn't want a trip to Europe or a million dollars. I wanted a plain ol' job, doing what I'd done before.

Now, I had to shift to Plan B.

Earlier, over lunch at Muy Bueno with Maggie, a Funsister friend who'd worked with me when we were teenagers at Amazing Adventureland, the local theme park, posed, "Why not try temporary jobs?"

I'd never considered working as a temp. I'd quirked my eyebrows upwards. "Temporary?"

"Sure." She'd beefed the idea with enthusiasm. "That way, if you don't like the job, you don't have to go back. And you can continue to look for buying jobs until the right opportunity opens up."

Maggie was right. Temporary jobs would pay the rent and provide cash for food—and chocolate—until I'd found the position I truly desired. An extra selling point was learning new skills and networking. Luckily, another friend, Trixie, owned the employment agency Jobs Inc. and placed people in permanent and temporary positions. I could be one of those. And after today's disheartening interview, I should call her to launch implementation of Maggie's Plan B.

Hugging the annual to my chest, I surveyed my assets. I was doing all right, in fact, as well as any peers. I'd purchased a gently used couch in blue-and-khaki check from a consignment store, the club chair with matching ottoman, and a leather-topped coffee table were garage sale finds. All paid for and not on credit.

A Chinese-styled armoire had been retrofitted with shelves and housed a flat screen television. An old farm-styled table with chairs painted white had been placed in the dining area. In my bedroom was my grandmother's iron bed covered in a beautiful blue and white toile ensemble my mom had crafted. I'd draped a coordinating, striped fabric over the bedside tables. Another antique armoire held clothing.

I heaved a sigh. "Wish all my dreams would come true." A job I loved. A man I adored.

"Don't we all, darlin'."

Jenny's small smile, just a tip of the corners of her mouth, showed how much she sympathized.

I said, "Just like the fairy tales."

"That may not be the best example."

"I know." I extended the squishy balls toward her. "Wanna try?"

"Nah, but leave up poster boy—just in case." She stood and slung an arm over my shoulder. "Let's eat."

I dropped the book on the couch, and we made our way to the kitchen counter. I stroked First Fish, my beta, whose bowl sat on the bar counter top. Jenny had named him. When I'd first brought him home in his clear plastic bag, he was silver-colored with magenta fins. I guess they starved him at the pet store 'cause he ate good fish food and turned electric blue.

My finger dipped in the water to stroke my aquatic friend while I contemplated dinner. As if on cue, my tummy growled. I wandered over to the kitchen cupboards to check for nourishment. Found nothing. No huge surprise since I had little cash.

Jenny peeked inside the fridge. Found nothing.

Well, not exactly nothing-nothing. A rotten head of lettuce and a jug, which undoubtedly contained old milk, were inside. She passed me the container. "You do it."

"No way." I pushed back. "You do it."

"I did it last time."

She had. Squeezing my eyes shut to avoid what I knew was forthcoming, I unscrewed the green plastic top. Bravely, I sniffed, instantly gagged at the repulsive scent, and rushed the container to the sink for emptying. My free hand flapped the air with vigor to clear the unforgettable odor. Helpful Jenny turned on the Vent-a-hood.

Considering the lack of promising contents inside the fridge or cabinets, I lifted my shoulders in an uninspired shrug. Because of the heat, I didn't really want to prepare anything anyway.

No one would ever say I was a great cook. I didn't like to. In desperation, I could follow a recipe with minimum, but edible, results. My best culinary skills extended to making tuna sandwiches, adding chocolate chips and pecans to a brownie box mix, and ordering pizza. After such a rotten day, I decided only one thing would cure everything—a soda and peanut M&Ms.

Jenny, who wasn't a good cook either, pulled out bags from our hidden stash and passed me one.

Because today could be labeled a red letter, never-forget-me kind of day, I needed a double dose.

Chapter Three

At last. Another *fun* day had passed, and Thank God in Heaven, I was home. I took in cleansing breaths, exorcising the workday blues. A couple of days ago, I'd pressed forward with Plan B by calling my girlfriend, Trixie, at Jobs Inc. for a meeting.

She'd tossed her shoulder-length, dark hair while flashing her round, blue eyes. A petite woman and conservative dresser, she had a calming influence and always a practical solution for her clients. "Someone with your experience will be an easy placement in a temporary position, however, probably not in your preferred field of retail."

Pivoting away to stare out her office window, I'd barely mumbled, "Darn."

I didn't want to work temporary jobs. Sitting while typing in a stuffy office all day long sounded bo-ring. I wanted to be at market and writing orders for the latest and greatest merchandise. Or zipping around town in my fun car, visiting the stores.

Temporary jobs seemed…ordinary.

But I had no choice, especially when I'd balanced my checkbook yesterday and found the sum of $150.53. Anxiety to be gainfully employed, even if temporarily, had taken root inside me and bloomed to catastrophic proportions.

I'd bitten my lip to hide my disappointment while

half-listening to Trixie describe a position in the claims department of Buy Rite Automobile Insurance Company, where I'd be employed as a data-entry specialist and all-around gofer. My hiring would replace a long-time employee who had died quite unexpectedly several months prior.

With a flick of her hand, she'd said, "Hattie, your skills are up to speed for this particular job. It entails entering data into the computer, copying, filing, answering phone calls, and other relevant office tasks."

She'd quizzed me on other areas of expertise, and suddenly, I possessed all kinds of new talents I didn't know existed, such as processing outgoing mail or inventorying paper stock for the copier and printers.

She must have seen the reluctance shaping my frown because she'd said, "Remember, Hattie. It isn't forever. You can leave the position if it becomes unbearable."

I'd left Trixie, storing her life raft of advice forefront in my mind as I drove to the interview.

****

Buy Rite's offices were situated near the intersection of two major highways which bisected Sommerville. The building had been wrapped in a copper glass skin with a decorative limestone archway highlighting the façade. Stoneware planters filled with pink and purple petunias and white begonias were prettily positioned near the entrance. Live oak trees had been planted next to the building's sidewalk, and larger ones had been scattered randomly amongst a few islands in the parking lot to provide needed shade.

To say Buy Rite's offices were on the cutting edge of interior design would be wrong. Two areas divided the space. The metal boxy furniture resembled what I called Early Dental, a style of primary-colored, vinyl and chrome furnishings popular in offices decades ago. The Berber carpet in oatmeal off-gassed a smell of formaldehyde, and—I sniffed—something like cat urine? *Ick.*

The area to the right belonged to Opal Brown, Executive Assistant, soon-to-be my supervisor. The bigger office behind Opal's belonged to Lester Johnson, B.R.A. Branch Owner. Off to the left, the section, which resembled a hefty closet without doors, housed the copier and filing cabinets. The desk in front of the filing space would belong to me.

Trixie had said Lester and Opal requested a "little visit" before I began my short-term position—most likely, them checking me out for the weirdness factor. However, when seated across from Lester and adjacent to Opal, I wondered if I should be the one doing the checking.

For the most part, Opal conducted the interview. While perusing my resume, she glanced over the top rim of her bifocals. "Hattie, I take it, is short for Harriette?"

"Yes, Ma'am."

"I prefer whole names, not nicknames."

Well, goody for her. My mind raced over variations on her name—Op, Oppee, O-pull, or O-Pal. Perhaps, her odd mind-set aimed to intimidate me, but instead, put me off. Considering her attitude, and because I didn't really fancy a temporary job and could care less about the interview's outcome, I took a different stance from my normal shy one. "I prefer Hattie," I answered with a firm tone. However, my shaky hands were clenched in my lap. If her intent was to not hire me because of my name, now would be the best time to know.

"Humpf."

She made this funny addendum, sounding like punctuation, which I soon discovered she used frequently.

"Tell us about your professional experiences."

"As you can see from my resume, which Trixie at Jobs Inc. provided"—I pointed to the papers Opal held—"Tuckers Department Store recruited me upon college graduation. I rose through the ranks, until recently."

"And?" she asked, lifting her black penciled brow.

"I was laid off due to department reorganization in an economic downturn."

"Humpf." She stuck her head back in my file. "I didn't know a Bachelor of Science in Fashion Merchandising degree existed."

I mentally rolled my eyes. *You and my mom.* "I also took lots of business courses like Economics, Accounting—"

"And why would you want to work for Buy Rite?"

Her brusque manner sounded...rude. Why should I brown-nose them in order to get this position? "You need a temporary and I need a job." Which was true. The sooner this freak show-slash-interview hit the road, the better. "I'm a fast learner and a hard worker. You won't be disappointed. So, what's the decision? Am I hired?"

"Why, yes, Hattie." Lester hadn't said much during Opal's grilling. He hoisted forward his large frame, spilling his enormous belly over the desk's top. "This is just to get us acquainted with each other. Right, Opal?"

He didn't see her shoot me the wicked squint.

"Yes, Lester."

"Do you have any questions?" Lester's bratwurst-sized lips spread into a grin.

"I'd like an idea of employee guidelines."

Opal handed me a piece of paper. "I just happen to have a copy."

Not a big shocker here. Obviously, she'd prepared for every scenario.

BUY RITE
AUTOMOBILE INSURANCE COMPANY
Employee Guidelines
Compiled by Opal Brown

1) Be on time. Our working hours are from eight to five.
2) No gossiping. Make personal phone calls only during lunch hour.
3) Show initiative. Do your work and do it well.
4) Dress professionally. No short skirts.
5) Lunch is one hour. Other breaks as needed.
6) Report to the Executive Assistant.
(all rules strictly enforced)

As I listened to Ms. Just-so-Perfect recite the guidelines aloud, I scrutinized the handout which documented Buy Rite's rules to exactness. And hey, if she wanted to fire me over any of these rules, fine by me. If Trixie could place me here, she could elsewhere.

"Any questions?" she asked.

I would have to be as dumb as a doorknob not to understand. "No questions. Everything seems crystal clear—"

"Yes, well, if that's all, Opal..." Lester interrupted, "Hattie, welcome to the Buy Rite family."

I took his proffered paw and shook it, taking in his sweaty palm. *Euew*. Without him noticing, I slid my hand over my thigh to wipe it dry. After a cursory glance around the office, I determined the place seemed clean and uncluttered. The salary didn't turn me off, approximately the same earnings I'd made with the assistant buying job, but with normal working hours. My gaze cut to Opal whose glare bored into me. "Thanks. When shall I start?"

He tilted forward, placing his hands on his desk. "How about tomorrow?"

Opal crossed her arms and shifted back in her chair. "Humpf."

****

Once home, I made my way to the kitchen in search of something to squash the growing hunger pains gnawing my insides. As I mulled over my limited dinner choices, I heard the doorbell chime which struck me odd. I hadn't spoken with anyone all day and didn't expect drop-bys.

At the door, my self-defense training automatically rolled into operation:

Can of wasp spray by the door? Check

Umbrella with pointy tip on peg rack? Check

I opened the vintage door viewer and found Officer Whatshisname?, aka Detective Wellborn, aka Allan Charles Wellborn, standing on the threshold. *Since when do policemen make house calls?*

Taking a longer peek—yep, I'd guessed right. I grinned. He was the same Allan Wellborn, Sarah Anne's brother. The same Allan Wellborn who did no wrong. The same Allan Wellborn my mom yammered about with her "What a Nice Boy" talk.

Rising to the tips of my toes for a better look, I noted how his jeans enhanced his long legs. A navy-and-white-striped Polo shirt showed off broad shoulders, and the same sunglasses continued to give off the mysterious and sexy impression. He appeared to be freshly laundered and shaved.

Okay, the truth. Probably, I'd looked harder than I wanted to admit.

After work, I'd changed into a floral-splattered sundress in shades of pink with ribbon straps of fuchsia and a matching belt. I glanced in the strategically hung mirror by the front door. Leaning closer to view possible imperfections, I ran a finger under the shoulder strap and did an adjustment. "Not bad." I plumped the hair and did a quick finger spit wipe-up under the eyes and squinted again. "Better."

The doorbell sounded a second time.

Having had no prior experience with a policeman at my front door, I hesitated, a slight paranoia overtaking my thoughts. *Why is he here? What if he's evolved into a stalker? Or a murderer? Or a rapist?* I would have to use my good judgment, which for years now, Dad jokingly claimed I didn't possess. Suspicious of his motives, I followed the self-defense training and carefully turned the knob. The hooked safety chain prevented the door from opening more than four inches.

"Howdy!" I said with levity through the slit.

A. Wellborn shifted around. "Hi! Do you remember I pulled you over the other day for a taillight out citation?"

"Are you going to frisk…" a little wariness crept in

43

my voice, "and arrest me after all?"

"No frisking. No arrests." He chuckled. "Sorry I didn't call first. I've something to show you."

He sounded slightly official. However, the frisking and arresting talk made me nervous. Remembering the cops and robbers television programs, I wondered where his questioning was headed. "Is this legitimate police business? Are you sure you didn't come here to cart me off to jail?"

He shook his head. "Not official police business. No handcuffs. Trust me. I have something for you in my truck."

No frisking and no arrests were—so far, in my book—a good thing. Knowing he was Sarah Anne's older brother, I found eliminating him from the stalker, murderer, and rapist categories easy. The *something in the truck* line sounded similar to approaches used in past dating experiences. For instance:

"Want to come up and look at my etchings?"

Translated: A roll in the hay.

Or the ever popular *"Would you like to meet Mr. Lizard?"*

Translated: Mr. Wiggly Worm.

"How about coming to my place for a drink?"

Translated: To ply me with multiple drinks and the requisite roll in the hay.

I hadn't fallen for those then and wouldn't be a sucker now.

He stuck his hands on his hips. "I know what you're thinking. I'm not a stalker, murderer, or rapist."

Apparently, he could read minds. "Just a minute." I closed the door enough to release the chain, then re-opened it. "Why can't you just tell me whatever *it* is?"

"No. I want to show you—"

"Not a Picasso?" I asked.

"No."

"Not an iguana?"

A perplexed expression crossed his face. "A what?"

"Not your pet worm?"

"What pet worm?"

"Not—"

"Look, I don't know what you're thinking. The only worms I know about are for fishing. I have something stashed in my truck. I think you'll be surprised."

I drummed my fingers on the door frame. *Oh, why not? He can't be that scary.* I slipped my feet into my favorite pink sandals, snatched my keys, and just in case, the can of wasp spray because in this day and age, a girl couldn't be too careful. After locking my door behind me, I trailed A. Wellborn who strode with determination toward a Toyota 4-Runner painted granite.

I paused briefly to admire his gleaming truck. *What a cool ride.*

"Dammit." He roared this frustration after reaching the rear of his vehicle.

My curiosity instantly perked. With widened eyes, I peered around the truck's fender. "What's wrong? Where's the surprise?"

I sensed A. Wellborn's glare from behind the sunglasses. His hand flung outwards in a hard, angry gesture toward the truck. "It's gone."

"What is gone?" Clueless, I crept closer to the bed and took a small peek. "I don't see anything."

"Pretty observant for a girl."

His words and tone sounded mean, upset, but I seemed to be the only person who didn't know why. "What's so all-fired important that's causing you to have a tizzy fit?"

"I wanted to help." His head dropped in a hang-dog manner. He waved his hand toward the truck again. "Your taillights and your bumper are gone."

I peeked again and found he was right. Nothing. I considered in some strange, odd way his bestowing a girl with recovered car parts could be construed as romantic. But what seemed more remarkable was how did A. Wellborn get my taillights and bumper? *Very interesting, indeed.*

I took a few steps backwards to regroup, my grip tightening on the spray can.

His hand reached toward me. "Hey, it's okay. Don't go. I'll explain. I felt crappy about pulling you over the other day."

My head cocked as I overlapped my arms. I leveled a questioning eye on him. "I don't see any taillights and bumper. And why would you have my car parts? They were stolen, remember?"

"I made a call to a friend, who has a friend, who called...uh, somebody—I didn't ask—to locate a bumper from a Jeep Wrangler. And guess what?"

I had no clue where this was headed. "What?"

"He found it."

"That's great!" I narrowed my brows. "But how did you know it was my missing bumper?"

"When the part was described, I assumed it was yours from the sticker plastered on it. Didn't you work at Amazing Adventureland during your senior year?"

"Yeah..." All of the sudden, I truly had a major revelation. I stabbed my finger right at his chest. "Wait a minute. You did know it was me when you stopped me the other day. Why didn't you say something?"

"I did."

"Nuh uh."

"Yes, I did."

"No, you didn't."

He shrugged. "Remember? I said maybe you do."

Men! The great communicators. Heaven forbid he would use more than his manly two thousand daily word allotment.

I tossed my head ever-so lightly. "Well, your remark confused me. I remembered you"—I pointed at him—"when I read your name on the citation." I lifted my chin and threw back my shoulders. "And FYI, I put the sticker on my bumper 'cause it looked cool."

"I'm sure it did."

I had to admit possibly the bumper sticker had looked cool…when put on our cars in high school.

To christen my new ride, Maggie had gifted me with a basket containing the sticker, a memento every Adventureland guest received upon parking, local and state maps, a cup of tissues for the cup holder, a clip-on visor mirror, and glass and leather wipes. I didn't want to hurt her feelings by not using the sticker and stuck it on the bumper instantly.

"Some people get rather upset when they're acquainted with a cop who gives them a ticket," he said. "I didn't want to embarrass you anymore. You looked wiped out. You'd said you'd had a really bad day."

I nodded, recalling a red letter, never-forget-me kind of one, and how today had gone as well. The very same. "So, where are the taillights and bumper now?"

"I don't know." A. Wellborn paced a parking space. Disgust oozed with each step. His fingers shot through his short dark hair.

Instantly, I was entranced. What a sexy move—*Sexy?*

"I had the tailgate down to haul the parts, which anyone could have seen while I drove around town. Someone stole the stuff while I was at your door." He slapped the truck's fender. He yanked off the sunglasses, revealing chocolate brown eyes. "Dammit. I knew better."

And when did he get such gorgeous eyes the color of my favorite food group and long eyelashes? Girls paid good money to acquire those, which reminded me I should buy the new, lash-lengthening mascara I saw advertised last night on a cable shopping show.

"You need to call the police again," he said with authority. "You did report the theft?"

I was not liking where this whole exchange was going, the whole passing the responsibility thingy. I fisted my hands defiantly on hips. "You know I did, De-tec-tive. When you checked your voice mail, you would have heard the messages I left the very same day you ticketed me. And just so you'll know, I called my insurance company, too. The adjuster said the check will soon be in the mail."

His hair distracted me, looking so cute, stuck up like Alfalfa's from "The Little Rascals" television show I'd watched when staying overnight with my grandmother. My hands itched to get in the beautiful silkiness and mess it up. Preferably during sex.

Oh My God in Heaven. First sexy, and now, sex?

Where are these wild thoughts originating? Flicking a glance his way, I hoped he hadn't heard that. "It seems to me, you need to call the police. The parts were lifted from your truck."

"It gets...tricky since the taillights and bumper are recovered stolen parts. This goes against all the rules about doing business with..." A. Wellborn's finger rubbed his chin as he looked skyward, searching for the appropriate word, "interesting people."

"Oh." Not being a total airhead, I understood very well the implication of what he'd done. Through friends of friends, a policeman dealt with "interesting people," something he didn't ordinarily do, to recover my car parts. I asked the question all inquiring minds wanted to know, "Why did you do it?"

"I wanted to help. Cost me fifty dollars to recover the parts."

His quick look made me blush to my toes. *Shoot.* At the precise moment, my checking balance of $150.53—$150.53—$150.53 flashed off and on in my head like an orange neon sign on the fritz. I didn't have an extra fifty dollars to reimburse him. Something else to sort out.

Feeling humbled, I fumbled for an answer and said, "Umm, thanks for trying. I'm a little embarrassed to...ah...admit I don't have the money right now to... ah...pay you back. I'm doing temporary work for a while."

A. Wellborn's shoulders dropped. His anger seemed to have settled. "Which explains what you meant when you said you had a terrible interview. I hope it works out. I should've called and asked, but when the parts were located, I decided to surprise you."

"You're so sweet."

Our conversation stopped, and a silence blanketed us.

"Well, thanks for trying," I said. "See ya." Giving a small wave, I tucked the container of wasp spray under my arm and turned toward my apartment, pulling my keys from my pocket. Then, I overheard another loud "damn." Swinging back, I said with a teasing tone, "Now, what's wrong? Was calling you sweet a horrible thing?"

He pulled his head from inside the truck cab. "No, my pizza was stolen off the front seat of the truck."

My head cocked to my right. Surely, he hadn't said what I thought he had. "Your what?"

His cheeks blazed fire-engine red. "My pizza was stolen."

"You left a pizza in your unlocked truck this whole time?" *Amazing*. What resistance. What willpower. Which were two characteristics I didn't possess when thinking of pizza because pizza had been elevated to the sacred foods list.

Extra-special foods, not normally eaten, but could be eaten, on a regular basis, like peanut M&Ms, cheesecake, homemade lemon meringue pie, whipped cream, even the canned kind. Consuming these selections seemed almost—I was mortified to admit— sexually orgasmic.

Naturally, I regularly revised my list to add newly discovered items. "Why didn't you lock your doors?"

His look could best be described as condescending. *Don't go there*, it read. I locked my doors. Maybe he forgot this one time, just like he forgot to lock the truck's hatch.

He said, "I brought a pizza along with the thought maybe..."

This sounded good. My insides got a little excited. "Maybe what?"

"Maybe," he sighed, "you could join me."

My heart melted. Wow, car parts and pizza. Just like Mom used to preach, Allan Wellborn was sooo nice. I set a finger to my chin and pushed it up and down like I was in a faux deep thought. "I dunno. What kind did you get?"

"Pepperoni."

My mouth curved into a girly grin. I ran my tongue over my lower lip. "I like pepperoni."

Eyes fastened on me, A. Wellborn swallowed deeply. One handed, he palmed his cell phone. "I need to make some calls."

"Who to?"

"First, to the friend who has a friend to ask him to locate the bumper again. Second, I'm ordering another pizza. You want some?" He gave me a questioning squint.

Staring at the darkening sky, I tapped my toes, deciding. The Funsisters and I have rules about food and guys:

Rule One: Do not turn down food when unemployed.

Rule Two: Do not turn down food when unemployed and invited to share by a hunky, thoughtful man.

"This isn't a life or death answer, just say yes or no."

He sure sounded impatient. What the hell. I won't have to scrounge for something to eat, and A. Wellborn had proven to be interesting, a nice note to end a complicated day. "Yes."

He punched a number on his cell. "What do you like on yours?"

How considerate. "I like pepperoni, but my fav is Canadian bacon and crispy bacon."

He frowned. "Aren't you concerned about cholesterol?"

"Not today."

Chapter Four

Since A. Wellborn had asked if the pizza delivery could be dropped off at my door, I had about two seconds to get my apartment ship-shape. I wasn't going to let the perfect opportunity to get to know him better go to waste. I raced to the kitchen and snatched poster boy from the wall, burying the paper in the trash under Frito pie remains. *No-no-no, would not do for him to see his picture hanging on my wall with divots puncturing his face.* I surveyed the kitchen for any other tale-tell items. All looked good.

With a plan of attack in mind, I got to work. I stacked white dinner plates on the table, silverware, cloth napkins embellished with blue stripes, and matching placemats discounted fifty percent from a Bed, Bath & Beyond clearance sale.

When he came in, I looked up.

He asked, "Can I help?"

"Set the table?"

"Okay."

I searched the fridge for drinks. "What'll it be? I have soda, water, lemonade, old wine..." I took the bottle from the fridge and sized up the well-aged contents "...but no beer."

"Soda's fine."

I dumped the beyond-drinkable vintage down the drain and threw the bottle in the recycling bin. I squished the two cans in coozies, laying straws on the placemats. After the pizza had been delivered, which A. Wellborn kindly paid for, he sat at the table. The place settings had been arranged neatly with the dishes, forks, mats, and napkins. Before joining him, I added a pizza seasoning jar and parmesan cheese, the kind in the shaker can.

While unfolding a napkin across my lap, I admired his stellar effort at table decorating. "Thanks for fixing the table. You do this often? I might consider hiring you."

He grinned and put a couple of slices on his plate, after which he lightly licked his fingers. "My mama told me to always mind my manners."

I knew this was true because his mom had polite *little talks* just like my mom. Only his mom had seemed way scarier than mine.

Snagging a slice of pie, I took a bite. I closed my eyes and sniffed, savoring another nibble. Mamma and Pappa's Italian Bistro consistently made the very best pizza. The crisp, thin crust had been covered with the right amount of richly spiced tomato sauce and not too much cheese, loaded with thinly sliced Canadian bacon and liberally sprinkled with coarsely chopped, crispy bacon.

"Mmm," I moaned, not realizing the sound had slipped out.

"You really like Canadian bacon and bacon pizza."

His comment broke my reverence. Heat covered my cheeks. How did a girl explain the whole sacred foods-being-orgasmic theory? And while eating, she might overtly enjoy the experience?

One more item to add to the ever-increasing

embarrassment list.

To disguise my discomfort, I ignored his comment and proceeded with the standard conversation breaker. Drawing a deep breath, I fired out questions like an automatic weapon: "So, what have you been doing the past few years-I didn't know you were a policeman-How long have you been one-I think I remember my mom saying you were an accountant-Why the change-Was accounting unbearable?"

Staring at me, he washed down a substantial mouthful with soda.

"Where did you go to college-Was it the same place as Sarah Anne-I can't remember-Do you hear from her regularly-She used to call, but not much anymore-Now, I get the rare email-She's so busy with the baby-How are your parents?"

His hands rose. "Whoa, lil' lady. Let's start at the top." Using the napkin, he swiped his kissable lips and dusted off his hands.

Kissable? When did I start thinking of A. Wellborn having lips? An all-too-familiar warmth flushed my face.

"I attended Southern University on an academic scholarship. A top-ten accounting firm recruited me. After a couple of years, crunching numbers didn't interest me. The accounting background didn't turn off the police department. I was hired."

I'd always known accounting wasn't exciting. And his explanation solved the mystery of the disappearing pocket protector.

"I was a patrolman and recently, made detective."

Without doubt, his fast rise to detective was due to him being an exemplary policeman, which could also explain the confusing part of my phone conversation with the woman at the station. Reminded of my exchange with her, I asked, "Why were you writing citations the other day?"

"I did a favor for a friend who needed a few days off."

Isn't A. Wellborn nice? He did me a favor and a friend a favor which would score points in Mom's tome of Desirable Characteristics in Men. Tilting my head, I examined him further. *Migh-tee fine.*

"You're staring." A. Wellborn's eyes and hands examined his shirt for possible dropped sauce.

"Sorry." I shook my head. "I can't help it. You look different, not anything like your senior photo in the Sommerville yearbook. No glasses, no trombone, no protector sleeve with pens."

His eyebrows elevated. Glints of amusement twinkled in his eyes.

"And was the other item a pocket level?"

"Busted. Sarah Anne constantly teased me about that and the trombone. In college, I discovered weights. Gained some height and changed glasses for contact lenses."

I screwed my napkin into knots with the notion his potential appeared very satisfying—*Huh?*

"You looked me up?"

My gaze flicked to where poster boy had hung. I was embarrassed to admit I had, but once again, I'd been caught red-handed. This appeared to be the story of my life anyway. "I read the citation and my head went ding-dong. So, I found the old Sommerville annual and checked."

A corner of his mouth quirked up. "Have I

56

improved?"

Fishing, fishing. As if I would tell all. My gaze shifted to the ceiling as I sipped soda. Interested in discovering more, I entered the uncomfortable, but *Necessary For All Girls Getting To Know Single Guys* part of our conversation. I toyed with the straw. "So, how's your love life?"

He choked, spewing soda everywhere.

Unperturbed, I mopped the table with my napkin. "Are you okay?"

He coughed. "F-fine."

Truth be told—I pressed my hand to my lips, holding my girly giggles—perhaps, he felt ill-at-ease being asked personal questions. Maybe my inquiries were a little abrupt and from left field, but nosy me just had to know. "Seeing anyone special?"

His face colored pink. "I keep busy."

A nice side step.

He stabbed a finger at me. "How about you?"

Now the proverbial shoe seemed to be on my proverbial foot.

"I mean, what have you been doing?"

So, I gave him the song-and-dance version of my life, omitting the social part. Interestingly enough, I hadn't experienced much of a real love life before college. In high school, geeks rarely dated, the exception being geeks dating other geeks.

They didn't ask me either.

I'd invited seven different guys to escort me to a club dance my senior year. Talk about a real blow to a girl's ego as one after another they turned me down.

And for my senior prom? My date dumped me two weeks before the big event. Incredibly furious, I came close to punching him over and over like an inflatable rock'em sock'em boppin' clown toy. Teaching the moron a lesson before he dumped another girl in the same manner would have been extremely satisfying. Women world-wide would have thanked me for this, too.

The real lesson was, on occasion, I'd picked loser guys. Inexperienced me didn't know what lay hidden under their handsome facades.

At State Tech, I'd been involved for a couple of years with College Boy. But at age twenty-two when he'd proposed, I'd said no. Deep inside, I didn't feel ready for a long-term commitment and possessed a desire to explore on my own. I had no regrets.

Anyway, that twenty-two year old wasn't the person I was at... I could say… a little past a quarter of a century. I liked the age I am now better.

I'd dated a reasonable bit since college, but nothing resembled anything like a long-lasting relationship. Right now, I experienced the natural consequence of having an unwanted, dating dry spell: Nundom.

Nundom wasn't self-imposed; rather, these random interludes came and went. The Funsisters and I reckoned guys in the same rowboat went into Monkdom.

Like A. Wellborn, I believed I'd improved over the years in the looks department. My pleasantly shaped face had an upturned nose. A wide, impish grin complimented by straight white teeth and smiley brown eyes. I didn't think my looks broke any mirrors, and I thought myself to be a fairly interesting conversationalist. Sometimes, I could be a little quiet.

Guys noticed when they saw how tall I stood while

wearing high heels. At an Amazing Adventureland employee reunion, a co-worker had said, "WOW! You've grown," and followed that with, "What happened to your glasses?"

Based on those remarks, I felt certain I'd improved. Did I relay any of this information to A. Wellborn?

Not me. No way.

Besides, Mom had lectured, "You shouldn't talk about yourself."

"I can't believe you haven't been snatched up," he said. "You look fantastic, even better than you did in high school." At his gaffe, he shaped his nose and mouth into the classic *uh-oh*. "I didn't mean, uh, you know, you might have been ugly in high school. Never thought you were—"

"Thanks," I interrupted. I knew what he meant, and my whole being felt flamey.

Not acquainted with anyone employed as a police officer, I had to know more. With undisguised interest, I leaned closer. "Is being a policeman dangerous?"

"Yes." A somber glint tinted his eyes. The crinkles disappeared. "But I've been lucky—so far. No weirdoes have shot at me. I know other cops who have been though."

I tucked in my lower lip before saying a small, "Oh?"

"It's part of the job, and we know it going in. Mom isn't happy, but accepts this is what I want."

I wished my mom was as understanding as his. "You don't miss accounting?"

"Not really, certainly not on a day-to-day basis. I file tax returns for a few friends and keep books for Daisy's Dress Shoppe."

"Small world. I know the owner. Her daughter went to school with us."

"Yea," he chuckled. "Kristi hits on me every month when I go to the store."

"Really? How"—I scrunched my nose—"awful."

"Yep. She's loud, really loud. A huge turn-off."

"Poor thing. But why the need for a change?"

He shrugged. "I wanted to do what interested me. I can always go back to accounting later."

Mom had said something similar to me the other day. "It's never too late to take up accounting." She presented me with a course catalog and outlined a plan to help pay for more schooling.

Not in this lifetime.

We finished our pizza in silence. Call me a pig because I devoured four slices. Afterwards, like long-time companions, A. Wellborn and I cleared the trash, collected the dishes, and tided the kitchen. When finished, I said, "We could watch a movie, maybe *Strictly Ballroom*?" I could quote all the lines and sing the songs, although it wasn't exactly a guy picture.

"I should go."

Rats. Sure would be nice if he could stay longer. "Something else? Unfortunately, I mostly have what you he-men call chick flicks like *Pride and Prejudice*."

With laced fingers, he stretched out his arms in front. "Some other time. I want to think about the missing part issue."

Darn. Maybe if I'd suggested *Die Hard* or *Terminator* or *The Great Escape*, he would have stayed. I accompanied him to the door.

Before turning the doorknob, he stopped and pivoted my way, tilting his head. "Would you like to do this again?"

"Again? Which part?" I asked with a teasing voice. "Writing me a citation? Stealing of the bumper? I didn't like those parts. I like eating pizza best."

"Eating. The bumper's already stolen, and I don't think you want another citation."

I stared into his eyes; the liquid essence mesmerized me—*Mesmerized?* I blinked and shook my head. "No. I wouldn't want another citation, but I would like pizza." I meant it, too. He was interesting and fun. He may have always been fun to be around, but I was too shy to notice back then.

"Or maybe a movie," he said.

I smiled. "Or maybe a movie. Thanks for dinner and for helping with the table and stuff."

"You're welcome." His fingers touched the strands of my hair near my temple and followed the length to my chin. "I like your haircut."

"Thanks." Waves of discomfort rippled over my body. Desperately, the need to fan my flushed face hit me. Pleased with his touch, I tried to maintain my cool, a certain j'ne sais quoi. "And thanks for trying with the bumper and taillights. You might get into heaven for being so nice."

He snorted. "I could use the extra boost."

I seriously doubt A. Wellborn required additional help. His mom thought him a saint, and my mom thought him the ultimate in perfection.

After exchanging polite good nights and closing the door behind him, I jumped up and down in delight. My toe caught on the carpet, causing me to trip and I collapsed against the wall. No wonder I hadn't been a cheerleader.

My hand crept to my hair, to the place he'd touched at my temple. A. Wellborn, a great looking, nice and thoughtful guy, wanted to eat pizza with me! And most important of all—again! *Wow.*

I fingered my sore ankle which undoubtedly would bruise and swell with a knot the size of a small grapefruit. A rap on the door caused me to jump. I peered through the peep box and set eyes on A. Wellborn. Holding my breath, I opened the door.

"Are you all right?" he asked. "I heard something. I was worried you might have fallen."

He really is nice. However, embarrassment never ends. I improvised, "I'm fine. Stupid me stumbled on the carpet. But thanks for checking."

"Anytime." He turned and walked away. "See ya."

Anytime. Oh, yeah.

Chapter Five

I was right.

My new job at Buy Rite Automobile Insurance Company was beyond boring.

Two days later, I wanted to pull my hair out because of the tedium.

But boring paid the bills.

Thank goodness, I wasn't a spendthrift. I would rather use my pro-shopper skills to buy clothing, or anything for that matter, as a bargain. Mom had taught her girls how to get the best value with limited funds. Now, with an experienced eye on the bottom line, I searched for highly coveted items at low-low prices.

When I'd worked at Tuckers, my salary had seemed adequate to cover the necessities of life, including enough for the required chocolate and a bit in savings. I'd taken full advantage of the employee discount, and if a highly desirable item could be found on clearance, more the bonus.

I didn't have much cash saved. However, I had salted away a fifty here and a fifty there for those really big emergencies like car repairs. Just not wads. I'd refrained from spending my sparse savings and working as a temporary would replenish the coffers.

In some respects, the Buy Rite position shared similarities to the assistant buyer's job. I clothed myself in proper business-like attire of trendy suits and blouses in fine fabrics, coordinated with handbags and matching heels. For Buy Rite, I traveled to the copier, to the file drawers, computer, and water cooler. I employed a professional demeanor while answering the phone. Each message, mostly a question or complaint, received courteous personal attention.

The people who worked at Buy Rite were, at first glance, nice folks who appeared not to have any higher aspirations than a job. At best, they seemed eccentric.

Opal Brown, a single, short and chubby, peroxide-dyed blonde, was around fifty, I guesstimated. She habitually flung her page boy-styled hair away from her face. Her plump thighs rubbed a *swish, swish* sound when she walked. Around her neck hung thick tortoiseshell bifocals fastened on a handmade beaded chain. Opal tended to examine me over the top rim of her glasses when I asked her questions.

Even thinking about her caused my eyes to roll. She was smart, simply not up-to-date. Her clothing of choice was impenetrable, wash-and-wear, double-knit pantsuits. I wouldn't touch the dreadful stuff, not even with a ten-foot pole. And hot! Hot enough to trigger menopausal flashes, which were possible considering her age.

She shot interesting comments my way about the care of my outfits, implying I spent too much on them and should consider polyester stuff like hers. "Is your blouse silk? And your skirt is cute, but I bet you have it dry cleaned, and dry cleaning is so expensive."

Truly, I believed she was jealous.

Exceedingly dedicated to her job and our boss, Lester, she called herself his Executive Assistant over the passé term of secretary. Her fingers flew in incredible proficiency across the computer keyboard. Her work appeared faultless. All the files aligned just so. All the labels on the files aligned just so. And the file drawers were aligned just so. And she spoke with the kind of condescending "*I know everything and you know nothing*" intonation. However, she did make herself exceedingly available when training me.

Too bad her niceness didn't last.

Over thirty years ago, Lester Johnson had established his career in Sommerville when he opened this branch of Buy Rite Automobile Insurance Company. According to Opal, his peers consulted him for his expertise in claims management and often recognized his contributions to the insurance industry. Numerous plaques covered his office wall, a testimony to the fact.

Dressed in a suit and tie, Lester looked like Jabba the Hutt, a bad guy in a *Star Wars* movie. He stood as tall as he was wide, wrinkly, bald, and kinda oily like an unsavory cartoon character. He wore Western suits to work, but threw off the coat, usually a unique variation on tan, the minute he hit the doors, then released the top collar button behind the loosely knotted tie. Only he chain-smoked those funny cigarillos which smelled unbelievably nasty, staining his fingers and teeth a putrid brown.

Typical of his generation, Lester stated he "wasn't into the computer age," even though the latest and greatest desktop sat on his desk. He preferred work to be executed in a "reliable" way with paperwork and files.

From the get-go, I realized Lester hired me because he liked the idea of having a decent-looking woman in the workplace. My predecessor, June Short, had looked to be a tall, bony gal. Her wiry, black hair, streaked with gray-and-white frizzy strands, curled into its own thing. I'd noticed this when examining the photo of her holding an adorable looking pet Lhasa Apso, the frame inscribed with "Mike."

At Opal's request on my first day at Buy Rite, I'd packed June's possessions in a banker's box for someone, presumably a family member, to pick up. Tears had overtaken her voice when she'd said, "I couldn't bear to do it."

I, too, had been filled with sadness as I stowed away June's belongings.

According to Opal, June had picked up the slack from the other two with great efficiency. "She did all the claims data entry in record time."

I'd concluded from Opal's insinuation I didn't nor wouldn't ever be June's equal.

The automobile claims used a software program especially created for data entry. The relevant information was entered on a preset form, sorta like fill-in-the-blanks. For example:

#500010. Stephen Schwartz, date, address, phone number, 1998 Honda Accura crunched on June 1 at the intersection of Ralph and Jupiter Roads by sliding on wet pavement and hitting pole.

#500011. Pamela Morris, date, address, phone number, 2002 Jeep Cherokee, stolen right door panel while parked in her employer's parking garage.

A Buy Rite claims adjuster received the details via email. He held the information on hand and after inspecting the vehicle, wrote the repair estimate for Buy Rite's customer. After the adjusters entered their findings, our computer received a file which automatically generated a copy. More mumbo jumbo was entered in the program for the insurance company files, but basically, that was all. Only oodles and oodles of these things were received by email, fax, or snail mail every single day.

The work seemed to be a chore to keep up with, but someone had to, which was me. Using my outstanding alphabetizing skills, I organized the copy, the estimate, and a photocopy of the claim check in the respective customer files. All of this could be stored solely on the computer. The hands-on action was the time-consuming and outdated portion of the temp job Lester required.

On occasion, I photocopied or printed off pertinent documents for someone who lost stuff or to fill other requests which arose. Precisely at noon, I covered the phones for Opal who went to lunch always, everyday, precisely at noon.

Being precisely on time was another of Opal's attributes.

Lester didn't like voice mail. "It's insensitive," he'd said on more than one occasion. He wanted Buy Rite's customers to speak with a real, live person, what he called "Customer Service."

A real live Hattie answered the phones, which I didn't mind as this task broke the daily monotony. I conversed with other people, mostly customers, and wrote messages. Sometimes, I had nice chats, acquiring off-the-cuff information. I knew Ms. Morris and her husband were adopting a baby girl from China, and Mr. Schwartz, a Nordstrom's shoe salesman, alerted me to an upcoming sale too good to pass up.

What a job. Nordstrom had the best shoe department—like Disneyland for shoes.

After Opal returned from lunch, I grabbed my handbag, making a quick exit for my date with high school girlfriend, Kella. Because New Yorkers say "r" on the end of words ending in "a," my friends—aka The Funsisters cause we act like sisters and have fun—and I call her Kellar which rhymes with stellar. She was also known as Killer, fearless in exterminating humongous roaches. She was slender, medium height, and her ash blonde hair had been razored short. Her sea green eyes glittered. We'd worked together at Tuckers before graduating from college. Intelligent and highly organized, she moved from accounting to the new field of financial planning, already managing our group's small investments. Another accounting whiz-kid.

Kellar and I hooked up at our favorite Mexican restaurant, Muy Bueno, which means "very good" in Spanish.

"You could eat at other Mexican restaurants in Sommerville," our friends often reminded us.

"Why bother?" I asked. Having speedy service every single time, Muy Bueno was consistently first-class. The hot sauce and thin, crispy chips were to die for. The king-sized frozen margarita was the specialty drink. However, I couldn't drink a whole one because too much margarita caused me to act silly.

We sat at our usual table to play catch-up. After setting her handbag on the floor by her chair, she asked, "So, what's new?"

I shared the shoe sale morsel, and we discussed our upcoming book club meeting. She asked about my temporary job at Buy Rite, and I gave her the lowdown on Lester and Opal. We didn't spend much time discussing my co-workers because I remembered something she would find more riveting. "I haven't told you about A. Wellborn and the stolen car parts."

"A. Wellborn, A. Wellborn..." she mused, her eyebrows drawing into a V. "Do you mean Sarah Anne's brother, Allan?"

I nodded, and we dunked the fresh-from-the-warmer chips into the zesty picante sauce.

"That guy?"

"Yes, that guy, the same geek from high school whose sister is Sarah Anne. But he's not geeky now, he's migh-tee fine. I didn't recognize him at first, which could have been because he wore sunglasses, but more likely, because I haven't seen him in years. His body looks buff. His legs are long, a nice behind, beautiful dark eyes and hair, and a great smile."

"I'm impressed with your report. Have you checked him for sexy neck?"

Some girls were partial to butts, biceps, or long legs. I found the back of men's necks and the part right below the ear to be particularly scrumptious. The Funsisters often kidded me about my fascination. After a fresh haircut, the skin was smooth and hair free, especially smoochable.

"Hattie," Kellar called me back from daydreaming.

"Sorry." I sipped my soda, sending thoughts of good-looking men down the sink. "Maybe I'll get a chance later."

She waved her hands, causing the charms on her bracelet to clink-clink. "I have a question. Why do you call him A. Wellborn? It sounds funny."

"I don't know. Maybe 'cause his name tag said A.

Wellborn. Saying his first name seems too..." I shrugged, "intimate."

"Chicken," she said.

I stuck out my tongue.

"I'm guessing it's 'cause you like him."

My grin seemed best described as elusive.

We munched on our second basket of the highly coveted chips. "Back to the original conversation... So, he's the same Allan Wellborn? What does he do?"

For a minute, I hesitated, mostly because I felt embarrassed to say I'd received a traffic citation from a cop I knew. On the other hand, she was best friend Kellar, and I should never be embarrassed with her. She'd already heard many—really all—of my secrets. "He's a cop and gave me a citation for a taillight out." My fingers shaped the in-quote thing.

"You weren't given a warning? How mean." Kellar frowned. "Is it the end of the month?" She leaned forward. "You know, I hear the police have a quota to fill, and the pressure is on to write more citations at the end of the month. The other day, I saw a team of motorcycle cops parked on the side streets off of Boston. They were tagging motorists with radar guns and flagging them over." She took another bite. "I've always wanted to shoot someone with a radar gun."

"Me, too." Or pretend to with a hair dryer or electric drill. The idea of that kind of power seemed thrilling. "I don't know about the quota stuff. What I do know is he pulled me over with blinding, flashing lights, which everyone in Sommerville could see, which included the biggest rat fink of all eternity, Suzanne."

"Euew," Kellar said with sympathy. "She's such a big gossip. I'm surprised everyone we know didn't get a call when she spotted you."

"Me, too, especially one from my mom. I would never hear the livin' end. And was I thoroughly embarrassed when Rat Fink honked as she flew by? Thank goodness, I'm not pulled over every day, even if by a cute cop."

"You'll get over it. Eventually."

Kellar was right. Time did heal all wounds. Eventually.

The waitperson served our meal. I ordered the number four—two cheese tacos and one crispy, puffed beef taco.

Kellar ordered the number six—a chicken and spinach quesadilla. She passed the fresh basket of chips.

I piled some on my plate. "The good news is he didn't write me a citation for the stolen bumper and taillights."

Her eyes widened, and she nearly choked on a bite. "Did you say your bumper and taillights were-were stolen?"

"Yep. Nearest we can figure, the bumper and taillights were lifted on Tuesday night while parked in my apartment lot. I remembered seeing all the parts when Dad and I changed the oil last Sunday." I broke my taco over the cheese tacos for my own version of a taco salad. "You remember the huge splatter of bugs smashed on the windshield from our last road trip?"

"Do I? Your car looked like you'd taken out every one between here and Canton."

"After I cleaned off the mess, which took a while because the dried bug stuff had to be scraped away, I remembered the taillights and bumper were on the Jeep then." One bite of taco filled my hungry soul.

"What does Allan Wellborn think about the stolen parts?"

"He asked all kinds of questions. Oh, here's another thing. When I called to report the theft, the lady who answered called him Detective Wellborn, not Officer Wellborn. Why would she do that?"

"Which is he…Detective? Or Officer?"

"Detective."

"Could he have been undercover, investigating stolen parts? Articles have been written in *The Sommerville Express*."

"I haven't read the paper in weeks. All I know is he said officer and she said detective. The other night, he told me he'd made detective last year."

"All this officer-slash-detective stuff confuses my brain." She signaled a waiter and requested a second margarita.

Obviously, she held her liquor better than I.

Picking up her fork, she toyed with her guacamole. "You called your insurance company?"

Frustrated, I pitched my napkin on the table. "Hello? I'm not an incapable child. The police took a report, and the insurance company gave me the same ol' line—the check is in the mail."

"Understandably, a busy day."

"Not a red letter A+ one, but rather a red letter, never-forget-me kind."

"I've had those."

I forked another bite of my concoction. "He came by with pizza."

"I have high hopes for a man who cooks his own food. Maybe, someday, I might meet the same type." A dreamy look possessed Kellar's eyes. The waiter deposited her drink in front of her, and his stepping away roused her back to life. "So, he just dropped by with a pizza?"

"Sorta." And I explained about the recovery and loss of the bumper, the loss of the pizza, and the ordering of the replacement pizza.

"A man who brings food is worth hanging on to. Remember the Funsister's rules about food and men." She sipped her drink. "Is he seeing someone?"

"I don't know. I tried asking about his love life, and he turned the tables on me."

"Not great lately," she said, pointing her fork at me. "Nundom."

Astonished at her frankness, I reclined in my chair. "Hey! I thought you were my friend."

"It's the truth."

"Anyway, the good news is he asked if we could do pizza again."

"That's not good news; that's excellent news. Surely, no one else is in his life if he asked you."

My girly chuckle warmed my face. "Me thinketh you exaggerateth."

Her green eyes twinkled. "What else does he cook?"

"Possibly burgers or Chinese?" I said this in jest, implying he only knew how to order takeout. Kellar and I took a break in our conversation to eat.

Parts of me are overwhelmingly shy. Mom said she never understood how I couldn't go in the grocery store to buy bread or milk.

Like other teenagers, we didn't confide our innermost feelings with our parents. Dad didn't tell his daughters anything about guy behavior, and Mom had barely mentioned the facts-of-life. My sisters and I had discussed our feelings while lying in bed late at night, massaging our legs aching with growing pains.

As an adult, I did better conversing with the Funsisters regarding personal situations. However, I was reluctant to admit anything about wanting to see A. Wellborn again. I didn't want to sabotage a possible…something.

"You know you're you going to see him again."

I blinked. Kellar wasn't shy, and if she really wanted to know the truth, she cut to the chase. "Sure, why not?" I left out the jumping up and down and tripping on the carpet. "Maybe he'll bring something to eat, anything, as long as I don't have to cook."

"What a relief! Nundom might be over."

Chapter Six

Like a babysitter faced with the horrible task to change a poopy diaper, I dreaded what I had to do.

I decided to take a stand and fight the citation in court. After all, the parts were obviously stolen; therefore, I technically didn't have a taillight out. Yet, A. Wellborn's theory involved having no taillight meant it was non-operational. Tricky, but I wanted the matter resolved...by someone with authority...and in my favor.

As a consequence of my decision, I had to request time-off from work on the following day. My job at Buy Rite was a new one, and with all new jobs, new rules applied. Opal's guidelines didn't cover personal matters; so I wasn't positive how everything operated. To be safe over sorry, I had no other choice but to ask her. *Oh joy.*

I consulted the list of frequent fines referenced on the back of the citation. Paying it outright cost $190.00, a big chunk of change for a semi-employed girl. Considering my finances and the saving-me-moola scenario, I might as well try my fate in traffic court.

Funsister Maggie had explained sometimes the judge levied a smaller fine if I showed in person. She'd said, "You could get lucky."

"I'm likin' the sounds of this."

"If the officer doesn't make an appearance, it is my

understanding, in some circumstances, the citation will be dismissed."

This was indeed supreme info...if it was the case.

"'Course I don't know this for a fact as I haven't been to traffic court."

Drawing in a deep breath, I approached Opal who sat at her desk, fingers racing over her keyboard. I tried to get a handle on her mood for the day so I could determine how to work her. I sure didn't want to alienate her any further. "Opal?"

"Hmm?" she murmured and inputted one last number.

"I'm sorry to disturb, but I need to speak with you about a personal issue."

Swiveling her chair in my direction, she examined me over the top of her owl-like bifocals and asked in her special prim and proper way, "What seems to be the problem, Hattie?"

"Before I came to work here, a cop wrote me a citation for a taillight out. I need to take time off tomorrow morning to fight it in court."

"And why do you feel you need to fight the ticket as opposed to out-and-out paying the fine?"

"It's a long story."

Opal rocked her chair away from her desk and crossed her arms. All eyes focused on me. "Try me."

"First of all, the taillight couldn't have been out as it had been stolen. Secondly, I don't have the $190.00 to pay the fine."

While she pondered my predicament, she extracted her favorite letter opener, the one resembling a dagger, from her pen jar.

"Hattie, did you read the Employee Guidelines?

You haven't been employed long enough to take leave for personal matters," she said, her tone conveying her annoyance. "Why can't you reschedule for a later date?"

Obviously, she didn't want to give me a break. Weariness clouded my words. "Yes, Opal, I read the guidelines you so thoughtfully provided. I'm aware I haven't been with B.R.A. long enough to warrant time-off, but I don't want to reschedule. I want this thing settled now. If you feel inclined to dock my pay—fine. If you want me to come in earlier or stay later on another day—fine. I am not paying $190.00 for something I didn't do."

"And why do you not have savings set aside for these situations?"

Excuse me, but when was it Opal's business how I used my money? Exasperated with her opinion, I crossed my arms and contemplated the cracked popcorn ceiling, trying to find a tactful way to say my financial status wasn't her concern.

Placing my hands on her desk, I leaned closer. "I've been unemployed for several weeks. By fighting the citation, I'll be saving money. I understand how inconvenienced you'll be by my being away for a few hours. I'm sorry, but it can't be helped. I want the situation resolved right now." My index finger rapped her desk firmly, emphasizing *right now.*

Opal's letter opener beat a light staccato on her desk while she considered.

She didn't appear too offended which looked good for me. "And it isn't any business of yours, but I do have some savings set aside. If I don't have to, I won't use the money. I might have an expensive medical issue arise and need the cash in that case."

"Which is the most sensible thing to do."

She thought so hard, I could almost envision the cogs churning in her head.

Finally, she said, "Fine. I'll inform Lester of your plans. I'm sure if a problem arises, he'll take it up with you."

"Great. Thanks for your indulgence. I will make it up to you."

"Humpf." She polished the opener with her shirt tail. "Yes, you will."

****

The next morning, I drove downtown to the municipal courthouse for traffic court held in the old police station. I was especially familiar with that part of town from my days at Tuckers and knew where to park, which I did easily. I berthed the fun car and made my way to the four-story building with fancy columns which framed the doorways. The building would have been considered impressive when constructed in the twenties and could be now—if the city had renovated it.

What I wasn't knowledgeable about was exactly how to fight traffic citations and how the whole court system worked. Since I'd begun driving, I received only two other citations for exceeding the speed limit. I'd paid those fines instead of going to court because like George Washington, I couldn't tell a lie. I'd been speeding.

Dad had instilled in his daughters an insurance fear which nearly paralyzed us. He'd shaken his finger in our faces and said, "Too many citations make your insurance rates increase." Translated, this meant spending hard-earned money unnecessarily. Dad was about saving money, saying, "All a houseful of women does is spend my money."

Memory of his preaching invaded my head. "You need money for this or that..." Yadayadayada. At this point, we'd tuned him out while he tiraded a money-saving lecture. Afterwards, he'd reluctantly, but almost always, would hand over some cash.

When I'd received the other citations, I paid the amount listed on the slip, saving me time and aggravation in the long run. And with full-time employment, I had more cash in the bank to do so. But not now.

Since I wasn't sure about the exact procedure, I'd consulted everyone I knew. Unfortunately, they'd offered limited advice. None of them had fought a ticket and admitted to taking the easy road—paying online or by check.

The Funsisters had suggested I show up well prepared. Using my camera phone, I photographed my Jeep from several angles which showed the absence of taillights and the bumper and printed the pictures. I obtained a copy of my driving record and the insurance company's estimate of damage. I'd assembled this information in a manila file folder which I carried with me to court.

Multiple times, I'd reviewed my thoughts and facts regarding the day. Rehearsing should help make me feel comfortable in telling my story. Not much, but what I had was better than nothing.

For a brief, itty-bitty nanosecond, I'd considered calling A. Wellborn and asking about the process. Without a doubt, he'd attended traffic court as a patrol cop. Truthfully, I wasn't comfortable with phoning him, much less asking his advice. Just knowing A. Wellborn would be in the court room, possibly laughing at me, was embarrassing enough. Since some kind of ethics thingy had to be involved in asking the policeman who wrote the citation for inside information, I'd passed on the thought and decided to wing it on my own.

I pushed open one of the twin art deco bronze and glass doors to the courthouse and took the elevator to the second level. Following the directional plaques posted along the hallway halfway lined with banded marble, I heard the tapping of my black flats on the terrazzo speckled floor as I wound my way to the courtroom.

I detoured to a nearby restroom to inspect my appearance in the mirror in case I'd forgotten something, or I needed to go, or my skirt's hem was tucked in my undies—all things I checked when facing an unusual predicament. I wore a black tee-top and a coordinating, pinstripe skirt in a chiffon fabric. My pertinent papers were stored in a black leather tote along with my latest romance read. With no stains on the clothing and no toilet paper trailing my shoe heel, I passed *GO* and exited.

At the courtroom doors, the roly-poly bailiff requested my citation and informed me I would be the third person called before the judge. He pointed to the wooden benches inside where he informed me in a routine, but kind voice, "Take a seat and wait for your name to be called."

"Thanks." After I settled on the bench, I studied my surroundings. On my left, sitting behind a heavily carved, wooden table was a business-like city attorney who scribbled away on a yellow-ruled pad. The presiding judge sat behind a raised desk, a name plate inscribed with *Judge Thomas H. Miller* in front of him. An open-work banister with a gate defined the area between us. Hand-crafted paneling lined the walls. Two-thirds of the way up, molding crowned the paneling. A western mural from the WPA era decorated the space above.

Wise beyond years was the phrase which came to mind while studying Judge Miller. Probably in his early fifties like Mom and Dad, he was heavy in the shoulders. Thick strands of black hair crossed the top of his balding head. He wore a black robe and gold, wire-framed glasses.

The bailiff called the first person, a middle-aged woman who sat two rows ahead of me.

Judge Miller asked her to step forward. After they conferred on her complaint, he directed her to speak with the city attorney.

Her leaving meant one person down and one more preceding me.

An elderly man, sitting off to my right, did the same thing as the woman in front of him. After his consultation with the city attorney, he left.

Anticipating my name being called next, I squeezed my tote's handles and readied myself.

"Ms. Harriette Cooks." The bailiff stared at me.

I rose, and when Judge Miller motioned me forward, I pushed my way through the gate in the banister to stand in front of him.

Judge Miller eyed me over his bifocals. "Good morning, Ms. Cooks."

"Good morning, s-sir." I sputtered my words nervously.

"Ms. Cooks, I understand you have a citation for a taillight out on your Jeep."

"Yes, sir." Politeness was a helpful piece of advice given by the Funsisters who said being respectful impressed judicial officials.

"Was your taillight out?"

"Sorta, sir. The taillights weren't out, but rather stolen, as well as my bumper. Therefore, I had no taillight to be a taillight out."

Judge Miller bent his head to his chest, a sign of having heard similar stories. "I suppose you wish to present your case?"

I bobbed my head. "Yes, sir."

"You understand procedure dictates you'll have to come back after the court clerk schedules a date with the officer who wrote the ticket, who would be..." he consulted his paper, "Officer Wellborn?"

"Yes, sir."

"Do you want a jury trial?"

"No, sir, it isn't necessary."

"The court clerk will phone you with the date of your next appearance. Then I'll hear both sides of the story."

"Thank you, sir."

Judge Miller nodded his head in dismissal.

With dullness in my chest and relief flooding my limbs, I walked back through the gate and to the door leading into the hallway.

Once outside the courtroom doors, I released a deep whoosh of tension which had ratcheted inside my body. I inhaled another lungful. I did have good news— Mom would be pleased she didn't have to visit her daughter in the clinker. When I ascertained I could function normally again, I walked from the building to the parking garage to go to work.

I returned to the office where Opal commented on my story by saying, "humpf." Later in the day, on my way back from visiting the ladies' room, I took the message she passed me which noted the court clerk's call. My next appearance had been scheduled for the following week. Detective Wellborn was expected also.

Oh, goody. My eyebrows arched at this thought as my mouth curved into a smile. I would love to see him. Of course, our meeting could be embarrassing. Yet, I should be used to being self-conscious with him around. Embarrassment appeared to be our common link.

After handling another business call, the notion smacked me about having to ask Opal for more time off. *Great.*

With my chin resting on my propped arm, I determined the best way to inform Ms. Plump-and-Proper of my revised plans. I didn't want to have another semi-unpleasant confrontation. Standing, I squared my shoulders and zigzagged around the furniture to her desk. No little squatty-bodied woman would intimidate me. If I had to, I could take her out.

"Excuse me, Opal."

Without moving her head, she raised her eyes a fraction.

"I hate to interrupt."

"What's your problem now, Hattie?"

"Regarding my personal matter… As you might have guessed from the message you gave me, I have to go back to court next week, which unfortunately means I'll need additional time off."

"And why is that?" Tilting back in her desk chair, she fixed on me a glare.

A tinge of sarcasm hovered in her words. She'd sounded so superior. Not so surprising. "I decided to let the judge hear my case. Hopefully, I won't have to pay the $190.00 dollar fine."

"Of course, you did."

Opal's holier-than-thou attitude was maddening. Why should I feel terrible about doing something which seemed good for me? Life—*my life*—wasn't all about her or Buy Rite.

"So…What you're saying is you need more time off from work next week to go back to traffic court."

Mom would say being pleasant was a good virtue. I put into practice her *Be Nice and Polite* little talk, hoping to win over Opal with my dazzling smile and courtesy. "You understand exactly what I mean. On the bright side, I was gone for only ninety minutes today. I expect to be gone about the same amount of time and can easily make it up."

"I still don't understand why you won't pay the fine."

Thunk, the sound of my politeness chucked out the window. "As I told you earlier, I don't have the money. And frankly, it isn't your business how I handle my business." In response to her disapproving look, I added, "I apologize if I offended you."

"Humpf." She stood, jerking down her hot pink polyester Mumu top to cover her round belly. "I'll discuss your situation with Lester, although you've already committed yourself to your cause and will have to be let off." Her flabby thighs *swished-swished* to Lester's office where she closed the door while she consulted him.

Yeah. Round Two and I won.

I think.

Chapter Seven

What in the wild world of animals were drivers doing out there? No rain, no sleet, no snow, and yet, claims for Buy Rite continued to pile up—which meant they had to be entered into the computer, which meant more copying and more filing, which meant the tips of my fingers nearly had blisters from typing.

Summer must be the busiest month for stolen parts or stolen cars. Even Cousin Patti's sedan had been swiped and subsequently, used in a gas station hold-up, afterwards recovered all dirty and violated. When the police tracked down Cousin Patti's car, they'd left fingerprint dust all over the interior and exterior. She wouldn't touch her baby until professionals had detailed it to perfection.

I didn't like the violated part.

I entered these claims:

#500012: Caroline Smith, date, address, phone number, red 1999 Jeep Cherokee, door believed to be stolen when parked at Body Style Athletic Club.

#500013: Mike Dattar, date, address, phone number, black 2002 Ford Frontier pickup, front bumper crunched in a car crash at Boston and South Briery Road.

I felt sensitized to the "Parts Missing" section of the program as my own taillights and bumper had still not been located through A. Wellborn's friend-of-a-friend association. Wouldn't a bumper with an Amazing Adventureland sticker plastered on it be an easy find? Maybe it had been stripped off.

Since so much time had passed, my car parts were, without a doubt, a lost cause. Or maybe A. Wellborn didn't want to be involved in an "illegal"—my word, not his—activity again which was understandable. Fortunately, I hadn't been pulled over for another taillight-out citation since. I continued to wait for the insurance check covering the replacement parts, which considering the amount of time passed, now seemed to be lost in the mail.

From the data entry, I noted lots of cars, but mainly Jeeps, in Sommerville had problems similar to mine. Intrigued, I knocked on Lester's door frame and interrupted Opal and him, presumably conferring over the monthly office supply list, to inquire about the rash of stolen parts. A gray smoke cloud wafted toward me. "Hey, Opal. Hey, Lester. Can I ask a question?"

"Sure. Have a seat." Lester set aside a file I'd placed in his "IN" basket earlier. "What can I do for you, Hattie?"

"I'm doing data entry and a lot of the claims belong to Jeeps. Is it normal for one particular brand of car to be singled out?"

Lester rotated in his chair, his body twisting like he was exercising his waistline via the reducing machine from the infomercial. "Thefts of cars and car parts can go in cycles. Typically, in the summer, young delinquents are the culprits, but the pros work year round. A lot of cars are stolen, sold, and shipped to other countries, never to be found again."

I always thought if my car had been stolen, I would

never, ever want it found. The interior would be dirty with stinky trash tossed in it, not to mention, the smells and stains which came from God-knows-where and I didn't want to know the where. A destroyed car took the novelty out of owning a new vehicle. I would sell.

Lester flicked ash in his Buy Rite commemorative tray. "Car alarms are only somewhat effective. Alarms notify people when the car is broken into. When stolen parts are lifted from the body of the car, not the interior, the alarm may, or may not, be triggered. These guys are pros. They live and breathe alarm systems, sometimes acquiring the blueprints even before a new model hits the street. Very little deters them."

The safety factor we consumers believed we had with alarms wasn't reassuring after all. The thieves found a way around or weren't bothered by them. "What about the system which can shut a car down via satellite?"

"Like ConnectLink? It's effective, but not all cars have the system installed."

Pretty interesting information about car parts thefts. However, I held the everlasting desire to pound the crap out of the guy who'd vandalized mine. Preferably with an umbrella and/or pointy-toed, spiky heels.

Something seemed wrong, triggering a niggle deep inside me. Sure, other car models had been stolen; however, the preponderance of stolen cars and parts seemed to belong to Jeep vehicles. "All of these claims feel fishy," I told Lester and Opal. "Why would so many claims be Jeep products?"

Their reaction was to look at each other and shrug.

"Sport utility vehicles are *the* car right now," Lester said. "They're an exciting and affordable SUV.

More are sold, making the demand high, and when the demand is high, so are the cars and parts."

He was right about this information. Basic economics of supply and demand. Just the other day, I'd seen a special on local news station WSOM about four-door SUV's being a popular target of auto thieves. Some years, the crooks favored small foreign sedans. Other years, something else. "Could a gang be stealing parts off the cars?"

Lester and Opal's spines elongated at my question. He said, "It's possible, and considering the circumstances, probably true. Since the SUV is the hottest thing on the road, like I said, the demand is high."

My curiosity jacked up a notch. "What do we do when we suspect something is going on? What is normal procedure? Do we call the police?"

"We've had thefts happen before on a smaller scale, but it has been—oh, let's say—five years." Lester took a hit off his icky cancer stick. "Normal procedure dictates we inform Buy Rite's investigative squad for an internal examination. They consult with the local authorities." He exhaled the gross smoke in my direction.

Inhaling some of the fumes, I made a cough-cough in my fist. Ever so subtlety, I passed my hand in front of my face to clear the air. "I know a police detective. I could call him or give you his name and number. Maybe he could help."

"No!" Opal said. "That won't be necessary. Excuse me." After she blew her nose, she walked around Lester's desk to sit in the chair next to mine.

Lester and I glanced her way to see if she'd

recovered. Then he refocused on me.

"Opal's right, Hattie. Law enforcement assistance isn't needed." He shook his head and crushed the butt in the ashtray. "But thanks for the idea. I'm sure your friend has more important cases to work. You're right, though. Buy Rite's best interest should be our main concern. I'll call the internal division. Depending on what they say, we may need to bring in the police."

Sounded like a good, sensible plan.

"Hattie, if you have too many claims for data entry, let me know. I would be more than happy to pick up some slack," Opal said with her patronizing attitude.

Leaning across the arm of my chair, she moved in so close, I could feel her breath on my face. *Nasty.* Garlic and coffee were her best friends. The woman needed a breath mint, maybe more like thirty.

Opal patted my arm. "I began my career in claims and remember how difficult a new job is until the learning curve kicks in," she added smugly. "Entering data is my specialty."

What isn't her specialty? Opal's offer to divide my workload could be an answer, but I didn't want them to think I wasn't capable of completing my job. Since I owed them overtime, I could catch up.

"Thanks, Opal." I made sure my voice oozed warmth. "It's nice of you to be concerned. But for now, I have a handle on the situation."

Her finger stabbed the bridge of her glasses. "Humpf."

****

The very same afternoon, Lester called me into his office and astounded me by proposing a full-time position with Buy Rite Automobile Insurance

Company, even though I'd been processing claims data entry for such a short period of time. I was pretty sure my jaw had smacked the floor in disbelief.

"Hattie, you're a great asset to Buy Rite," Lester said.

His inference being I was more than welcome to June's job. Once again, he swiveled his chair from side-to-side, trimming his waist. He mentioned a salary which sounded highly desirable.

All my monetary worries could be dissolved with a simple *yes*. However, saying *yes* would mean saying *no* to the dream job in retail—if it ever showed.

"I appreciate the offer; however, I'd like to think about it," I said, still in shock.

"Take your time," he said with a tap of his hand, dropping ash on his paperwork. He flicked it away before a fire could start. "Take your time. It's a good idea to consider one's future. We're not in any hurry."

The Buy Rite proposal didn't put me off, and the job was easy as long as Lester didn't burn down the joint. On the other hand, the thought of working with Opal and him for forever needed...digesting. I could get cancer. I could end up wearing polyester outfits.

Standing, I said, "I'll get back to you in a day or two," and left his office.

As I passed Opal's desk, I found her peering over her glasses' rim, studying me in an almost menacing way.

"So..." she said, "Lester talked to you about the position."

Obviously, nothing escaped Opal's supersonic hearing. "He did."

"I told him you weren't ready."

Not surprising. "Oh?"

"Taking it?"

"I said him I wanted a few days to think about it."

"Humpf. It's a good job, and a girl like you should be considering all options," she said not too kindly. "Nice men come into the office, and maybe you could meet one of them. It's been known to happen."

Opal's turn of the phrase *a girl like me* sounded derogatory. So far, the only man I'd met was the UPS guy and—I'd checked—he was married.

****

Another day done and another dollar pocketed. My Jeep hummed along the road to my refuge from the insane world: Home Sweet Home.

When the signal turned red, I stopped. At the same light, a police car drew even with my auto on the passenger side. I glanced over the way folks do while waiting for the light to change. Catching my fleeting look, the policeman smiled. As he held the steering wheel with his right hand, he fashioned his fingers in an up wave.

A nice cop. Relief surged through my limbs, relaxing my bunched shoulders. Thank goodness, he didn't appear interested in giving me another ticket considering my parts hadn't been replaced because the insurance check had yet to appear. We, meaning all citizens, should make every effort to be nice to the boys in blue.

Smiling, I made an up-wave back.

Astonishingly, the policeman pointed behind him.

Weird. I glanced over my shoulder, wondering what he'd pointed to, but I didn't see anything. Could he be—*No, what a wildly stupid thought.* But I couldn't shake it. Could he be hitting on me?

I continued to smile, the light changed, and I drove on, careful not to exceed the speed limit in case he trailed me.

As I made my way merrily down the road, singing along with rock tunes from the seventies and eighties, I pulled my vehicle to a stop at the next red light. Fed up with the endless waiting, I looked around, only to find another police car next to mine.

The policeman driving made a finger-up gesture while his partner saluted from the passenger side. They pointed over their shoulders.

What the hell? Looking in my rear view mirror, I couldn't see anything. My body twisted and turned as I tried to determine what they were indicating and I hadn't seen. Nothing was noticeable, and no emergency vehicles were in sight.

Maybe they were being sociable.

Once again, I returned the smile, the light went green, and the cops drove off. Still feeling confused, I hit the accelerator with caution, and the Jeep proceeded through the intersection.

At the next light, and for the third time, another policeman gave me a finger-up wave. I wondered in exasperation if a cop tradition existed I didn't know about.

After I waved for a fourth time, I gripped the steering wheel tighter when the friendly policeman pointed over his shoulder. "This is outrageous!" I mumbled to no one in particular. My head crooked to the rear with a small hope I'd discover something, but I didn't see anything. "Why are these policemen waving and pointing?"

Are policemen stalkers? The idea sounded far-fetched, but in this day and age, who was to know? Or perhaps somebody had attached an unknown tracking device to my car which flashed *Follow Me*.

I sat at the light and reviewed the events with deeper thought. With my right hand, I did a *cops waved*. With my left, I *waved back*. Right—*cops pointed to something unidentifiable behind me*. Left—*baffled*.

Then truly, *Bing*! I flinched, grasping a gigantic, light-bulb revelation, probably the biggest, most enormous eye-opener of my entire lifetime. My hands slapped my cheeks, mimicking the "Home Alone" kid screaming. Actually, I wanted to scream.

They knew. The policemen knew about A. Wellborn and the citation. They knew about my bumper and taillights. And to make things worse, they recognized I knew they knew. I stole another glance only to find this guy rocking with laughter.

All the cops in Sommerville knew about my car and the stolen parts. And the only way they could have known was when A. Wellborn—I whacked the steering wheel—had told these guys about my taillight and bumper mishap. Whack! Whack! Undoubtedly, he'd shared my problems in the locker room.

Could I *be* any more embarrassed?

Thank God, the light changed. I stomped the gas, racing for home with an eye open for the police who seemed to materialize out of thin air.

While I pondered the fun-waving, but not-so-funny predicament, I felt my embarrassment evolve into hysterical rage. When faced with my hysterical rage, A. Wellborn should be really, really scared, maybe even terrified. Verbally armed and certainly dangerous described me best.

After I threw open the apartment door, I stalked through the living area to the kitchen. I flung my canvas handbag, and the bamboo handles clattered on the counter. I stared at First Fish who floated in lazy circles around his bowl.

I wanted to kill—*No, too easy.*

Maim—*No, I'd carry a huge guilty burden. And how would my mother explain to his mother what I had done?*

I'd-I'd—I'd figure out something.

Jenny popped out of her bedroom to investigate. "What's up, sweetie?"

She laughed and laughed after I'd told her the sordid details. She laughed so hard she clutched her ribs and doubled over. I expected more sympathy. I lived to be funny for my roommate, friends, and now, I could add cops.

"Should I make another A. Wellborn poster?" She grabbed a box of cheese crackers and tracked a hasty retreat to her room.

"Hey, no fair," I protested. Cheese crackers and milk made an excellent dinner. "I want some."

I turned my attention back to First Fish who fluttered to the bottom of his bowl at my touch. *Why is this stuff happening to me?*

Lately, nothing seemed to be working easy. Certainly, not the life I'd planned. Not the car. Not the job. Not the romance department. I did all the right things like my parents had advised me and look what came my way—a big, fat nothing. Nothing—except a stupid job at a stupid company.

Stupid.

"I am a good girl," I muttered. I contemplated overdosing on peanut M&Ms, desperately needing the restorative and curative powers they contained. Funsister Maggie had quoted a recent study which said chocolate stockpiled antioxidants. Good, because I needed preventative saving.

The doorbell rang, cutting short my pity party. I stalked to the door, accompanied by my friends of frustration and irritation. Ignoring my self-defense training by not checking thru the square door viewer, I flung the door wide and found A. Wellborn and another unsolicited visit.

Did I look surprised? *Hell yes.* In all probability, the police fraternity informed him they'd seen me, and I seemed a little out-of-sorts.

"What. Do. You. Want?" My hostile stance blocked the open doorway. I knew I didn't sound very nice, but then, I didn't feel very nice. Mom wouldn't be pleased with the yelling, trotting out a variation on her "Nice Girls Don't" little talk.

"Not the normal kind of greeting." A. Wellborn removed his sunglasses. "From the tone of your voice, I'm guessing you're a little...upset."

"'A little upset?' Yeah, you could say that. A *little* upset doesn't begin to explain how embarrassed and humiliated I feel right now, thanks to you."

His hands opened to show everything. "What did I do now? Why would you be embarrassed? Is this because I didn't call before coming over?"

I craned my neck forward and gave him the evil eye. "Aren't you funny? As if you don't know."

After thinking about this for a sec, he shook his

head with a negative. "I haven't a clue."

"Don't mess with me; you know."

"Nope." He sighed. "For the first time in my life, I'm clueless."

"I'll give you a hint. Cops."

His right eyebrow lifted in question, and once again, his head shook.

I thought I'd given him a good clue, but obviously not. So I reached into my bag of tricks and found another. I demonstrated the finger-up wave. "Several cops in police cars pulling up next to me at red lights gave me a friendly gesture."

"Not *the* finger?"

A. Wellborn really should work on his wit when dealing with irrational women. His dismal example of cop humor left me feeling unamused.

"Maybe they're friends of yours?"

His finger rubbed across the dent above his chin. "Maybe. I think I need another hint."

"They all pointed behind me."

"Pointed behind you?" He paused over this nugget for a moment. His finger did a back and forth wiper thing in my direction. "Uh oh, now things are making sense. You were driving around, and some of the guys saw your SUV with its missing bumper and taillights."

Quite agitated, I tapped my foot while I observed him using his unbelievable deduction skills. No doubt his little brain cells had worked overtime on this one. No wonder he'd made detective. No wonder he'd been promoted so quickly. "You think?"

"You've been a very busy boy." I launched into the promised hysterical rage. "You haven't been talking. You've been gossiping. Thought girls were the only ones who, for lack of a better word, gossiped. I wasn't aware cops talked about that kind of stuff. I thought men's locker room discussion centered on who, what, when, where, and how satisfying.

"Is your life *so* boring you have to chat about my problems with your band of brothers in blue? I've never been so humiliated in my whole life. Four times today, different cops pulled up next to me, waved, and pointed to the back of my car. I wondered what the hell they were doing. I was afraid they would throw me in the slammer. But duh..."

At this point, I jiggled my arms up and down like a marionette, dancing a lame imitation of *ho-ho-ho, look how stupid Allan Wellborn's friend is*. "Silly little ol' me couldn't figure this one out.

"I looked like an idiot." I fisted hands on my hips. "Then after they drove off laughing, I finally had a Thomas Edison moment. Their good buddy Allan Wellborn told them what had happened to my car and the stupid citation you wrote me."

"Look." I lowered my voice to a he-man's depth. "There's the girl Wellborn ticketed. How stupid can anyone be not to notice missing car parts?" I stabbed my finger on his chest. "They were laughing hysterically at me and my poor car. Did you think I needed an extra kick in the butt? Did you think I needed to be shamed by every policeman in town?"

He just stared.

He was probably glad I ran out of breath. In exasperation, I threw my hands in the air. "What?"

Instead, to my amazement, A. Wellborn slid a hand over his mouth to stifle his amusement.

Apparently, no sympathy would come from him,

and obviously, my hysterical rage had little effect.

Sobering somewhat, he shifted his feet a bit, then crooked his head to his right and choked back another laugh. "Sorry, Hattie. I didn't mean for you to be embarrassed. I was thoughtless and tactless. You're a little shy, and I shouldn't have said anything. I'm really, truly sorry."

"Yeah, right. Nice try." An edge of sarcasm edged my words. I continued to remain planted in the apartment doorway, arms crossed. Tap, tap went my toes.

He stood on my apartment threshold grinning.

Nice. Polite. His being sensitive wasn't easy to extract much hysterical rage on. No wonder Mom thought him perfect. I didn't quite know how to feel or what to do; so I continued to stand in the doorway, my gaze focused on the ground while I pulled my act together.

"Hattie, I'm sorry."

"If that is all," I emerged from my black hole and said in my best prim and proper voice, "I'm going to overdose on my favorite chocolate right now. They're full of..." I searched the porch ceiling for the right word, "antioxidants." Distressed with my lack of cognitive thoughts, I added, "And peanuts."

"My sister eats lots of chocolate, especially when it's..."

Now, this intrigued me, mainly because his sister was my best friend, and I knew every freakin' thing about her. "Go on. Finish. When?"

Putting his hands in his pant's front pockets, A. Wellborn rocked back on his heels and his eyes rolled heavenward.

Apparently, he needed God's help.

"When?" I asked pointedly again. "Girls bond through chocolate and chocolate stories." This was a tried-and-true fact.

"Uh." His pause was lengthy and he swiped his hand over his head. "When it's her time of the month."

Dum-dah-dum dum. Not the best response to say to a highly agitated woman. I stared at A. Wellborn. He was still unbelievable and still a geek! Despite him looking sexy in his turquoise polo shirt. The fury within me spewed forth. I gave the door a hard shove. It slammed so loudly, Jenny popped from her room for a second time. I slid the chain home.

Banging sounded on the closed door. "Dammit, Hattie, open up. I'm sorry I said the wrong thing. A-gain. Open the door and let me explain."

"On behalf of women world-wide, let me think about it—N period, O period."

"Hattie, please. A simple misunderstanding. Open the door."

My glance shifted to Jenny who lifted a questioning eyebrow. I knew her look too well. She wanted to know if I needed her help and would I ever invite A. Wellborn in. I shook a negative and thumbed my chest. Her damage control wasn't required. A big girl like me could handle him perfectly fine on my own. Thank you very much.

Jenny went back to her bedroom doorway, just in case I yelled for help.

Hell, she was watching and waiting because this scene was better scripted than the television program blasting from her room. By letting A. Wellborn stand on my doorstep and apologize for an hour, he'd learn a hard lesson in dealing with women, especially enraged ones. And remembering his sister, hormonal ones, too. "No way."

Leaning my back against the door, I curled my fingers inward. I examined the nails on my right hand. *Oh my. That fingernail could use a touchup.*

"Please."

I bet he thought I didn't recognize this kind of tactic. I checked the nails on the left hand and flicked a hangnail on the little finger. I'd treat myself to a full-blown manicure just as soon as he left.

I glanced down the hallway to Jenny. Her dark eyes narrowed to slits. I gave my shoulders an inquiring up-shrug, and she nodded.

Oh, all right. She'd better not be feeling empathetic toward him. I blew out a *whew*, as I opened the door a bit, looking sideways through the little slit. My hand flapped a shoo-shoo motion. "Allan, I've had enough for one day. Go away."

His face relaxed in relief. "Hattie, let me make it up to you. I want to take you to dinner."

Darn him, he'd done it again, causing Funsisters' Rules One and Two about dinner offers to roll into operation since I was still sorta unemployed. And hungry.

"Well..." I said, which, hopefully, would cause him to sweat more while considering his suggestion.

"This sounds promising. Come on. Say yes. It'll be fun."

Fun—*huh.* I tapped a finger against my jaw. This girl power stuff was great stuff. Little did A. Wellborn know, I could easily have him stringing along for another ten minutes. "I'm thinkin'."

Oh, what the hell. I could file my nails later. I unfastened the chain and opened the door slit wider. "No cops?"

"No cops."

"No weird stuff?"

"No weird stuff."

"Scout's honor?"

His right three fingers formed the Boy Scout salute. "Scout's honor."

I giggled, feeling audacious. "I get to pick the restaurant?"

"Yes, yes, yes." A. Wellborn's impatience tinged his words. "Your choice."

"Okay. I'm picking and you're buying." I opened the front door all the way. And the lesson I learned was by becoming angry more frequently, I'd get my way more often.

Grabbing my tote, I winked at Jenny and closed the door, rattling the pictures on the wall. Pretend rage could cause a girl to do interesting things.

A subdued A. Wellborn trailed me down the sidewalk, mumbling mostly to himself, "But don't think you can manipulate me like this again."

I loved when men groveled.

Chapter Eight

Dinner went better than I'd expected.

Since I'd demanded to select the restaurant, I chose one in an old part of town, which with Somerville's tax dollars at work had revived. However, the real reason I picked this restaurant was because of my two favorite items on the menu—a grilled chicken sandwich and queso with chips.

Familiar rock and roll songs from the primetime of the sixties and seventies played in the background. After we settled in the pew-like benches at the tile-covered table, A. Wellborn passed me a laminated menu and a beer coaster. The server brought our requested drinks.

Due to a lack of chocolate, I main-lined my soda in one gulp. The server went to fetch a refill while A. Wellborn decided if he could converse and still retain body parts. With amusement, I observed him do a mental checkup. Arms, legs, hands, and chest all survived the—I would now admit to myself, but not him—highly illogical woman whom he'd encountered earlier.

Hey, it was justifiable.

I gave him a cautious smile. "Thanks for bringing me here. It's my favorite."

"Like you gave me a choice." He sounded sarcastic, but his smile softened the tone.

The server placed a plastic basket in front of me and gave A. Wellborn his double burger.

This restaurant made the best chicken sandwich. Before taking the first bite, I inhaled the sweet combo of soy and pineapple. The tang of onion. The charcoal from the grill. I bit into it and chewed deliberately. *Lordy.* "Mmm." As I experienced another orgasmic moment, I closed my eyes. Good thing Mom wasn't here to deliver the "No Talking While Eating" little talk, another something perfect ladies didn't do.

"Any news on your stolen car parts?" A. Wellborn asked.

This must be his lame attempt at tentatively testing the conversation waters. I shook my head and took another bite.

"Did you get your insurance check?"

"No." I patted my mouth with the paper napkin and shook my head, sending my hair to brush my shoulders. "No car parts and no check. Have you heard anything?"

"Sorry, nothing from the friend-of-the-friend. I'm thinking the bumper is officially gone this time."

"Me, too." Since A. Wellborn was buying dinner, I should be nice. Soda could be considered a wonder drug for hysterical rage, right up there with peanut M&Ms. I snagged one of his cheese fries coated with bits of crispy bacon.

His hand clamped on my wrist. He fastened on me a quizzical, raised eyebrow look. "We can order you some."

I shook him off. "You have plenty to share." My mouth curled into a devilish grin, traced with a *challenge me* expression. His retreating hand showed he'd caved. I asked, "Are you still writing citations?"

"No, I did the favor for the one day. I'm working cases again."

"Oh?" I took a drink. "What kind?"

"A while back, the chief of detectives handed me a high-profile one."

Interesting. "Can you talk about it?"

"A little. It involves the murder of an older woman."

"Oh my. What is this town coming to? Who would have thought we'd have murder in Sommerville?"

"I know. It's usually pretty quiet here. Only taillight out problems."

"Very funny."

A. Wellborn dragged his cheese fry through the ranch dip. "A single woman who worked at an insurance agency was found murdered in her apartment about three months ago."

While he talked, I mentally reviewed the case's details. Something jangled in my head. "How...weird. I've been temping at an insurance agency. An older, single, female employee died three months ago."

He stopped mid-bite and fixed on me a hard, intent look, one almost intimidating. He swiped his mouth with his napkin before asking, "That is weird. Are you, by chance, working at Buy Rite Automobile Insurance?"

I set down my sandwich and stared. "I'm temporarily doing automobile claims data entry. I replaced June Short, the member of staff who passed away." I screwed my face into a puzzled, eyes-narrowed look as I asked, "How did you know?"

"I didn't." His lips flattened into a tense, grim line. "How long have you been employed with them?"

105

"I've been at Buy Rite"—I stared at the old timey photo mounted on the wall behind his head—"for a few weeks." I refocused on his face. "What's up with the twenty questions?"

"First, tell me about your job."

I explained I worked with automobile insurance claims which had been caused by wrecks, and auto or parts thefts. How my boss was Lester and his assistant was Opal, and how Opal's hose *swished-swished* when she walked.

Confused, tiny wrinkles framed the corners of his eyes. "*Swish-swish*?"

"It's a special sound." I brushed my palms briskly against each other. "You know, when large thighs rub together."

"Oh. Learn something new every day. How much longer will you work at B.R.A.?"

"B.R.A.—that's hilarious. I work at B.R.A." I returned my sandwich to its basket. "I don't know. If I work, I can pay bills. If I work, it's harder to find time to search for the job I really want—a bonafide Catch-22. I just don't know." Halfheartedly, I admitted, "Lester offered me a permanent position."

Hand poised at his mouth, ready for the last bite of burger, A. Wellborn paused. "So soon? Are you taking it?"

"No... Yes... Maybe." I flung my hands skyward. "I don't know."

"You sound as if it's not-so great."

"It isn't, which is why I don't want to stay. Although the salary is all right and would solve my financial worries, claims data entry isn't my job career of choice. And I wouldn't want to work with Lester and

Opal for years on end."

"That terrible?"

"That terrible. The minute I walk in the office, I'm positive my IQ has been lowered by fifty points. And I can only take so much of Opal's swishing and his cigarette addiction." I chuckled, then sobered. "I'm not desperate, not yet anyway."

"What do you really want to do?"

"You won't tell?"

His face took on a serious expression as his finger swiped across his chest in a familiar manner. "Cross my heart and hope to die."

"And…"

"Stick a needle in my eye."

"I've never told anyone this"—I leaned closer—"I'd love to open my own shop. But need to save a bit before I could try. Show the bank I have some dough to put down. That I'm a reliable risk..."

"I'd help you. You would be good."

Wow. I lengthened my back and looked at him in a new light. I had no idea he thought that highly of me. "You think so?"

He nodded.

"Thanks. Means a lot to me." I scooped the last bit of queso on a chip. Covertly, I watched him for a moment while he chomped down a cheese-loaded fry. Nice and polite.

He finished off the soda. "You're a hard worker. You have fantastic taste. I'd back you in a minute."

A surprising glow spread through me. *Oh dear.* At that moment, I understood the warm and fuzzy feelings I'd experienced. *I like him.* I contemplated while my hands shredded the paper napkin in my lap into strips and my surging emotions. *I really like him. Where are these thoughts coming from?* Suddenly, I felt transparent, as if he could read my innermost soul-searching contemplations.

"Hattie?"

I jumped. As I collected my wits, I rubbed my finger on my temple. "Oh, sorry. I was thinking. Let's see… Where was I? Oh, yeah, today I had a chat with Lester and Opal about a possible auto theft ring."

A. Wellborn perked up. "Tell me about it." He wiped a ketchup plop from his chin.

I possessed a moment of tempting pleasure at the thought of touching my finger to his lips. I shook it off and continued, "While entering claims data in the program, I noticed many Jeeps have missing parts or are stolen. I asked Opal and Lester if something should be investigated."

"And they said..."

"They said it was possible. Lester said he would call B.R.A.'s fraud division. Maybe they'll do an investigation."

"Normal procedure." He stared at the straw he twirled through the slushy ice. "About how many claims did you say?"

"Since I began, I'd say along the lines of forty to fifty." My brow wrinkled in question. "Why?"

"Nothing. I'm just thinking."

"Casually," I shrugged one shoulder, "I mentioned knowing someone who could help Buy Rite. But Lester said he would prefer to wait until he heard from corporate headquarters."

"And your "someone" would be me?"

This boy was on the ball. He'd showed off those

brilliant detective traits again. "Well," then mortified me who couldn't meet his eyes said, "yeah."

"I'm flattered."

"You're the only cop I know."

"Let's go." He rose and picked up the check.

I waddled to the exit and snagged a peppermint from the hostess stand. I had to contain the onion breath just in case he kissed me.

Kissed?

After the short drive back to my apartment, A. Wellborn walked me to my door.

My key rotated in the lock. I turned to face him Now, knowing I had a small tendre for him, would our relationship change? Would he kiss me goodnight? Did I want him to kiss me goodnight? I swallowed before saying, "Thanks for dinner. Sorry I yelled at you earlier. I was a little...upset."

His smile revealed straight teeth and desirable lips. "A little?"

Desirable lips? I blinked. I swear to God my brain traveled the one-way track to sex.

"Sorry I embarrassed you."

I swallowed deeply. "Thanks. I think I'm probably over it. The perfect soda has curative powers."

He laughed. "So I've heard." Taking a step toward me, he leaned in like the love interest did in a romantic comedy movie. Our gazes locked.

His right hand skimmed across my left cheek and into my hair, bunching at my neck. My gaze centered solely on his eyes. Closer. Closer. *Please kiss me. Please.* Without any instructions from my brain, my lips parted. All I could think about was how his head lowered to mine. How much I wanted to kiss him. How much I wanted to feel our bodies meld.

We were barely a liplock apart. "Allan," I asked with unsteadiness in my voice, "what are you doing?"

"This." He pulled me tight and showed me.

Since I was a wholly sworn member of Nundom, I hadn't been kissed senseless in a while. I swore his was "The Kiss to End All Kisses." His mouth felt soft, tender, and moved with...intensity?

My lips responded instinctively, pressing and pulling across his. Feeling the tenderness. Taking in the wetness. Swiping lightly with his tongue. All time and space suspended. My eyelids fluttered when we parted. Unsteady, I teetered a bit. "Wow."

For a second, he grinned at my groan, then pulled me back into his arms, and started again.

My arms circled his neck. Instinctively, our bodies moved even closer, touching at the hips and chest. A slight scrape of his beard roughed my jaw. His lips moved to the left side of my neck below my ear. My head tilted for better reception. I moaned again, releasing a breathy, "OhmyGod."

Pausing, his head tilted aside. "Is that…bells?"

Bells? He's got me in his arms, and he hears bells? A soft chime caught my ear. I turned my head. *Why bells? Where?*

Thankfully, he didn't pause for long, and his mouth captured mine, squashing all thoughts to the far blue yonder.

"Wow." The only word I knew in the English language. Call me Gumby cause my bones became pliable and it wouldn't take much to manipulate me like a little rubber toy. Fortunately, Nundom didn't appear to be a permanent condition.

He continued to control my mouth and mind, pressing my body into the door frame. His hand ran down the side of my left breast to my waist.

More, my body asked for as my chest lifted. Somewhere, out there, in the far-off distance, I heard a "Guys?"

"Hey, guys."

"Guys! You have to stop!"

Strong words penetrated our senses. We stopped, his forehead resting against mine. Our bodies heaved, pushing our chests against each other, and sending incomprehensible swirls to race through me as we released small gasps through parted mouths. Who knew there was such a thing as aerobic kissing?

Slowly, our heads moved bit-by-bit toward to find Jenny, all messy in her nightie and looking a little rattled, standing behind us, waving for attention.

She pointed to the door frame. "You-are-ringing-the-doorbell."

A. Wellborn barely mumbled. "What bell?"

Like she instructed kindergarten kids, Jenny stabbed her finger on the button, the same one he'd rammed into my back when he pushed me against the doorframe. "The-door-bell. It-is-ringing. Hattie-is-leaning-on-it."

He shifted me to the left. "Oh. Sorry."

Releasing a yawn, she flapped her hand. "Continue."

My eyes were mesmerized by his dark chocolate ones as he pulled me closer. His magic manhands wrapped around my upper arms, wanting to pick up where we'd left off.

The moment broke at the *whump* of the closing

111

door. My body froze as if a pan of ice-cold dishwater had been dumped over me. Awkward sensations took control. I pushed at A. Wellborn's chest—*oooh,* it felt really firm. "Wait a minute."

His grip tightened.

"Stop." Under normal circumstances, I wouldn't want to be let go. I adored hold yous. This wasn't normal. I shoved hard. "I'm thinking you need to go right now."

"What? Go? Right now? Why?"

"You have to go right now."

A. Wellborn squeezed my upper arms for emphasis and kissed my hair along my temple. "But I don't want to go. I like what we're doing."

A tough call because, I, too, liked what we were doing. However, the myriads of thoughts surging through my head at this spot of time and place had made me self-conscious. Pushing back his arms, I broke free. "Because this isn't right. This isn't what normal people do in normal relationships. Today, I've been embarrassed by you, your buddies, and now, I've been caught in an awkward moment by my roommate. I just have to go." I groped behind me for the door knob, twisted it, and backed inside.

He reached toward me. "Hattie."

I closed the door. Mega-sensory overload caused my head to go woozy. The heat, the man, the smells, the everything. With my back resting against the closed door, I fanned my hands vigorously in front of my face.

The door knob jiggled. "Hattie. Hattie, open up," he demanded. "Dammit, Hattie. Open the door."

Too much was too much. I tipped my head from side-to-side to regain equilibrium. "No. Go away."

A. Wellborn muttered, "I can't believe I'm doing this. I was trying to be a nice guy."

I agreed with him and felt my lips fashioning a small secretive smile. Occasionally, he was a nice guy, a very nice guy.

"And she's such a hottie."

Did he say I was a hottie? *Cool.* I'd never been called a hottie and could get used to this hottie stuff. I glanced in the mirror to see what hottie Hattie looked like. Huge eyes, untidy Bridget Bardot hair, swollen lips, pink-skinned.

"Hattie."

Loud. I didn't answer.

"Hattie."

Louder.

"Hattie!"

Loudest.

"You'll get over it!"

His manattitude—what guys said when they thought they had a handle on life and women didn't—tinged his words. I slammed the security chain home, demonstrating his approach would not fly with this gal.

I examined my nails, thinking I had time to do polish them after all.

I wiggled my toes. And maybe toes, too.

Chapter Nine

Thank God for the weekend because I didn't get a wink of shut-eye last night all due to kissing. And remembering the kissing.

Over and over like a stuck DVD, my mind replayed the evening with A. Wellborn. And the kissing. Which alternated with the police laughing. And more of the kissing. And who could forget the embarrassing and awkward moments? Which were followed by even more kissing. The doorbell ringing and Jenny discovering us.

With my tossing and turning destroying my bed, I rolled to my back and stared at the white ceiling. *Oops, a cobweb in the corner*. I hadn't been kissed senseless in a long while. A. Wellborn was good; so extraordinarily tall-lean-and-mean good, he consumed my thoughts. As a result of the lack of sleep and the carousel of mind games, my body felt beaten, black and blue. I surrendered with a moan, "Oh, I can't do this."

Rubbery limbs dragged me to the bathroom where I stood a long, long time in front of the mirror, hands resting on the counter. I tried not to contemplate my predicament and more importantly, new—yet scary—feelings about him. Mom was right. A. Wellborn was perfect in every way. For me. *How had I never known?*

Reluctantly, I looked at my likeness in the mirror and jerked back. If I could summon the energy, I would have screamed. The girl reflected looked used and abused. My eyelids were swollen. My face all lined and smashed. And my hair stuck out like I'd been electrocuted.

With a rough grab, I pulled off my pink and green paisley pajamas and stepped into the shower. After adjusting the water temperature to a bearable stinging hot, I stood under the spray, numb to the pain. As a stream coursed down my nearly comatose body, the heat penetrated and relaxed my muscles. *Better.* I roused and rolled my shoulders. *Much better.*

My hand fumbled the bottle of floral-scented shampoo. I lathered my hair, relishing the sudsy foam and the therapeutic massaging of my scalp. I soaped my body with the sparkling grapefruit-scented shower gel with a foam body scrubber. With a long, slow blink, reality seeped in.

A. Wellborn.

What more could a girl hope for? Not only good-looking and well built, he was intelligent, funny, caring, and kind. He helped with my car problem, provided food, and was dependable and strong. And had an undeniable twinkle in his eyes.

There was a very good reason I had all those attraction feelings.

I wrapped myself in a lightweight, terrycloth robe and a towel for my wet hair. After grabbing a detangling comb, I went to the kitchen where I found Jenny sitting at the table, drinking her morning café au lait.

Once upon a time, Jennifer Arbuthnot and I had worked together at Tuckers. She'd been hired from a neighboring competitor to be our luggage buyer.

Because her cubicle was located near the men's division, she and I had become fast friends.

My old roommate had relocated to another city. I needed someone to share the rent. Jenny and I talked and decided to give it a go. She stood about five-four, had bright, reddish brown hair, a great grin, and acted most helpful in a crisis.

While sipping her morning brew, her gaze scanned me with a sparkle in her eyes. She flashed the great grin as she took a bite of whole grain toast smeared with sugarless strawberry jam. "Bad night, darlin'?"

I discerned from her sarcastic tone she didn't seem too concerned with my condition. Jenny was just plain curious. Staring right back, trying to determine where to begin, I asked, "When I told you all the gory details yesterday, didn't you think they were gory?"

A perfectly tweezed eyebrow arched. "Gory?"

"Yes, gory. And when you found us with the doorbell rammed up my back, didn't you think I would be embarrassed?" I dropped onto a kitchen chair and my forehead fell to rest on the table top. "Yesterday was full of horrid embarrassment. I can't begin to describe how I feel." After a small reflection, I raised my head. "Well, that's not altogether true. I do feel better after a shower."

Jenny showed nerve by laughing. "I'm so sorry you had a crappy day, hon. Frankly, it could be worse." She said this matter-of-factly as she sipped from her cup.

"Like what? Like what could be worse than all the weird-ass stuff I've been through? I can't even imagine."

"Like terminal cancer. A hurricane. A plane gone missing. Et cetera, et cetera."

Jenny had a way with words, and deep down, I knew she was right. Dying was worse. I stood and made my way to the fridge with slow awkward steps, retrieved a soda—my favorite remedy for any ailment. From the pantry, I seized a box of saltines. What I wouldn't give for a couple of Ibuprofen to magically appear.

Returning to the table, I chewed and drank and considered. *Who is in control of my destiny?* Me. Maybe I shouldn't dwell on the past, but look to the future. Nodding, I swallowed a drink and crunched on two crackers. I pulled a comb through my wet hair.

Jenny grabbed the cracker sleeve and removed one. "Honestly, Hattie, it wasn't horrible. Telling you embarrassed me."

"You have an odd way of showing it."

An enigmatic smile flashed. "I'll have some interestin' tidbits to tell at book club today."

"Over my dead body."

"Which could be arranged."

"I wasn't aware you know any hit men."

She laughed.

"Isn't anything sacred?" But I knew better. I took another drink. "Guess I'll go get the paper." Taking a deep breath, I rose carefully, testing each major joint for pain. With shuffling steps, I worked my way to the door, released the security chair, and twisted the knob.

Plop! A brown paper bag tied with a balloon tipped inside the open doorway. With a hand pressing on my aching back, I bent over and examined the bag, inscribed with "Hattie" in black marker.

"What's takin' so long? What are you doin'?" Jenny asked.

117

"Check this out."

She joined me. "A gift! Lordy, I haven't seen one of those since the passin' of dinosaurs. Who gave it to you?"

"I haven't a clue."

"Girlfriend"—she nudged me in the side—"I do believe you have a secret admirer."

My insides were shouting woohoo. "Who could it be?"

We marveled the floating Mylar flower pot filled with colorful daisies. My finger plucked the string tying the balloon to the bag, causing it to bob and weave. Rare novelties like this should be savored. "I like the balloon. It's colorful and happy."

"Why a Get Well balloon? Are you sick with somethin' I don't know about?" Her voice dropped to a concerned level. "Do you have some kind of sex disease?"

"No! I'm not sick. You have to fornicate in order to get those diseases and how would I get any if I'm in Nundom?" I nudged my toe against the bag. "It's cute."

"Maybe I should shoot a photo for posterity." She dug her cellphone out of her pocket and captured the Kodak moment. "Smile."

"Since this hasn't happened to either of us recently, I think I'll remember." I shoved her arm. "And don't go posting that picture to Facebook."

"Remember the pot of red tulips last Valentine's Day?"

As if I needed reminding. What a horrible blind date. I needed to settle a score with my friend Maggie for the huge mistake, undoubtedly one of her rejects. Despite popular belief, not every man looked good in a tuxedo. Most did, but this one hadn't. "Yeah, but we burned the note 'cause the guy was creepy."

"He really was." She tilted her head. "What are you waitin' for? If you don't hurry and open it, I will."

I picked up the sack and untied the balloon which she took from me. Then, very cautiously, I opened the bag and took a peek. *Thank God, no bombs.* Crammed inside was a one-pounder package of peanut M&Ms, my favorite chocolate. Buried underneath, I found a white note card, decorated with a festive, pink heart. I extracted the card and unfolded it with care.

"Hurry up!" she said. "Who's it from?"

"Hold your horses. I don't want any more surprises."

The card read:

Hattie, I'm sorry things were difficult for you yesterday. I would like to try pizza again. Call me. I hope the chocolate's "restorative and curative powers" will help me.

—Allan

Jenny took the note card and scanned it. "Thoughtful."

"Yep."

"Nice."

"That's what everyone says."

"Goin' to call?"

I grinned. Chocolate and a dinner invite were the ultimate combination. I'd come to the conclusion A. Wellborn was a pretty decent guy and found I'd suffered no serious—only dramatic—side effects from being with him. So what if he thought he knew what was right.

Giving another of my infamous jumps, I tripped on

the carpet as I came down. My shoulder hit the door. Remembering the last time, I checked the parking lot in case somebody might be watching and then slammed the door shut.

Ouch. The pain in my ankle was excruciating. I hobbled to the couch where I elevated my injured foot to rest on a pillow on the coffee table.

Jenny gave me a bag of frozen peas—something she unearthed in the dark recesses of our freezer—to curb the swelling. She headed for the shower.

Stuck with sitting for a while, I perused *The Sommerville Express*, the daily paper. I snapped it open to straighten the folds, and gasped an *OhmyGod!* Right on the front page was an exclusive article: Police Focus on Stolen Autos.

For obvious reasons, my attention had been grabbed.

This column detailed how the police were investigating a gang which had stolen parts off SUVs and sold them. Or they'd stolen the whole car and stripped the parts. Or they'd sold the stolen cars which were shipped to foreign countries for a specific customer.

Lester and Opal had shared this same information with me. "OhmyGod. Jenny," I called. "Come here. Quick."

Dripping wet and grasping a white bath towel round her middle, she emerged from her bedroom and shuffled closer. "What is it?"

"You have to read this article. You won't believe it." I punched my finger on the paper emphatically. "Look. Look right here."

"Oh my," she said, her hand propping the towel

turban on her head. "How very interesting."

"So it appears."

"What else does it say?"

"A gang of thieves is operating in Sommerville, stealing cars or car parts. You know what I'm thinking?"

"You're wonderin' if your beloved auto could be involved."

"Yep," I said.

"It says the police are conducting an investigation into the matter."

"Yep."

The turban fell to the floor. She tossed her wet hair which flung water droplets everywhere.

"Hey," I protested.

"Sorry, the article got me excited." She took the paper and rapidly scanned. When finished, she asked, "Hattie, did you ask Allan 'bout this?"

I crossed my arms and huffed. "I'm wondering why he didn't say anything about these parts thieves when he knows about my Jeep."

Her brow creased. "He didn't say anything?"

"Not a thing." I backpedaled my thoughts to the citation writing incident. "He did say something odd when he pulled me over."

"What?"

"He said, 'I've been waiting for someone just like you.'"

"What the hell does that mean?"

"I'm not sure. He was parked in an obscure spot, like the cops sometimes do, to zero in on speeders. Maybe he waited for someone with missing car parts to drive by so he could investigate."

"Are you sure it isn't coincidental?"

She had a valid point. "It could be, but I have a funny feeling. I think my car's somehow tied to the stolen parts ring."

"So, why didn't he say somethin' when he pulled you over?"

"I'll ask him next time I see him."

"If you get to."

I picked up her towel and passed it to her. "I closed the door a little hard. It didn't mean anything."

She slung the towel over her shoulder. "Tell that to the Marines."

"Maybe book club girls have some advice."

"Go get 'em. I have to finish getting ready." Jenny reminded me to do the same.

****

I wish I could have said *yes*, meaning *Yes! Yes! Yes!,* I'd accepted A. Wellborn's pizza offer. But I didn't. This particular Saturday had been set aside specifically for book club. However, the returned call provided an excellent opportunity to ask about my car baby, and if it could possibly involvement in his investigation, the one he hadn't talked about. Rather mysterious when I thought about it.

Off the record, we book club girls called ourselves "The Women Who Want to Use Power Tools." Did we know how to use power tools? Not really, except for Maggie who could use a hammer, and on occasion, a screwdriver, and I didn't mean the drink.

Yeah, she used that kind, too.

All of us were proficient in duct tape. Last year for Christmas, Kellar received the book *101 Uses of Duct Tape You Didn't Think Of* and a roll of the indestructible product. Trixie amazed us by crafting a handbag. I'd requested a pink clutch.

Book club was *fun* and because we cherished each other like *sisters*, we called ourselves *Funsisters*. Our group, friends from high school, college, and work, bonded over favorites like mysteries. We craved them and didn't discriminate against passionate romantic suspense or humorous crime thrillers.

Funsisters used each other as pseudo psychiatrists, hashing out numerous problems and leaving the rare secret between us. We encouraged our dreams and goals, wanting the best for our friends. On occasion, we connected on road trips to exciting places like Tulsa and Houston.

Balancing imaginary scales, I considered A. Wellborn vs. Book Club. A. Wellborn vs. Book Club. I harbored ambivalent feelings regarding yesterday, despite the excellent mind-numbing kissing. I called his cell, leaving a voice mail, which sounded a tad haughty, when he didn't answer. "Thanks for the dinner offer. However, I have Book Club today."

I didn't say anything about getting together again. Maybe my omission could be construed as playing hard to get.

Remembering my well-schooled manners, I thanked him for the chocolate and the balloon. I added, "I want to ask some questions about stolen car part thefts."

Jenny and I drove to our meeting at Trixie's house.

Exiting her car ahead of us was Maggie. She waved. "Hey." With red-gold ringlets and big blue eyes, Maggie reached the same height as me. She'd married her college sweetie and fulfilled a lifelong dream of becoming a doctor. When the Funsisters took road trips, we felt extra safe with our own personal physician. Fortunately, we were better patients than her real ones.

We waited for Kellar who had pulled in behind us. "Hi, guys."

At the door, we were met by Trixie. Her nickname, Cesspool, was a contradictory term because she was beyond sugary sweet and kind. "What took you so long?"

Inside, we found my younger sister, Tracey. While growing up, Tracey and I'd shared a room. She'd cut her flaxen hair short. Tracey acted and looked more like me. Shoes were her obsession while handbags were mine. She dressed a little on the edge while I favored well-tailored suits.

Like me, she had attended State Technological University. Only God knew from where my sister had inherited the accounting gene.

I plopped on the sofa. "Did you girls see the front page of *The Express*?"

Maggie's blue eyes widened. "I did. Your predicament came to my mind. What else do you know?"

Disappointment festered in my belly. I let my mouth deepen in a frown. "Nothing. The article said basically, the police are investigating a gang stealing parts or cars."

"That's all?"

"They interviewed Allan Wellborn, the detective in charge of the investigation. He didn't divulge much information, only to reiterate we should lock our cars, keep an eye open, and report anything suspicious to the police."

"What a big, fat no-help."

"Yep. He's good at being closed-mouthed—"

"Come and get it," Trixie interrupted.

I dragged myself behind the others as they made their way to the food. I knew one more place I could go to retrieve what I needed, straight from the horse's mouth—A. Wellborn.

He wouldn't know what hit him.

An important element at book club, other than what to read, was food. Sometimes, we planned a theme around the selection, sometimes a dessert orgy, or sometimes we brown bagged. This month's read, a mystery taking place near a beach, mandated a seafood theme. Trixie prepared pasta with chunks of shrimp and crab, Jenny fixed tuna salad, and Maggie made homemade, French bread, crusty from the oven and spread with butter.

The second important element was our ritual drink, mimosas. A mimosa, a mixture of well-chilled, bubbly champagne and freshly squeezed orange juice poured equally into wine glasses, guaranteed plenty of silliness and lots of relevant discussion. Our group required two bottles of champagne. The ritual dictated we gather into a circle and clink our glasses in salute, cheerfully raising the toast, "Woohoo!"

The third important element was a truly decadent dessert, usually chocolate. For this particular meeting, I had the honor of providing the epicurean delight. I brought the gourmet—God, I'm mortified to admit— one pounder package of peanut M&Ms, the ones A. Wellborn had gifted me.

I'd flaked out.

After such a terrible day yesterday, I had completely forgotten about dessert. Compounded with the time I'd spent with my bruised ankle propped on a pillow with the cold pea pack, I didn't have time to prepare anything anyway. My goof didn't matter as any chocolate would be received with great rejoicing from this group.

The meeting began with the mimosas, and never ones to let a perfect opportunity pass, we imbibed a healthy share. After filling our glasses for round two, we settled at the table and moved to the food orgy. We used this opportunity to intimately examine each other's pimples, scars, and war wounds, also known as our intimate love lives. After thirty minutes, we hadn't said a word about the book.

"Hattie is seein' someone." Jenny dropped a nuclear bomb.

All heads twisted in my direction. My world screeched to a stop. Way beyond dumbfounded best described how I felt. "I. AM. NOT."

"He's a cop and she knew him in high school," she said.

Heads swiveled to her and then back to me. With a little practice, the Funsisters could compete as Olympic synchronized swimmers.

"I caught them in a heavy-duty makin' out session with the door bell ringing 'cause he'd pressed Hattie against it."

Heat flooded my face. These embarrassing situations never would end. Twilight Zone seemed to be a better description of my feelings. I sighed.

"Who is it?" the Funsisters chorused.

Kella snapped her fingers. "Is it the guy who wrote

you a citation? The one in the paper?" Snap. "Who was the guy?" Snap, snap. "I know. Allan Wellborn. The one from high school?"

The Funsisters looked pleased with her memory.

"Since you haven't mentioned him lately, except for today's paper, I thought the romance was off."

More synchronized head swiveling to Kellar and back to me. Yep, their practice had paid off: eight point seven out of a possible ten.

Needless to say, all hell broke free. "I'm—I'm..."

Ignoring my protestations, Jenny and Kellar filled in the Funsisters on my exciting love life.

Love life. How funny. An interesting phenomenon occurred amongst Funsisters. We lived vicariously through each other's. Theirs seemed to be in the toilet, and today, this lucky victim took a turn under the microscope.

Jenny appeared more than happy to share the gruesome details, horrible embarrassments, and awkward moments. After all, she lay in the trenches as an avid observer, complete with camouflage clothing, binoculars, and helmet. Her flamboyant storytelling had been enhanced with colorful language and hand gestures.

Should I be jealous? Nah.

Her hands clasped to her small bosom with a melodramatic flair, reminiscent of the heroines from World War II films. She also passed along a detailed, yet spot-on, description of A. Wellborn. "He's tall, has broad shoulders, brown almost black hair, and intense dark eyes. He exudes sensuality and strong male authority."

"Aah," said the Funsisters as they nodded.

Wow, Jenny's intel came from one little glance on a dark night. She had to have borrowed night vision goggles from the Navy.

Loud, roaring laughter accompanied her vivid rendition of the doorbell ringing episode.

"What?" I raised my palms in question and cast a glance around the circle. "Hasn't that happened to you?"

They shook their heads. Obviously, klutzy episodes were confined only to me. The crown of my head leveled with the table top. Today, I required additional mimosas.

Jenny was unstoppable. She told a lively rendition of the surprise gift bag, Get Well balloon, and the subsequent sore ankle stories from this morning.

To quote Daffy Duck, "Shoot me now, or shoot me later." *Someone, please have pity and just shoot me.*

When in motion, this kind of machinery appeared unstoppable. As a recipient of similar discussions in the past, those times hadn't warranted as much consideration as this one. Or maybe we weren't drunk enough to find them interesting. Usually, the other Funsisters' love lives were far more entertaining than mine.

I wished they were today.

God, please help me.

Truth be told, I had a good reason to be reluctant to discuss A. Wellborn. Deep inside, a small, private piece of me wanted to keep him to myself. Not share anything with anyone, even my best girlfriends. I coveted the idea of a relationship with him. I just didn't want anyone else to know right now.

As a guideline, I had three dates with a guy before

the friendship terminated. Some of the partings were their idea, and some were from desperation on my part. If I'd shared A. Wellborn with anyone, well... Anything I desired—wished—hoped for would be jinxed.

Certain aspects of being with him—the thoughtful, nice, kind, and kissing parts—made me feel flushed and squirmy, but the right kind of squirmy. The stupid parts like "get over it," cops waving, doorbell ringing, et cetera weren't ideal, but eventually, forgettable. Anyway, a relationship with him was doubtful since I'd tossed him out the other night. On the other hand, the surprise gift bag could be a positive turning point.

Oh hell.

Chugging more mimosa, I raised my gaze to study the ceiling, tuning back into the conversation when the volume died.

"I like the candy touch," said Trixie with sweetness and sincerity lacing her words.

She, also, seemed to have a soft spot for chocolate.

"It's a good sign when a guy funds the chocolate bank. Men like him are hard to find. He's special to think of you in that way, Hattie." Her hand coursed the side of her body with a dramatic flair. "Besides, think of the things a body can do with chocolate." Here was how the nickname Cesspool came into play.

"Oooohhh," the Funsisters said.

"I want some action," Maggie said.

"You always want some," Kellar said.

"But I never get it."

"Everyone says Hershey's the best," Maggie said. "I like the fudge topping from the ice cream store."

"I've never done chocolate," Trixie said.

The Funsisters gave her an eyeful.

"What?" She tipped her hands upwards. "I like whipped cream. You know the kind in the can?"

Biting my lips, I sat up and paid attention. One of my favorite orgasmic foods was whipped cream.

"Whipped cream," the Funsisters chorused. Tongues dampened lips in delight while they imagined finding the delicious, white stuff in delectable places.

I listened in amazement to the chatter about dairy products. This seemed to be one of those times when I'd acquired way too much information about my friends.

"It comes in chocolate flavor, too." Trixie was full of useful whipped cream tidbits.

"I'm all wet," Maggie said.

I so didn't need to know this.

When I heard Tracey say my name, I jumped.

She asked, "Did you really throw Allan Wellborn out and tell him to go away?"

This sounded like a trick question. I nodded, but not a full-fledged one. More the head-tilted-aside-with-a-wary-look-in-my-eye one.

Vigorously, my sister shook her head at my stupidity. "You shouldn't have done that. Mom will be disappointed when Mrs. Wellborn shares this news. She has always wanted big plans for you two. They have been cooking and scheming all these years."

Interesting. This is the first I'd heard of her intentions. I cocked my head in the other direction. "Like what?"

Her stare implicated I'd arrived from another planet. "Please, Hattie. We all know you aren't a doofus. She wants you two to get married."

All moms wanted their daughters to be happily

married. It seemed mine thought Allan Wellborn was my desirable, happily-ever-after match. "Arranged marriages are out of vogue."

Trixie pointed a finger, the nail painted a rosy pink to match her toes, in my direction. "It has been six months since you've seriously dated anyone. You are in Nundom."

With the facts slapped in my face, I felt icky like I'd contracted pond scum or some scary scarring disease. I didn't want to be in Nundom; I was just having an ordinary, run-of-the-mill dry spell.

"You know how close your mom and Mrs. Wellborn are. Those old PTA connections never die," Trixie said.

Tracey nodded. "She'll see Mrs. Wellborn at the grocery store, and over bananas, they'll talk and talk. The whole story of how you yelled and slammed the door on him will eventually come out."

No, please God, no. I crossed my chest, even though I wasn't Catholic, and clasped my hands in prayer. "You can't tell Mom. Please, promise me you won't say anything." Desperation hung in my words.

"Why not?" Tracey asked with an exaggerated eye blink.

I didn't find her innocent act the least bit funny. She knew why not. But I had to make sure she was convinced my way. "You know why. I'll get a phone call from Mom, followed by her little talk on *How to Treat Men* which is based on her memories from the good ol' days. I don't need this lecture because I've had this long..." my arms stretched wide, "loonnng one numerous times. It's embedded deep in my memory." A finger pressed to my temple indicated where.

I pointed at Tracey. "And I can repeat it verbatim, even in my sleep. If you require a reminder..."

Tracey's mouth snapped shut.

I knew she could repeat Mother's lecture word-for-word as well. We'd always wished Mom had taken up a cause such as World Peace or Save the Sea Monkeys on which to sermonize. It wasn't meant to be.

We grew quiet while contemplating this fact. The other girls nodded as their moms had their own versions of a little talk and were prone to trot out theirs on occasion.

Jenny broke the silence. "Allan Wellborn will call again. He's a masochist."

Chapter Ten

Know-It-All Jenny might be right. A. Wellborn may be a masochist.

Was his being a masochist a good thing or a bad one? If he was, I did weird things, and he liked it—which sounded really creepy. Or maybe we were sorta dating which made him one.

Me thinketh my roomie was being sarcastic.

Routinely, I checked my cell phone after returning from book club and reported the masochist had left a voice mail.

"Told you so. The guy has stayin' power." She toed off her shoe. "What did he want?"

"He said 'sorry, he missed me' and 'to phone back,' leaving his number. He wants to know about book club." I plopped in the club chair and crossed my arms secretly thinking I was sorta thrilled he'd phoned.

"You know you'll phone him."

Did she always have to be right? Say I was stupid. Say I was weak. I succumbed easily and returned his call.

"Hi, Hattie."

Either he was psychic or he had recognized my number.

"Can you come over? I have something to show you. I went ahead and ordered a Canadian bacon and bacon pizza, filled with your favorite ingredient, cholesterol."

Pizza bribery had to stop. However, my appetite had died at book club with all the attention focused my way after Jenny's eye-popping opener. So, I considered his offer for a moment, and once again, rules about guys and food won. And my tummy rumbled loudly at the mere idea of my favorite pizza. I told him yes.

"Okay." Like a GPS, A. Wellborn gave me perfectly turn-by-turn directions to his place.

After I hung up, I flew to my closet to choose an appropriate outfit. I rifled through the hangers and selected a summer dress or cool pants outfit, only to toss the rejects to the bed. After much deliberation, black capris embroidered with white flowers and a white twinset, the long-sleeved sweater looped around my shoulders in a classic style, got my vote. I slipped tiny heeled red sandals on my feet, a bracelet crafted from mahjong tiles on my arm, and put the essentials in a red leather clutch. As a last touch, I spritzed the back of my neck with Joy.

I looked at the mirror, and the idea of being overdressed bothered me. I took off the bracelet. With a damp washcloth, I scrubbed off the perfume.

I drove to his apartment and tried to distract myself by tuning to Hypnosis Hour on the classical radio station. A long time ago, I found classical music soothed my mood. Worries flitted and floated away on a puff of a breeze as the peaceful tones crept into me. After the book club fiasco, I needed a major distraction. However, the music currently playing featured an organ, sounding like something sinister from a thirties horror flick. I turned off the radio and popped my back up CD, Vivaldi's "Four Seasons," in the player. I sounded just like the birds singing the chirpy parts. "Do, do, dada, dada, do do."

I was a "tweetie."

A. Wellborn lived where unattached, and on-the-prowl people resided. Longtime Sommerville residents called this part of town Swingerville. Nearby, trendy restaurants, fashionable boutiques, and night clubs catered to the demographic. Swingerville wasn't far from my favorite upscale shopping mall. Or my apartment.

Thanks to his outstanding directions, I located A. Wellborn's place easily and parked the Jeep. As I moved toward his door, an unpleasant notion crossed my mind: He could slam the door on me. And no, it wasn't funny.

I'd barely knocked when he flung the portal wide.

"Hi." A dazzling smile crossed his face. "You look amazing."

I grinned. I'd take amazing.

With a light touch on my wrist, he guided me inside. I found he looked his usual migh-tee fine, even when dressed in black cargo shorts. A ratty, yellow t-shirt silkscreened with the saying "Accountants Rule" stretched across his chest, revealing amazing pectoral definition.

I swallowed deeply. *Golly.*

Going to a guy's apartment always provided interesting insight into the male modus operand us. With a light inspection, a girl could evaluate if he was sloppy, how he cooked (microwave versus oven), what his habits and hobbies were (sports or hunting), and cultural influences like music, books, and magazines.

A. Wellborn's apartment appeared to be the same

as other guys' with great emphasis on the television. His had evolved into a huge, 3D flat screen. His media equipment had been stored on a store-bought shelving unit, instead of crammed onto a cinder block and plank shelf or tottering precariously on a microwave rolling cart.

I assessed the other areas and noticed a dark chocolate leather couch, end tables which matched a coffee table, ceramic lamps, remotes, et cetera. Most likely, his mom had assisted in picking the furniture as his stuff looked too coordinated. And my suspicions were confirmed when I found the needlepoint pillows she'd crafted laying about.

No visible stains or smells were anywhere. No underwear tossed about. The kitchen looked clean with wooden barstools pushed to the peninsula. His computer desk, placed in the dining area, looked well organized. Books and papers were piled in neat stacks. Gratefully, I didn't see his gun lying around, which led me to the relieving conclusion he had no plans to shoot me tonight.

A staircase had been positioned along the far common wall of the living area. My gaze followed the stairs' ascent which led to the bedroom loft. Which led my musings to other places. My cheeks went hot. "Nice place," I said, throwing out this original line.

"Thanks. I like it. Would you close your eyes while I get the surprise?"

A. Wellborn seemed very keen to show me something. I hoped it was nothing gross, and he would hang on to his underwear. While I considered the possible lack of undies, I experienced an unanticipated tinge of warmth, especially in my female spot, flare and surge throughout my body. In all likelihood, I could be persuaded to change my mind about the underwear.

I tick-tocked my finger. "Wait a minute."

Turning at my words, A. Wellborn halted at the bottom of the stairs. "What?"

I set my finger to my nose and let it glide over my lips to rest on my chin. "Let me get this straight. You're retrieving something from your bedroom, and you want me to close my eyes?"

"Yeah. What's the big deal?"

"The big deal is it sounds fishy."

"You make me sound like the stalker, murderer, or rapist thing again."

What was going on here? Coming here could be a big mistake. Uncomfortable with closing my eyes, for a silly moment, I pondered leaving. My right foot went tap, tap.

Oh, come on, Hattie, said Mr. Subconscious perched devilishly on my right shoulder, *you're being stupid. A. Wellborn's your best girlfriend's older brother. You've known him for forever. He wouldn't do anything to hurt you.*

Like before, he shaped his fingers into the Boy Scout salute as he gave a little laugh. "I promise. Nothing fishy's going on. Play along and close your eyes."

Oh hell.

"Please."

I shut my eyes. When he wasn't looking, I could always peek. His surprises could be way too interesting.

He said, "No peeking."

My harrumph sounded like Opal's. *Sick.* I exhaled, "No peeking."

"Promise?"

I rolled my eyes ceiling ward and did a fast cross the heart. "Promise."

He chuckled and continued upward. "I'm pretty sure you'll like it."

While I grudgingly shut my eyes and stood still, I heard the padding of brisk footsteps running the stairs to his bedroom. What did his room look like?

After a moment, I heard the thump, thump of his feet as he padded down the stairs. "Okay, open."

Cradled delicately next to his chest was a cat. A large, fluffy, gray-and-white-striped tabby. My mouth dropped in amazement because the last thing I'd expected to find in A. Wellborn's arms was a cat.

I smiled so hard, I was positive dimples I didn't have popped up. "A kitty. What a cutie pie." Moving closer to him and his new friend, I extended my hand. The cat sniffed my fingers giving me the go-ahead to pet his head and ears. Instantly, a roaring purr started. "How great. Can I hold him—her?"

"It's a him and sure." He surrendered the cat.

Cuddled upright on my shoulder, he didn't squirm or claw or do anything other cats do when they were first introduced to strangers. I stroked its ears flat and then moved to scratch under his chin. With gentle movements, I stepped to the couch and sat, releasing the furball to my lap. I ran my fingers along the cat's spine, and his back arched in response.

A. Wellborn sat beside me.

I gave him a sweet smile. "I love cats. What's his name?"

He shrugged with an uplift of his hands. "I haven't decided. I've tried a couple, but they sounded lame."

"Like what?"

"Killer, Tiger, McDonald. They don't seem to work. Have any ideas?"

McDonald? "It's definitely a him?"

"The vet said so. He had been neutered."

"I like him." The cat walked back and forth across my lap, his head bumping against my hand with each pass. I had a curiosity about the match since guys were usually into dogs. "Why did you get a cat?"

"I went to the golden arches for a burger. When I opened my car door, I saw him hunched by the wheel. He looked sad. I spoke quietly, and he came closer. I picked him up and stuffed him in the truck."

Which explained the burger store name. "You're fortunate he didn't go berserk and claw everything inside."

"He got in the floor board and just sat. Must be used to being in a car."

My gaze and mouth went tender. "You're a soft touch."

"Yeah, but don't tell any of the guys at work."

What a notion. The corners of my lips shaped into a mysterious smile. I could store this blackmail material as payment for the incident with the friendly waving cops.

"Hey, I know that look. Don't get any ideas." His finger shook in front of my nose.

The cat's ears flattened and he backed away.

"Anyway, he seems to like being held. So, I drove around the neighborhood, looking for lost pet signs, but didn't find any. After searching for a while, I decided to keep him."

Maybe I needed to wash my hands. I turned them

over and examined for weird, invisible, fatal feline germs. "Is he sick with anything?"

"Nope. The vet checked him over, under, inside out. He probably belonged to someone who had loved him and got lost."

"How sad. Think his owners will be found?"

"He didn't have a microchip." A. Wellborn scratched the kitty's ears. "I didn't find any signs posted on poles near the restaurant. It's a pretty safe bet they've given up or don't care."

Everyone knew this story. I wished my complex allowed furry pets. Cats were much better than fish at following. They could talk and have a sense of need, knowing precisely when to graze their body against a human's or sit in the middle of an unfolded newspaper for attention. They didn't have to be walked like a dog. They fed, bathed, and pottied all by themselves.

I said, "I lost my cat, Snuffer, when I was a little. I missed him for a long time. He was very affectionate and big. He bumped heads."

"Mine, too, a sheepdog. Baxter."

I stared, my jaw dropped open. For sure, I had misheard and felt stupid asking, but did so. "You named your dog...Bastard?"

A. Wellborn howled with laughter. He just about dropped down dead on the floor, laughing so hard.

Confusion swamped me. Undoubtedly, Mom had hit the nail on the head when she'd said loud rock and roll would ruin my hearing. Who would name a dog Bastard, especially one for kids?

Finally, his hysterics ended. "Not Bastard, Baxter. B-A-X-T-E-R."

"I knew I misunderstood." Trying to shake the

humiliation enveloping me, I moved on. "I don't remember your dog."

"We had him when we lived in California before we moved to Sommerville. A long time ago." He sobered and silence settled while we thought about our lost friends as the cat walked across our laps and then back again.

"So you're keeping him. Did you get a cat box and kitty litter? Food? Toys? A brush?"

"Yes, yes, yes, everything you mentioned but the brush. Cats like to be brushed?"

"Big time. They walk everywhere and rollover so you can reach their tummy. It reduces excess hair and fleas. And since his fur is long and silky, hairballs."

"Good to know. I'll get one."

"Isn't he lucky?" Lucky. *Hmmm.* Lucky just might be the perfect name. Softly, I sounded it out loud, "Lucky."

His gaze drilled into mine. "Lucky?"

"Yes, Lucky."

"Let me get this right. You want to get, uh, lucky?"

How embarrassing! How humiliating! How stupid! The horror of the double entendre. I fisted my hands to keep from burying my face. *Will these kinds of situations never end?* A. Wellborn thought I'd propositioned him. He'd completely missed my train of thought. I'd hit a big two-in-a-row jackpot of mortifying misunderstandings, winning the mother lode in Vegas.

If only I could disappear.

"Not that kind of lucky," I said in a squeaky voice. "I'm thinking the cat's name could be Lucky, as in isn't he *lucky* you found him?"

He laughed again. "Are you sure? I can arrange the other if you want."

I felt positive he felt positive he'd thought his offer magnanimous. I shook my head. We smiled.

"I knew it was almost too good to be true." A. Wellborn bumped the cat's forehead head with his. "Lucky. I think the name works for him, and it works for me. Lucky, you are pretty lucky." He scratched his new buddy's ears. "I do like the other kind, too."

It's a well-known fact, all guys more than like *that* kind of lucky.

Like the best of companions, we petted our feline friend. I glanced at A. Wellborn, flushed, and felt the shimmery, butterfly attraction in my chest return. Once, I'd read a magazine article which described how a guy treated his pets was indicative of how he treated his girlfriends. Tummy rubbing—pretty interesting.

Hunger rumbles rolled in my belly. How opportune when having a date. Mom had always said, "Stomach noises aren't very lady-like." I hadn't planned on this happening, but how did anyone stop it? Hopefully, A. Wellborn was slightly deaf or distracted.

"How about pizza? I promised your favorite."

Evidently, he read tummy sounds as well as minds. "With big bad-ass cholesterol?"

"Is there any other kind?"

I smiled and shook a no.

He handed over Lucky and went to the kitchen, pulling a flat box from the oven which he placed on the coffee table.

My favorite sacred food oozed a tantalizing aroma. I inhaled deeply, taking in the smell of garlic and bacon, almost through my skin.

Returning to the fridge, he grabbed two cans of soda, one of which he passed to me.

After releasing kitty, I cradled the cold can to my chest. "What would you have done with all the pizza if I hadn't accepted your invite?"

"Let's see… I could do breakfast, or lunch, and any left over could be for supper." He ticked off the meals on his fingers.

I laughed for all of us have had eaten pizza for breakfast at some point. Pizza smeared with sauce and bacon on top, instead of on the side, could be considered toast. Served with milk or OJ, it was the quintessential breakfast food.

The cat incident had warmed me, giving me a fresh attitude about A. Wellborn, one that filled my heart. All the embarrassing things which had occurred lately upset me. But who can stay angry for long with someone who continued to prove he was nice, thoughtful, food supplying, and now, a cat-loving hunky guy? He was immensely huggable and ultra-kissable. I began to wonder if he would kiss me into oblivion again. *Kiss me, kiss me* floated in my head. The butterflies returned to wreak havoc in my body.

Slyly, I watched A. Wellborn set a plate loaded with two pieces in front of me. A desire to explore the soft spot on his neck overcame all of my sensibilities. I placed an imaginary finger right below his ear. *Yeah, that one.*

"You're looking at me funny again."

Rats. He was too damn observant. My poker face had failed. On the other hand, being observant was a major component of his job. I tried playing nonchalant while taking a drink of soda. "I'm happy to be here."

Oops. Without a doubt, thanks to my big fat mouth, I'd fail Interrogation 101.

"I'm glad you're here, too." He wiped his mouth with a paper napkin and set another slice on his plate. "Tell me about your book club."

My *no!* pierced the room. "You don't want to know about book club."

"Sure, I do."

"No, you don't."

"I do. I want to know more about you."

Since the Funsisters confessed everything to each other, too many secrets were attached to book club. Anyway, as the discussion had revolved around him, I didn't want to share anything. Similar to the television commercial about Las Vegas: *What happened in book club, stayed in book club.* "I rather not. It's a girl thing."

"Okay, but I'd still like to hear about it."

"I'm telling you, you-don't-want-to-know." My voice grew loud to emphasize my point. "Take my word for it."

His hands went up in resignation. "Okay, okay, whatever you say." He pushed away his plate. "Looks like we've been called to court next week."

Thank God, he'd changed the subject. A blush crept up my neck to stain my cheeks. "I guess so."

"You aren't paying the citation?"

"I am not," I said with a crisp tone. My fingers crushed my napkin. "You know I didn't exactly have a taillight out."

"Ha."

"You think this is funny? Well"—I lifted one shoulder—"I don't, and I don't have $190.00 either."

"I forgot about the fine and your job situation. Well, court with you should be entertaining, I, uh, mean, interesting."

Maybe I should do the Charleston to prove how entertaining I could be. My eyes stretched into cat-like slits. "Glad to be a source of amusement."

"Can I ask you some more questions about work?" he asked.

"Fire away."

Chapter Eleven

A. Wellborn and I tidied the coffee table of the pizza crusts. A long time ago, I'd read the Aztecs followed meals with chocolate. I thought their idea superior, and regularly followed this belief myself, particularly with peanut candies, not plain. Plain tasted best when mixed with peanut.

Guys thought chocolate consumption a *girl thing.* Men went for vast bowls of ice cream. From his pantry, A. Wellborn fetched a bag of double stuff cookies.

I batted my eyes and blew a tiny sigh. Another sacred food, scoring more points in the Highly-Desirable-Traits-o-Meter.

He passed me the opened bag and a fresh paper napkin. "Are you still temping at the insurance agency, or did you decide to look for another buying job?"

I pulled three treats from the bag and returned it to him. "I hate to admit I've drifted into complacency at Buy Rite. I'm not looking for a buying job as hard as I should be nor any other retail position. The temporary job isn't difficult, just busy. Claims come in all day long, every day. Wrecked cars need repairing; stolen parts need replacing. There's filing, copying, answering phones, and other normal tasks."

"It sounds like ordinary office work. How are Lester and Opal?"

I rotated off the chocolate cookie top and took a

bite, hoping unattractive, dark goo wouldn't stain my teeth and lodge along my gums. I swiped my tongue over my front teeth before answering. "Lester can be very nice, especially when it's to his advantage."

When realizing I'd made a derogatory remark about Lester, I caught a cookie crumb with my tongue and backtracked. "Sorry. Maybe I shouldn't have said that. I've already described him physically, which by the way, hasn't changed. I might get lung cancer from all his cigarette smoking."

"Yuck."

"Opal still swishes."

A. Wellborn raised a questioning eyebrow. "Really? Maybe she should go on a diet."

"Ha. Not going to happen. She hides candy bars in her desk drawer and eats when no one is looking. Only, I see her. I guess she thinks swishing is an attribute. And she still wears bullet-proof polyester clothes. You know the kind?"

His head made a no.

"Bullet-proof polyester is a very thick, double-knit, wash-and-wear fabric, waaayy out of style. No ironing is required. It's so hot, you'd think she would dissolve." I could say other things, but I didn't want to sound like a whiner. "Opal leaves me alone, but I always feel creeped out, like she's watching what I do. It's a-a hovering feeling, one hanging over my shoulder even when she isn't in."

I twisted off another cookie top and licked the filling. "I don't know. Maybe she's waiting for me to make a mistake. She's such a perfectionist. I ask her about complicated claims, and she helps me with those. She offers to assist if I'm overloaded, but it hasn't been an issue—yet. I must be more capable than I look."

His lips twisted a fraction. "They sound spooky."

"They might be." After I popped half the cookie top in my mouth, I chewed, then swallowed. *Most excellent*. "I suppose I'm used to people like myself and my friends, and not used to people like Lester and Opal. At Tuckers, we dressed and worked differently because the clothing industry is poles apart from the insurance business, not attracting the same kind of employee.

"Lester and Opal take their jobs seriously. I'm not saying I didn't take my job seriously at the store. I did. I enjoyed the working environment at Tuckers more. It's what I'd always wanted to do. Lester and Opal have a life-and-death dedication which seems unusual, but probably typical for people passing middle age.

"Anyway, Lester has been employed by B.R.A. for thirty years. He looks old enough for retirement, although he hasn't said anything. He has a grown son who looks to have ten-plus years on me. When I saw a family picture on Lester's desk, I asked him who everyone was.

"Opal has been Lester's Executive Assistant for a long time. One day, she said something about eight years. I tuned her out. Sounded as if she has been with Buy Rite long enough for tenure. Nowadays, eight years of service with any company is quite remarkable." I paused and scratched my temple.

He cocked his head. "Something else?"

"I think I need milk."

A. Wellborn went to the kitchen where he poured two short glasses of two percent, perfect for dunking. He returned, handing me one. Most men would pass me a beer, but not this hunky one. I took a long drink.

He said, "You were trying to remember something else about Buy Rite."

"I don't know. I'm not sure." My brow furrowed while thinking about the oddities of my co-workers. "If I don't remember, it isn't important."

"Sure, it is. Tell me."

I watched him gulp deeply from his glass before replying. Was I the only person in the world who thought a man drinking milk looked sexy? Or maybe everything about him looked sexy.

Breaking a cookie in half, I said, "I thought it weird Lester and Opal took a long time hiring a replacement after my predecessor passed. The paperwork shouldn't sit around and collect. If the stuff isn't processed properly, it takes longer for a check to be produced.

"The clients inquire as to the claim's status. They get irate, and probably will take their business elsewhere if the complaints aren't fixed because in the long run, the claims business is about customer service and satisfaction. Could Opal and Lester have worked overtime to process the claims or maybe they had other temporary help—who knows? They never said, and I never asked."

"Are the customers dissatisfied?" he asked.

I waved my half treat in a negative. "Not really. We get a few complaints. I mean the stolen parts people are having trouble getting checks on time, just like me. Sometimes, the customers grumble about their settlement check, saying the amount should be more." All the talk about stolen cars made a thought in my head ding. I changed the subject. "By the way, my claim is handled through B.R.A. I accidentally found the file the other day. Nothing odd there. I asked Opal, and she said the check is in the mail."

He nodded.

"Still, Ms. Pamela Morris has waited a long time. Her car door had been stolen, and we talked about how much we love our vehicles."

"You spoke with Ms. Morris about her car?"

He sure does ask a lot of questions. "Of course. Every day I cover the phones precisely at noon when Opal goes to lunch. Ms. Morris makes her personal calls at lunchtime. We've had lengthy discussions about how long it's taking for her to get her check. Why do you ask?"

His finger ran along the rim of his glass. "What do you do when a customer hasn't received a check?"

"I told Ms. Morris I would track her check and determine if it's in the snail mail. I specifically asked Opal when she returned from lunch, showing her the message. I explained Ms. Morris really wanted to get her car repaired before she travels to China to adopt her baby girl. She'll need it fixed for when she returns."

"So, she's adopting a baby."

"Yes. She can't drive a child around in a car without a door. It has to be fixed, which makes sense."

"How many times has Ms. Morris called?"

"I would say three."

"Always at lunch?"

"Always at lunch."

"And do other people call several times?"

"Some, I never hear from again. Usually, they call one time to verify if the..."

And we said simultaneously, "Check is in the mail."

We both reached for the cookies. Being a gentleman, he let me go first. "Standard operating procedure," he said.

"Seems to be." As I lifted off another chocolate top, I gave him a curious look. "Why are you asking so many questions?"

"You make your work sound interesting."

He did his man thing, dunking his cookie in milk and munched. My dad dunked, too. Sometimes, late at night, we'd shared a glass of milk and a pile of vanilla wafers.

"Yeah, right." Quietly lost in our respective thoughts, our conversation paused. With the paper napkin, I wiped my mouth. At that moment, I remembered *The Sommerville Express* article and how agitated I got and how I needed to do some of my own probing. "I have some questions for you."

"Fire away."

"I read an interesting item in today's paper."

He stuffed his mouth and mumbled, "Oh?"

"Oh?" I mocked.

"I haven't read the paper." He drained the last third of milk. "What was so riveting?"

"The front page article about car part thieves operating in Sommerville."

"Car part thieves operating in Sommerville," he said gravely as he set down his empty glass.

"Yes, I'm curious about the police investigation."

"The police investigation?"

Sighing with annoyance, I set aside my milk glass and reached for my soda. When I realized what I held, I frowned. A Coke chaser after milk and cookies could be considered a diabetic overdose. I returned the soda to the coffee table. "Yes, the police investigation into the car parts thieves, remember? You are the lead detective."

He overlapped his arms. "Oh, yeah, that investigation. I am the lead detective."

Due to his lack of communication, I felt the innards of rising frustration. I leaned back and studied him. "You're being difficult."

Pointing a finger to his chest, he arched an eyebrow. "Me?"

Even a bird brain could figure out A. Wellborn seemed reluctant to talk about the article and didn't take my questioning seriously. But I persevered. I needed to know what he knew and for how long. And if my car was involved in his investigation. And if it was, why didn't he just say so? "Yeah, I'm curious as to why you haven't told me about an on-going investigation on stolen car parts."

His feet scuffed around. "Well, I have a very good reason."

How exasperating! I rolled my hand to move our chat along. "I can't wait to hear this. Which would be..."

"The police do not talk about on-going investigations."

I fastened a *same song, second verse* look on him. "What a convenient answer."

"It's true," he said, puffing his chest.

"Right. So are you sure you don't have anything else to tell me?"

He shook his head. "Nothing I can think of."

"Isn't it coincidental my car's parts are missing?

"Could be."

"And the police are investigating a theft ring?"

"Anything's possible."

"Were you on a stakeout, looking for vehicles with missing parts when you pulled me over?"

"Whatever gave you that idea?"

He examined me with a quirked eyebrow, like I had inside info. Clearly, I wouldn't be privy to any additional information. *Closed mouthed* cop was a lesson well taught at the police academy. I would have to uncover what I needed on my own.

Fine, for now.

As stimulating as this conversation seemed to be, the evening grew late. I yawned. Another *Something Girls do not do in Polite Society* according to Mom. At least, my hand covered my open mouth. "Time to go." I stood, collected trash, and carried it to the kitchen. "Thanks for providing dinner. Lucky is a most excellent surprise."

A. Wellborn followed with the pizza box and soda cans. "Glad you like him. Come visit us anytime." After setting his bits and pieces on either side of me on the counter, he circled his arms around my waist and pressed my back to his chest.

His body felt inviting and warm against mine. His man-heat began to seduce me, especially when his palms slid down my arms. I tilted into him. His breath bathed my ear.

"You don't have to go," he said softly. He pressed his lips to my hair right at my temple. "We could explore the lucky part."

Letting him have his way would be so easy. Too easy.

But no. I did my best to ignore his suggestion and

turned, breaking his hold. Lacing my fingers, I stretched my arms in front of me in a yoga move which forced him to step back. "I should go. It's been a long day. I didn't sleep well last night." *Oops, I didn't mean to confess another big one.* I stole a glance to see if he overheard my last remark.

"You didn't sleep well. Why?" he asked in a mischievous tone. He ran a finger from my eye level down the length of a strand of my hair.

I went still, not about to answer. With him, I'd been caught red-handed a lot. He was too damn good at detecting.

"I'm thinking you didn't sleep well because of me." He said this a little too confidently as his fingers grazed my cheek. He moved a bit closer, leaning in.

Golly. Hypnotic man-vibes radiated from him as I caught a piney, soapy scent wafting my way. Sucked into the moment, my head hit his chin, clearing the sensory overload before I'd succumb to manpower. I stepped around him. "Sorry."

Quickly, I walked to the sofa to retrieve my handbag.

He followed me to the door. As did Lucky whose bright blue collar with newly acquired vet tags clinked, clinked softly with each step.

I petted Lucky bye and gave A. Wellborn a traditional girly look, one saying *I'd never tell*. With my hand on the door knob, I said something, and immediately, had regrets about stating it, "Jenny wants to know if you're a masochist."

"A what? Why a masochist?" An expression of amazement crossed his face. "Oh, I get it."

Guess A. Wellborn wasn't a detective for nothing.

"You two are wondering why I keep coming back for more."

My lips buzzed his cheek. It seemed safer.

Chapter Twelve

I spent the remainder of my weekend in recovery. I stayed up late, captivated in reading a mystery about a murderer in the horse business. As a result, I overslept. I hung out at my apartment and caught up on normal activities like laundry and ironing. And, in case of a surprise Mom visit-slash-inspection, cleaned the bathroom.

The low-key aspect of Sunday primed me well for work on Monday. Highly energized, I settled at my desk and observed Opal as she opened the day's mail. She selected an envelope, examined the return address, and then flipped over the envelope. Her letter opener sliced with great ease through the paper. She extracted each document, stapling the envelope to the back of the letter, and set the documents in her sorted piles. The majority appeared to be intended for data entry, aka me.

Eeney, meany, miney, moe, I thought as I watched her. One for Lester. One for Opal. One for me. I will have plenty of claims to enter, files to file, copies to make. "Hey, Opal," I said, admiring the way her letter opener cut the envelopes.

"Yes, Hattie."

"Where did you get such a sharp opener? It slices thru the paper effortlessly."

"Oh." She twisted the item in question. "This ol' thing?"

She bestowed an admiring look as if the opener resembled an eighteenth century Turkish dagger. "Yeah."

"A few years ago, Lester gave these to clients as a complimentary gift for doing business with Buy Rite."

"Can I have one? All I have is this ol' thing." I showed her the one I'd found in my desk drawer. It resembled a flimsy miniature saw.

"I'm sure the one you use is perfectly serviceable." Rising, Opal gathered my mail pile and, without ceremony, dumped the correspondence in my inbox.

"Gee, thanks," I said with sarcasm.

"You're welcome," she replied sarcastically.

Picking up the first claim, I went to work.

****

A couple of days later, I consulted my phone calendar, checking my appointments for the rest of the week. For Saturday, I'd made a notation next to seven p.m. I clicked for details.

Oh, holy hell. I can't believe I forgot this party. I am in deep doo-doo. I knew better than to R.S.V.P. for two.

The parents of my boss formerly from Tuckers were throwing a big bash to announce their son's engagement. This to-do required me to wear a little black dress, and for my date—*darn, how could I be so stupid*—a suit and tie.

This event mandated an escort. I frowned, thinking *OhmyGod, what am I going to do?* Because of my current Nundom status, where would I unearth someone at the last minute? I couldn't ask Jenny as she already had a date for it, a big one. So did Kella and Maggie.

As I searched for a solution, I rubbed my forehead.

Then, like Jeannie from her bottle, *Ask Allan* popped out. My toes bounced a tap, tap. The idea wasn't awful. And the more I considered him as a solution to my dilemma, the more I liked it. Better than a good idea, it was an extraordinary one. Time for payback for the embarrassing situations, the cops, and the doorbell.

A. Wellborn. Because he owed me.

However, a big difference existed in *asking a guy for pizza* versus *asking a guy to accompany someone to an engagement party*. Men tended to become all weirdly freaked out, thinking their hallowed single status could be threatened. They had the stupid notion all girls were Hunting for Husband Material when asked to attend, for example, weddings or the company Christmas spectacular. This could be especially awkward if the guy escorted someone he didn't particularly care for.

I checked my phone's contact list and found the fortunate man's number, the one I'd saved after he'd invited me for pizza. A cop's home number could come in handy and this was one of those times. Calling on Wednesday didn't seem too early, and not too desperate time-wise to ask. If-if-if he hadn't already made plans. Cross my fingers, hoped not to die.

Shyness returned. So I rehearsed, gauging approximately how long the message would be. I punched a button before I chickened out and set the cell to my ear. Tap, tap went my foot as my anxiety mounted, hearing the rings go on and on. After a while, his voice mail picked up—*thank God*—and with relief, I exhaled. If I'd spoken with him, I would have said something stupid and embarrassment would take over—again.

After I heard his voice saying to "leave a message at the beep," I said, "Hi, Allan. It's Hattie. Oh, you probably figured it out from your caller ID. Anyway, I need a superior favor. A friend of mine is having a big—quote—to-do—unquote—on Saturday evening. Dinner and dancing. If you could pick me up at seven and wear a dark suit and tie, that would be super. Say 'Hi' to Lucky for me."

Clicking the off button, I knew I'd sounded desperate, never mind being presumptuous. *Dammit.* Oh well, too late to change anything. I sure wasn't going to act like a super-stalker girlfriend, and there was no way I could access his voice mail to erase what I'd said. Hopefully, I'd sounded like he had been forced to go and not too stupid.

I consulted Jenny for her expert opinion.

She said, "Allan's a masochist. He'll go anyway."

Her position sounded brutally honest, or she delighted in excessively teasing me.

Since the other evening, when I'd met Lucky and eaten pizza, had finished on a nice note, I figured A. Wellborn would feel compassionate. By Saturday, if I hadn't heard anything different and was about to walk out the door, I could go with the thought he wouldn't be accompanying me.

When I told Jenny, she reminded me, "You know what assume means."

I sighed. "I know, I know. Ass of u and me. It wouldn't be the first time." Yet, we always hoped it would be the last.

The worst-case scenario was him not going at all, and I could handle that. I'd attended affairs without a date before. We all had, and ultimately, survived. After all, Nundom wasn't far behind me, which didn't seem very reassuring now that I thought about it.

The real issue?

What to wear.

****

My next court appearance was scheduled for today. I reminded Opal where I'd be.

She scrunched her nose and said, "humpf," for once imparting no lectures or nasty looks. "You had better get going. You don't want to be late."

Well, well, well, what's up with her? Something went easy. Could it be she wanted me out of the office so she could review my work behind my back? I wouldn't put it past the little stinker.

I drove downtown and parked in the same parking garage in almost the same spot and walked the same path as before. I pushed open the large doors to the courthouse, and once again, I followed the signs to the elevator. A check of my watch told me I was Johnny-on-the-spot time-wise. Before entering, I gave my outfit the once-over. *Perfection.*

The roly-poly bailiff stood by the courtroom door and took my citation. As he smiled, he waved in a courteous gesture, directing me to the same wooden bench just like before.

I surveyed the courtroom, noting nothing had changed; however, I hadn't really expected anything to and found comfort in the thought. I pointed a mental finger. Judge Miller—there. The railing—there. The chair—there. And the gate in the banister—there. No one else was present, and especially and most importantly, the man of the hour, A. Wellborn. Maybe he was manning the streets again, looking for offenders.

"Ms. Harriette Cooks," the bailiff sang.

His voice caught me unaware. I rose and passed through the gate in the banister. Annoying Judge Miller wouldn't be the best idea.

"Ah, Ms. Cooks," he said, peering over his cheater readers, "back again?"

My nervous hands walked around the edge of the papers I held, crimping them. "Yes, Sir."

He consulted my paperwork. "If I remember correctly, you wish to discuss your taillight out citation."

"Yes, Sir."

At this point in the proceedings, the court clerk leaned closer to whisper in Judge Miller's ear. Something seemed to be up. After a short exchange, the Judge's attention returned to me. "Ms. Cooks?"

Something was definitely up. I could tell from his demeanor. "Yes, Sir?"

"Ms. Cooks, we have a slight problem."

Lordy. Not again. "Oh?"

"Yes, well, we'll have to reschedule your hearing until next week."

Reschedule? I frowned at this news. I'd have to deal with Opal—*Rats*. "May I ask why, Sir?"

"Detective Wellborn isn't available today. He's working on a big case and something terribly important came up. He apologizes for any inconvenience."

Big case? Apologizes? Just wait until I got my hands on him. "Oh, no," I said saccharine sweetly. "How unfortunate."

"It is. The court clerk will notify you later today of the next available date."

"Thank you, Sir."

Dismissed, I pushed through the gate, letting it close behind me. Postponement dragged out my situation and caused me to consider *things* weren't moving in a desirable direction. Confusion clouded my thoughts as I shoved opened the courtroom door and stood in the hallway, my body quaking.

What was the deal with Detective Wellborn anyway? Yeah, yeah, yeah, I hadn't heard from him. He hadn't even bothered to respond to my undeniably fantastic invitation to be my date.

My citation looked like chopped liver. He was too busy "working on his big important case," the one he hadn't discussed. So what if it involved the murder he'd told me about? My court case was—is—just as important.

Well—my heart sank—*not really*.

I wondered what Opal would say this time when I told her about round two. I crooked my mouth sideways.

I found my way back to the elevator. After stepping in the car and turning to face the closing doors, I glanced through the rapidly diminishing opening only to discover A. Wellborn standing outside the courtroom door. *Wait…* I thought he couldn't make it. I reached for the *open* elevator button, but was too late. *And why is he waving*?

I pushed the button several more times, but to no avail. The door closed firmly, and the car began its descent.

Just wait until I get my hands on him.

****

On Friday afternoon, my computer crashed. I punched various buttons, restarted, and tried all the tricks I could think of, which numbered few. Nothing happened. Data entry appeared to be wholly shut down.

"Damn machine." I sighed and, with a kick, pushed my chair away from my desk. Computers were meant to solve problems, not *be* the problem. I wound around my desk and in front of Opal's for a consult about repairing the freakin' thing. "Opal?"

She finished the last bit of her project and pulled off her glasses to better hear me. "What seems to be the problem, dear girl?"

Uncharacteristic sympathy oozed from her voice. And her *dear girl* epithet sounded like something the charming snake from the Garden of Eden would have said. I lifted one shoulder in a half-shrug. "I don't know. My computer is down. Crashed, I think. Everything just stopped."

"Maybe it needs to rest for a while."

I'd never heard of a computer needing rest before. But like the old saying goes, there's *always a first time*. "Maybe."

"Why don't you quit for the day. Start fresh on Monday," she said.

"You don't think we should call in a technician and get it debugged?"

Her head tilted while she considered. "Occasionally, we have similar problems, but they seem to work themselves out if they're shut down. Besides, you look tired."

"I am tired. Computer stuff is stressful." I shrugged. "You're the expert. I'll go with your suggestion and finish some other time."

"Do you think you can get caught up next week?"

I pondered, but shook my head. "Based on the

current activity, it'll be hard. I'd rather come in on Saturday. I'm free until my date later in the evening. This could make up for when I went to court for the citation."

Opal nodded. "When do you think you could make it in on Saturday?"

I referred to my trusty phone calendar. "Ten-ish."

She made a notation on her day-by-day calendar on the computer.

"I might as well tell you my latest news." I noted the *what now* question in her eyes. "I have to go back to court next week. I'm expecting a call from the clerk."

She flung her pen on her desk where it rolled around a bit before resting against her keyboard. "Hattie, this is outrageous. How much longer is this going to continue? If you had paid the ticket, you wouldn't have to ask for time off. It's inconvenient."

Right. Like I did this to personally hassle you. My fists went squarely to my hips. "You don't have to yell, Opal. I feel bad. I have a higher working standard than what you're thinking. I told you I don't have $190.00 to throw around, and hopefully, the judge will reduce the fine, or even better, I'd have no fine to pay. I didn't know I would have to go back and forth, back and forth to the courthouse. Who knew Detective Wellborn wouldn't show?"

A *nosy gal* expression crossed her face. "You sound as if you know the detective."

"Yeah, well, kinda, sorta," I said. "His sister's my best friend, and our mothers are long-time friends; so you could say we grew up together. I hadn't seen him in nearly four-plus years. After Detective Wellborn pulled me over and gave me the citation, we became reacquainted, and now, we're seeing each other—a little." Possibly, I divulged too much personal information.

Slowly, she shifted back in her desk chair, drilling a hard look on my face. making me uncomfortable. "Let me get this straight: You're dating the policeman who wrote you a citation?"

Opal had a way of making me uncomfortable. "Kinda. Maybe. Sorta."

"This sounds highly irregular."

"He is." Everything about A. Wellborn seemed highly irregular. Agreeing with her on something…anything sounded funny.

"Is this who you have a date with on Saturday?"

Could be, if he'd listened to his voice mail and called me, I would. "Yes..."

"Is this the same policeman you said could help us with the thefts?"

"Yes..."

"Hattie, your problem is getting in the way of our completing our work."

Another tirade. I set my hands on the edge of her desk and leaned in. "Look. I said I would finish on Saturday. I will. Take it or leave it."

"It'll have to do."

"I don't see what your problem is." Perhaps, I'd spoken a tad mean. I regrouped and in a lower register, said, "Next week, I'll tell Judge Miller if this merry-go-round continues, I'm not accommodating my supervisor. Is that good enough for you?"

"Fine. I'll go to Lester's office and secure a key." Once again, all five feet of Opal's blubber swished-swished to Lester's office, oozing her protest.

Usually, one of them arrived at work ahead of me; so I didn't need a key. I didn't know if June had had one. My finger stroked up the bridge of my nose. When I cleaned her desk, I didn't recall finding anything in her belongings. Perhaps, someone had picked it up, or it was lying around somewhere on a key ring, lost.

On occasion, Lester traveled to present claims adjustment proposals to prospective clients. When he did go, Opal stood at hand with her key. I assumed being a temp didn't entitle me to one. Not as if I would poke through their desks. I wasn't rude. If Mom had discovered I'd snooped, she would have been outraged, imparting the Three R's lecture—*Respect, Respect, Respect.*

Craning my neck, I watched my co-workers confer through the sidelight window next to Lester's door. I quit blatantly staring when Opal exited and swished-swished back. She passed me the key. "I'll see you on Monday?"

"Sure."

Her hand touched my sleeve. "Hattie, if you don't mind my asking, how long do you plan on temping with us? Did you decide to take the job?"

I had considered the work-slash-searching for work quandary regularly and understood her predicament. The truth was I didn't feel overjoyed working at B.R.A. and would rather be somewhere else. But the almighty paycheck called.

"I'll stick with Buy Rite until I'm more comfortable with my cash flow. If you feel it necessary to fill the position permanently, fine by me. My friend will place me elsewhere. I know you have to pay her weekly."

"That's right, we do pay her a little something, but so far, it isn't a problem. We're very"—Opal searched the ceiling for the right word—"pleased with your performance. Consider the job yours for now."

"Thanks. I'll see you Monday." *Un-be-lieve-able.* Turning away, my jaw slacked in shock. Opal had bestowed an off-handed compliment about my work at Buy Rite! I removed my handbag from my desk drawer and then walked to the office door, closing it behind me. *What's up with her?*

****

I woke early Saturday and took a short run. Once, I'd had a gym membership where I danced aerobics and ran on the treadmill. By canceling my membership, much-needed cash had been saved. I didn't consider myself a big runner, but I tried every now and again to counteract my chocolate consumption. I could tear through a pounder bag of chocolate-covered peanut candy bits like the Tasmanian Devil. My shoulders were burdened with guilt.

For now, foot action seemed to be the only athletic action coming my way. I dressed in baggy black shorts and a white v-neck athletic shirt, a pair of white socks, and running shoes. After a few warming stretches, consisting of lifting my knees like a drum major and side bends, I headed out. Tunes blasted through the headphones stuck in my ear.

The morning air felt refreshingly cool, the sky looked clean and clear, and combined with no traffic, I faced ideal running conditions. Avoiding the potholes and uneven sidewalk, I found my way to the neighborhood park with a quarter mile track around the perimeter.

I admired people whose running style mimicked graceful gazelles. But no matter how hard I tried, I didn't excel at running. I started with the idea of hoping to surpass a mile, reaching a little farther and farther each day. I tried everything, even Maggie's suggestion of interspersing the run with a walk.

My thoughts diverted to A. Wellborn and why I hadn't heard from him regarding tonight's date. Maybe he was playing games with me—the rat. Maybe he was working on his big case—double rat. Maybe he thought I wasn't worth it. The idea sounded depressing. My head bobbed from side-to-side and my limbs wiggled in a jiggly dance as I shed the gloomies. Whether or not he showed tonight, I would go with the flow.

Afterward the run, I took a restorative shower, rubbing a towel through my hair. Slipping on my robe, I opened my closet's louvered doors. While scrutinizing my wardrobe for little black dress options, shoes, and the perfect accessories, I considered, *which one, which one*, all the while praying for divine intervention.

Rules existed for selecting the right little black dress. I didn't invent them; they were understood by all women.

1. *The right little black dress caused jaws to drop, making a show-stopping entrance.*
2. *The right little black dress caused scandalous talk and hopeful passes.*
3. *The right little black dress was debated for weeks by envious women. And horny men.*

While detangling my hair, I reviewed my choices. Balancing the hanger of the tailored-to-fit, black linen sheath high on a finger, I flipped the dress from front to back.

Nice. This dress fitted my curves and the knee-high slit enhanced my lengthy legs. The black heels with little black bows across the toes completed the desired look.

I pulled out a new purchase, a short dress with no sleeves in black silk, I'd found on sale in the couture department at Tuckers. The square neckline, cut low, revealed a bit of bosom. The back tapered to a V where a small bow nestled at the waistline. This dress sexily beckoned *follow me.* Even I let rip a wicked grin. This, indeed, might be The One.

The small, teensy weensy problem: I had to be my skinniest to wear it. Rotating the hanger to view the back, I toyed with the idea of starving myself the rest of the day in hopes for the ideal fit. But one day of starvation didn't really work. I decided the bow shoes looked perfect, too.

Since no girl should limit herself to only a few options, I went back to the closet and found a couple of combinations which I laid on the bed as emergency backups.

I consulted with Ms. Know-It-All for her opinion. Jenny selected the number two dress, agreeing with me the *follow me* thought was the possible mantrap I most desired. She also agreed I had to be skinny to pull it off, suggesting the newfangled foundation garment which squished one's lumps and bumps into place.

Pushing aside my shoes, she sat on my bed and watched while I organized. "Have you heard from Allan yet?" she asked with tender concern as she smoothed away the nonexistent wrinkles with her hand.

I sensed a flush creep up my face at the mere mention of his name. "No."

"If you're concerned about going solo, you can always go with me."

And her date? *No way. Three is a crowd.* I waved one hand. "It isn't as if I've never gone anywhere by myself before. If he comes, I'll go with him; otherwise, I'll go alone. I'm a big girl and can handle it." My voice sounded full of confidence as I patted my selection. All was arranged.

Jenny pushed off the bed. "I just thought I'd ask."

"Really, I'll be okay. Thanks for caring."

At the bedroom door, she turned and blew me a kiss. "Don't chicken out. Go with that little black dress." She pointed to the short, silky selection.

I nodded.

"You'll blow his socks off."

Maybe I'd rather blow his boxers off?

****

The key Opal lent me unlocked the office door without difficulty. After turning the knob, I peeked around the door's edge and, when finding no boogey bears, exhaled a huge sigh of relief. This was my first time at the office all by myself on a weekend, and it seemed spooky, probably because of the lack of light. I dashed to the main switches and flipped on the overheads, illuminating the entire area. I skimmed my way to my work station and turned on my desk lamp. Shaking off my scary thoughts, I settled at my problem computer.

Recalling my frustration from yesterday, I said to my monitor, "You had better work." I pushed the desk top's main button. The appropriate lights pulsed in the right places and at the right times. Surprised, I keyed my name and password in the login boxes. The screen went through its warm up stuff, and the different programs' operational icons blinked.

"So far, so good." I rubbed my hands in anticipation. I selected the shortcut housed on the favorites bar for the claims data program. With a click, it opened easily. I picked up a claim from the top of the pile and began to enter the necessary information.

#500125: Ted Norris, address, date, etc. Red 2001 Jeep Cherokee missing mirrors.

#500126: Debbie Harms, address, date, etc. 2003 black Wrangler, missing front left fender.

#500127: Cliff Turner, date, address, etc. 2000 black Isuzu, in a wreck at the intersection of South and Pearl Streets.

I reflected on the completed entries for a moment. A funny feeling hit my gut. Like I'd told Lester and Opal, a lot of Jeep claims had been processed. *What if...*

My fingers scrambled over the keyboard as I ran the program to search by car manufacturer. Approximately fifty cars with missing parts or stolen vehicles—a lot in a few weeks time—were listed. I scrolled my finger over the screen as I read through the itemized list.

After examining all the claims entered over the past three months, I found other SUV claims. But on the whole, most of them were confined to different Jeep models. This seemed extraordinarily interesting.

I entered a print job to create a hard copy. As I stuffed paper in the printer, I wondered if I should ask Lester about this list on Monday. Of course, Opal would say, "Oh, Hattie...blah-blah bluh-bluh blah." She had an answer for everything.

As I waited for the print job to finish, I wandered

over to my co-worker's desk. A stack of mail in her inbox caught my eye. After picking up the envelopes, I flipped them round, rationalizing *what could it hurt?* The mail needed to be opened, and I could get a jumpstart on Monday.

I rifled through the letters, locating the envelopes already printed with our address. I sat in Opal's chair and extracted her prized letter opener from the pencil jar. It sliced through the envelopes with such ease, I nicked my finger accidentally.

"Ow!" I dropped the instrument of torture to the floor while blood flooded the cut. I reached behind me for a tissue and dabbed at my finger. I tucked another in a makeshift bandage around it until I could get a strip from the first aid kit. Once done, I finished my examination of the envelopes' contents and identified about fifteen additional claims for data entry.

Taking my stack, I returned to my desk. I typed in the required information for the new claims. I decided to reprint my list to include them. Afterwards, I scanned my report, feeling pleased with my resourcefulness which called to my mind *Buy Rite Guideline number 3: Show initiative*. I placed the report in a file folder. I would be fully informed, report in hand, ready for a conversation with Lester on Monday.

I clicked the mouse to shut down the computer, switched my desk light off. Turning ever-so-casually to survey the room one last time, I found nothing. No boogey man. No ghosts. No body parts. No one. With that thought, I speedily locked the door and ran to the elevator. I had a date—*okay, a possible one*—and just in case, didn't want to be late.

****

In the parking lot, I found a not-so great story—a flat tire. Unaware, I'd climbed in the car and had driven a few feet, sensing the car pull to one side with a whumpa-whumpa sound. Upon inspection, I discovered the tire lay flatter than a pancake, and no way could the car limp to a gas station for repair. A half-inch wide puncture was in the sidewall, not a nail or screw in the tread. *So much for not being late.*

I didn't have one of those flat fix-it cans, and I had doubts as to whether it would work in this circumstance anyway. With hands pressed against the fender, I considered my dilemma. I had no time to spare. In the past, when the rare car problems had required mechanical aid beyond my skill set, I'd called my dad who could fix everything.

Dad never admitted, but he loved to drop what he was doing and rescue his daughters. *Daughter Rescuing* was his last link to his off-spring for coping with the age-old problem of them as grownups. Knowing the lug nuts would be factory standard tight, and since I needed a change expediently, I sighed, pulled out my cell phone, and hit speed dial 3.

"Hi, Hattie," he said. "What's new?"

"I need a daughter rescue."

"Oh?"

"Seems I have a flat tire and can't undo the nuts." I heard Dad grumble, which was all show.

"I'm on my way."

Disconnecting, I searched the parking lot for a place to park my carcass while waiting. The lone oak shading my carbaby looked best. I sat on the curbing to pass the time. I fished around in my handbag and took out my latest read, a hysterical romance about a hysterical shopaholic. I didn't have enough cash for the shopaholic category, but the obstacle didn't deter this heroine. On occasion, I did fit the hysterical characteristic.

Searching for something to snack on, I found a box of breath mints. As I popped a few, I thought at three calories each, I'd have to consume six boxes to feel full. Then, I'd get gas.

Dad's large SUV turned into the lot. He'd broken land speed records for my rescue. After pressing a quick kiss to my cheek, he gathered his tools and squatted by the wheel. He fingered the slit. "Could be some kind of knife cut. Wonder what did that? Give me your keys."

I handed them over. "Probably some prankster."

"I don't find this funny."

"Me, neither. More like expensive." We loosened the lug nuts, making an *uh* over the tight ones. Once done, we jacked up my baby. The damaged tire was lifted off and set to one side.

When we daughters had first learned to drive, Mom had insisted we assist Dad with car maintenance to become familiar with what was required. While hanging over the fender, we were taught how to change the oil, which we never had to do with him around. Check the brake fluid, radiator level, and whatever else he wanted to tinker on. Pride filled our scrawny chests as we held his sacred tools like the adjustable wrench. And when he asked for a screwdriver, we knew which one to hand him, Phillips or flathead.

On Saturdays, we'd washed the cars with a soapy sponge and scrubbed the tires with a stiff brush. We were intrigued by the lambskin chamois used for drying. Dad would wipe away the water, and after a while, he would wring it out. To a kid, the material seemed like...magic.

I believe Dad had enjoyed these exchanges. We talked about all kinds of stuff, me asking questions about why "this" was "that" way. He'd asked about school, friends.

We shifted the spare into place, me handscrewing the nuts on as far as I could. He used his adjustable wrench to secure them firmly into place. He cleared his throat before softly asking, "You want me to pick up a new tire this week?"

I smiled at his offer. *He's so sweet.* "No, thanks, I wouldn't want to inconvenience you." Looking down his nose, Dad's expression read *this sort of inconvenience would never be an inconvenience* causing funny, odd feelings to consume my insides. To pacify him, I said, "I can get one at the discount tire place."

"You need some cash?" he asked in a casual tone. "I know you're still job searching—"

"No, Dad, I can put the new ones on my credit card. Quit worrying. The card has nothing on it—I know, I know, a miracle."

Dad and I shifted the damaged tire to the front seat to rest on an old towel.

I gave him a peck on the cheek while cleaning my hands on the wet wipe he'd handed me. "How about I pay you in chocolate chip cookies?"

A light flared in his eyes.

Good ol' Dad and his cookie sweet tooth. He'd taught us how to dip cookies in milk perfectly, and as a result, baked goods were sucked up at our house at warp speed, like a new-fangled vacuum cleaner.

"I'd like some. Mother isn't making them lately. She's on another—"

"Diet," we said together, then chuckled.

"Oops," I said after a quick glance at my watch, "I have to get beautiful for a date."

"Date?" He frowned.

"It's no biggie. Just with Allan Wellborn."

"Allan, huh. Your mom really likes him."

"Don't I know it." I gave him a sideways slant. "What about you?"

His fingers stroked his chin while he thought. "He'd be an ideal son-in-law."

"Dad!" I climbed in my car. Waving, I drove away and noticed his frown had returned. Perhaps, all dads disliked hearing about their darling daughters' romantic lives.

Chapter Thirteen

As teenagers interested in beauty stuff, my sister and I'd created The Overhaul.

The Overhaul involved a long bath or shower and shaving the legs and underarms with care. Afterwards, we rubbed on lotion, brushed a peel-off mask on our faces, and thoroughly moisturized. We plucked eyebrows and attacked the dreaded zits. The finished "overhaul" made a huge improvement in conquering "the uglies."

My sister had nicknamed me Ugly.

Now, my unique ritual included a nap. With one, I could party-hearty longer. Mom would be happy to know I didn't yawn in my date's face, thus not embarrassing myself.

My bedside clock read three. Plenty of time to prepare. After shaving, I soaked in a delicious, delectable bubble bath. After a brisk drying, I rubbed lotion over my body. The zits were corralled, and all was pronounced beautiful.

I put on underwear and an oversized t-shirt emblazoned with "Every Night I go to Bed with a Good Woman—Me!" I must have been overly tired because I woke at six, according to the alarm clock. I'd overslept. Definitely not great. I had to hurry with no time to be super picky over makeup and hair.

I puffed on Chanel No.5 scented powder. I touched

the back of my neck with a drop of the same scent from a miniature bottle, a giveaway from the cosmetic department at Tuckers. I'd stashed three other bottles in a drawer for future use.

Sitting at the vanity, I turned on the makeup mirror and began working. After a thorough examination, I found nothing I could do anything about without extensive plastic surgery.

I brushed on black mascara and smoothed on a pale beige foundation. Swiping on two shades of brown eye shadow, I went for a slightly more dramatic look. A dark rose blush highlighted my cheeks. I finished with a dusting of face powder and Dazzling Bordeaux lipstick.

Pursuing beauty seems to be a crap shoot. While turning my head aside to examine my efforts, I had to admit, this time the results looked impressive.

Hair next. Using the curling iron, I rolled a small section, continuing this process over my whole head. I picked and bounced the curls into the style I aimed to achieve, examining for any needed re-curling.

I stared at my reflection and determined the hairdo worked and glued everything with super freezey hairspray. Sure, this seemed like a lot of spray, but I didn't like to re-comb my hair. Besides, combs didn't fit well in small handbags.

Next, I examined the little black dress for wrinkles. Usually, I ironed my clothing before storing them in my closet. I didn't have to figure out what to wear or make a hasty change in the morning as I wasn't known for coordinating well in a semi-awake state. Anyway, ironing saved me an extra step and a headache.

I had an outrageous theory television had been invented for ironing. Hours quickly passed while watching old movies like *The Thin Man* or the bygone dramas of *Bonanza*, *M*A*S*H*, et cetera. The addition of satellite brought a wide selection of food, craft, and decorating shows.

Fortunately, my dress looked wrinkle-free. I slipped on the garment and slid my feet into the heels with the black bows. I fastened the pearl earrings Mom and Dad had given me for high school graduation. After clasping the matching bracelet around my wrist, I studied my reflection in the mirror. The jewelry accessorized the little black dress with a sophisticated, yet sexy, look à la Audrey Hepburn, and perhaps…hopefully…an irresistible one?

At ten 'til seven, gowned in her short black confection, Jenny popped in my room. "My date's here. Are you ready?"

"Almost. You look amazing."

She gave me a pearly grin. "So do you."

I turned around. "Can you zip me?"

"Sure." The zipper rasped as she pulled it up. "No Allan?"

"Not yet."

"Well, give him a few. If he doesn't show, I'll be waiting at the party." Jenny gave me a light touch on the back after hooking the bow.

She was fabulous at boosting my confidence. "I'll see you there." As the front door open, I heard a *Wow* and *Thanks*, soft laughter, and the *shump* of the door closing.

I wandered through the apartment, pausing by the sound system to adjust the iPod to Adele. How I wished I could sing like her. Her voice sounded spellbinding. I pushed a button and changed to Diana Krall. "The Look of Love" crooned on in her deep, sultry voice. I wished I could sing like her, too. My attempt sounded lame.

The clock read seven-o-five. *What did I expect?* I hadn't heard a word, and it was time to go. Retrieving my handbag and sheer scarf embroidered with colorful polka dots off the sofa, I walked to the door, taking great pains to avoid tottering. I checked my appearance in the mirror one final time.

At the moment I turned the knob, a faint knock made me jump. Opening the door, I found A. Wellborn. *OhmyGod.* I sighed, yet my heart pounded harder. God shouldn't have created such a handsome man. Good would have been an understatement. Somehow, I managed to snap shut my gaping mouth.

"Hi." He smiled, looking even taller, leaner, and not meaner. His bright, white shirt enhanced his tanned face. A pale blue and yellow-striped tie and a dark blue suit pulled together his look.

I never understood why some men hated wearing a suit and tie. In my opinion, they were utterly irresistible. I couldn't take my gaze off him. With a quaky hand, I tucked a strand of hair behind an ear. My heart thumped so hard, I heard it. "Umm, do you want to come in?"

"I think I'm late." Stepping inside, Allan glanced around the room, his gaze resting on my face. "You looked surprised to see me."

"I didn't know you were coming."

He frowned. "Didn't you get my message?"

He'd called? I frowned. "What message?"

"The voice mail I left on your phone."

Crap. My gaze flitted toward my handbag. *Had I given him the correct number when I'd called him?*

Who knew? I'd been so nervous and busy with work and the tire changing.

I patted his sleeve. "It's okay. I'll check later. We should go." Besides, my legs felt like Jell-O and needed to move quickly before my body slid to the floor in a puddle.

He allowed me to pass first. I locked the door behind us. I stared at him in wonder as his hand looped with my arm to escort me to his truck. "Thanks."

"Last Saturday, you tripped and hopped around like a baby chick. I want to make sure you don't hurt yourself on my watch."

"I'm fine. Thanks—" I froze. *Now I get it.* After finding his surprise gift, he undoubtedly hung around and saw the jumping and the subsequent sore ankle results. "You were watching me when I found the bag you left at my door."

Obviously amused, the corner of his mouth quirked up. "Yep. Had to make sure no candy thieves were on the loose."

I didn't respond. It wasn't worth it, and no matter what could be said, I'd still felt, and maybe even looked, like a dummy. We resumed our short walk to the truck where A. Wellborn helped me inside. While I fastened my seatbelt, he slid in on the driver's side.

As we drove off, he asked, "Where to?"

I gave him the printed-out directions to the party. Quietly, the truck hummed along as he paid attention to the road, while I tried not to pay attention to him. But I didn't succeed. This was not the Allan Wellborn I knew. He was a…stranger.

Say you met an old friend, like one at a high school reunion. A lot of time had passed. You tried to find a familiarity to determine if this person really was the one you remembered. A laugh, a curve of a smile, a gesture…anything.

This was where I found myself.

I knew his family well, knew what they stood for, their values, and how they treated me as one of their own. I knew all about them—the voices, body shapes, and family dynamics. Gone was Sarah Anne's big brother. Gone was the shy, geeky boy. Dressed in a suit, he looked handsome, smart and direct, more expressive, and confident.

I knew A. Wellborn. The familiar heat from a blush reached my cheeks. *Sorta.*

I turned to stare out the window to hide. *God, I hope he can't hear my thoughts.*

My attention shifted to the elaborate invitation my shaky hands folded and unfolded. Friendships effortlessly flourished in Sommerville. My boss at Tuckers had become good friends with some of mine and vice versa. We met for happy hours, dinners, parties, movies, and ball games. His parents had piles of money and a big house where tonight's party was being held. The invitation said a buffet-styled dinner and champagne would be served. The rooms would be extravagantly decorated with flowers and dancing would follow on the patio. Guaranteed to be a swanky event and my friend's announcement of his engagement was worthy of it.

A. Wellborn and I drove along the boulevard in a historic neighborhood where the homes, nestled amongst towering oak and elm trees, looked majestic. The dwellings weren't just sizeable, they were massive and noted for a unique, craftsman style. The branches of the trees lining the street touched, creating a canopy.

At one time, the neighborhood had slid into decline. The old mansions had been bought cheaply by dual-income couples who transformed them into their original splendor through lots of sweat equity with up-to-date amenities. As a result, the neighborhood had regained its popularity.

Driving through this area at Christmas never failed to lift my spirits. The festive lights and elaborate decorations lit a warm glow deep inside me. One winter, a rare snow fell late in the afternoon, covering the street and homes in a deep layer. As early evening approached, the vintage street lights came on. I had the indescribable pleasure of being the first to drive along the picture postcard street.

A. Wellborn nodded to his right. "This must be it. Look at all the cars."

"Looks right to me." I checked the address on the invitation and pointed ahead of us. "The valet is at the end of the driveway."

We pulled alongside the stand. A young man approached the truck, politely assisted me in exiting.

Once again, A. Wellborn tucked my arm with his and escorted me to the front door as the valet drove the truck away to park it. He smiled at my inquiring look, making my face flame. *Is he issuing me an invitation to...?*

We rang the door bell and were greeted by the happy couple and their parents. A waiter with a tray balanced on his fingertips stopped, and we took glasses of chilled champagne.

I discovered A. Wellborn to be an excellent engagement party date. He made pleasant conversation with everyone he encountered. Behind his back, my friends whispered discreet comments, "When did you meet?" and "How long have you been seeing each other?" and "If..."

I had no answers for the friendly, but prying, examinations. Instead, I made agreeable noises and waved them on their way.

After locating places to sit at a table with Jenny and her date, we filled our plates at the buffet. The main entrée, an appetizing chicken and shrimp concoction, had been covered in a creamy rosemary sauce. Sautéed vegetables for the side. A salad of wild greens, apples, and dried cranberries with citrus dressing, and an assortment of dinner rolls accompanied. With full dishes in hand, A. Wellborn and I wove our way to our table. He nodded a *hello* to Jenny and a *nice to meet you* to her date.

Jenny's friend wouldn't break any mirrors with his va-va-va voom looks.

Since I'd finished the first glass of wine, I took another. I was an easy drunk and two glasses weren't the prudent thing to do. *Oh well*. Maybe it'll help me relax. I took another sip.

"You were surprised to see me tonight," A. Wellborn said this in a silky low voice.

His breath ruffled the hair around my ear. Terrified to look his way, I bobbed my head. "Yes, surprised." Another drink of bubbly, and the wine boosted my courage. "I'm sorry I missed your call."

I had a difficult time concentrating on eating, and instead, moved the delectable chicken and shrimp around my plate. At last, I speared a piece of oak leaf lettuce. "I threw the invitation at you at the last minute, and it was okay if you didn't want to attend a party for people you don't know. Perfectly understandable."

"My bad. I should have called again. My only excuse is running short on time. An inadequate apology. I wanted to come because it seemed important to you."

Oh my. Our gazes locked, bonded. I said from my heart, "I wanted to be with you."

"I wanted to be with you, too." We stared at each other for an indeterminable amount of time, taking in our deepest admission. Finally, a passing waiter broke our connection.

A. Wellborn manipulated his knife into a straight line and cut. "Some of your friends look familiar. Your roommate, Jenny, and those two girls over there..."

I squinted in the direction he'd indicated with a nod and found Kella and Maggie, waving. He did a little fork wave. They smiled and began whispering behind their hands.

Not trusting anything they would do, I gave them the evil-eye squint. I said, "You might remember them from high school. They're my best girlfriends."

"Now I do. Married?"

"Maggie is. Kellar isn't."

"Kellar? Doesn't sound familiar."

"A nickname. Her mother calls her Kella. We also call her Killer."

"Killer...She isn't a hitman-girl, is she?"

"No." I smiled. "Killer 'cause she came over one day and found drinking glasses turned upside down on the carpet in the living area to suffocate roaches." Jenny and I had found a humane solution for bug extermination—no spraying or nasty noise or body parts or bug juice.

He chuckled. "Most people squash bugs."

"It's not funny. I can't do that. Bug guts everywhere."

"Sorry."

"Kellar took off her shoe, picked up the glasses, and smashed the bugs. Now, we call her Killer, although Exterminator was an alternative choice."

"You're not into killing bugs."

"Suffocating isn't noisy."

He stared at me like I'd just made a fast run from Jupiter.

A corner of his mouth quirked up. "Women."

As an extraordinary quiet covered the room, I took a glance around and found hundreds—maybe I exaggerated—of eyes focused on A. Wellborn and me as if we were on stage. I glared the *give us some privacy* look right back. My friends really needed to find a life of their own.

Leaning into me, his arm grazed the side of my breast, sending a humming through my limbs. His very essence caused my senses to do a float and hover dance.

He said, "Have I mentioned you look stunning in black?"

Wow. I flushed and checked myself for spills. "You like it?"

"Like is not the word. Later, I'll show you the right word." His finger stroked my hair in his recognizable way—from temple to the tip. My body flamed hot. A rush coursed to my toes, and my breath evaporated. Inhale. Exhale. He certainly knew how to push my buttons. Inhale. Exhale. I swore to God I was delirious, about to faint at anticipation of what he would show me later. I choked.

He patted my back. "Are you okay?"

"Water." I took the glass he offered and drank deeply. "Thanks. Must have eaten something weird." *God, I am such a pathetic liar.*

With its own momentum, my head turned, and my gaze rested on him as he continued to dine. I didn't know what to think and stared, idly twirling my fork on my plate like filling it with imaginary spaghetti. I'd experienced strong attraction feelings for other men I'd dated. I'd had intimate relationships with some of them. Those had begun in the normal dating game way. We'd met at parties, through friends, and sometimes, on blind dates. After a while, everything was over. A girl knew whether or not to continue seeing someone.

My relationship with A. Wellborn had started off differently from any other. The unsettling feelings I had for him were scaring me. An alien inhabited my body. A strong hold played with my brain. My body grew shimmery everywhere. And I felt at loose ends, swinging between wanting to grab him and wanting to run. *Concentrate. Focus.*

Every girl always wonders if *this is it*, if *this is the one*. And we'd speculate what life would be like with one person to share everything, a best friend we married. I would be foolish to admit right now I had those very same thoughts.

Honestly? I did.

As much as I wanted to, staring at him throughout the party would look foolish. We needed to have some semblance of conversation. I searched my brain and found we could talk about his lack of appearance at traffic court.

Reaching for a third flute of champagne, I cleared my throat. "Why didn't you make a show in court the other day? As the elevator doors closed, I saw you standing outside the courtroom. Why did you do that?"

"Hattie."

My name sounded musical when he said it slow and deep and caused my bones to melt. I gawked at him with adoration.

His face softened. "I ran late. When I'd told the clerk what was going on, he said fine and would consult with Judge Miller who said we could reschedule. I really thought I could make it. I hated to miss, but had no other choice. Is there a problem?"

His words sank deep within me, slightly intimating I'd never come first. I laid on heavy guilt, but in a nice way. "You should know Opal's scolding me about missing work...again."

"I'm sorry." His mouth curved downwards at this news. "What can I do? You want me to talk to her?"

"No!" I said in horror. When I realized lots of people had heard and turned in my direction, I smiled back.

"I only want to help."

"I know. I wonder… You know we have to go back next week?"

Nodding, he took a sip of wine.

"We need to finish."

He touched his glass to mine with a smile. "Come hell or high water, I'll show. Is that okay?"

"Sure. Thanks." We resumed eating. I should say he ate with gusto. Under extreme conditions, guys always managed to eat. I picked and continued to move food from the right side of the plate to the left and back.

Hopefully, my edginess didn't show much. Under the table, however, a different story unfolded. My right foot had begun tapping.

I really wanted to know if he felt the same about me, like I felt about him. I thought he did, especially with the *get lucky* line from the other day, but still harbored some doubt.

With a clink-clink of a knife to their glasses, the couples' parents stood. The guests centered all attention on them. They made brief speeches and the delightful announcement. Afterward, we showered the happy couple with enthusiastic congratulations and stood for a formal toast.

Later, the groom's father said, "Please continue to celebrate with us over dessert and dancing on the patio."

The music started up. I recognized a Sinatra tune sure to entice guests to the dance floor.

A. Wellborn set his napkin next to his plate. "Would you like to dance?"

Because of my heels and the three glasses of wine, I ran a mental checkup to see if I was in proper shaking and jiving condition. *Not too ghastly.* I set my hand to his. He assisted me to my feet, and with his hand lightly placed on my lower back, guided me to the patio. With his thumb stroking my bare spine, I scarcely noticed the festive fairy lights, the music… Really, anything.

Smooth and flawless best described his dancing. One arm circled my back, pulling me close, while the other supported my hand. The rhythm wasn't only in the music. It filtered through my body. Being held in his arms embodied pure intoxication. Charged by the electricity arching between us, my entire being went hot. I liked the way he moved. I liked all of him.

He pulled me tighter and rested his jaw against the topside of my head. Occasionally, he hummed along with the music.

A fragrance wafted my way, and I took a small sniff, finding he didn't wear fancy cologne. Some guys I'd dated wore way too much scent. With a good night kissing session, the odor had rubbed over my face which meant my sinuses were permeated for days. I pressed my nose to A. Wellborn's neck and inhaled again. He smelled like…old-fashioned soap, the kind scented with crisp pine. *Mmm, divine.*

His embrace emboldened me. My left arm reached around his broad back for more. My breasts lightly grazed his chest, and throbbing began down low. I brought the other arm around and clasped both behind his neck. His irises deepened to almost black as he gazed intently into mine. His hands moved lower, resting at my waist, pulling me closer to... *Do I feel an arousal?*

He whispered in my ear, "You smell incredible."

So he'd noticed. *Thank you, Chanel No. 5.*

"Sorta like my mom."

Euew. That's...horrible. Well, maybe she had great taste, too. Leaning slightly back, I studied his face. He looked to be just as pleased with the way things were progressing. A happy glint in his eyes made the corners scrunch up. A baby smile lifted his mouth. We swayed with the music and stared deeply into each other's soul. A desire, especially when our bodies made contact at the waist and hips, intensified. When would he kiss me until my whole body tingled again?

For an hour, we forgot about the rest of the party

and concentrated on the two of us and what developed in our own little world. The comfort level let us explore each other. Lightly, hands moved here or there, touching an arm, a shoulder, my naked back—*Holy Mother of God*. My face pushed closer to his neck where once again, I took in the soapy smell. I felt an overwhelming compulsion to kiss the spot, so I did.

"Thanks."

I pressed a second kiss near his ear and whispered, "You're welcome."

Eventually, we stopped for refreshments and small talk with friends. Observing him fall easily into their company, I admired his warmth and personality, his humor, and his kindness. I held the dessert plate while he took a lemon bar, bit off a bite, and placed the rest against my lips. I took in a nibble and the tip of his finger, giving it a flick with my tongue. *Golly*, he even tasted delectable. A glance at my friends told me they were momentarily shocked.

We slipped away to the patio for the final dance. As I raised my right hand toward his, he clasped my wrist. "What happened to your finger?"

"Oh, I cut it with a letter opener today at work."

"You were working on a Saturday?"

"I had computer problems yesterday and went in this morning to finish. I opened a few letters intended for me with Opal's opener and nicked my finger."

He buzzed the small cut. "The letter opener was very sharp if you had to put on a bandage."

At the brush of his lips, I almost puddled on the floor. "It looks like a dagger from the Far East. She's rather picky about who uses it. I'm not allowed. Maybe because it's sharp."

Midnight had arrived, and the party broke up. A. Wellborn noticed my fatigue. "Time to go."

Greatly relieved, I retrieved my bag and wrap, said our goodbyes to the hosts, and we departed. Once stowed in his truck, I could barely hold open my eyes.

"How's the temp job?" he asked as we made our way home.

"Mmm?" I shook the fog from my head. "At the insurance company? I've already told you about this morning; so it's basically the same."

"Did you finish?"

"Yes. I felt funny...weird being at the office after hours. I wrongly sensed someone watching me."

"But you checked? No one was there?"

"No one. Just me having boogey man feelings." I remembered the flat. "And another thing. It's weird, too."

His brow veed. "Tell me about it."

"In the parking lot, I found my tire had a cut in the sidewall."

"How unfortunate."

"Yeah, I called Dad for daughter rescue."

"I'm sure he was all over it."

"He was. He changed the tire way faster than I could have."

"Are you okay otherwise?"

"I'm fine, though I have to buy a new tire this week." My head leaned against the headrest and then involuntarily rolled to the left for further observation. "When I entered more claims today, I found several SUVs had stolen parts."

His gaze zeroed in on this statement. "Tell me about it."

"I bet I found fifty or so claims involve Jeeps with missing parts or stolen ones vehicles. Sorta funny, but not ha-ha funny."

He bobbed his head. "I get it. What's next?"

I lengthened my spine. "Out of curiosity, I did a program search in the data entries, running a report which specifically focuses on Jeeps. I printed it, thinking on Monday I'd show it to Lester. Maybe he can make sense of the mess."

"Sounds like a plan. Any idea what Lester will do?"

"Nope."

He took a quick peek my way before flipping the turn indicator. "Did he ever call Buy Rite's internal squad?"

"I don't know. I haven't asked."

Becoming aware of my surroundings, I sat straighter. Something didn't look right. The proverbial dawn broke: we weren't headed to my apartment. We were headed toward his. "Hey, we're going the wrong way."

His mouth fashioned a small secretive smile. "I thought we could go to my place."

"Oh." I gulped. His place. His man-cave where all kinds of man things could happen. My nerves overtook, making my hands quake. My body tensed. "I see."

"I hope you don't mind. It could be crowded at yours." His grin deepened.

"And why would you be worried about that?" As if I didn't know.

He just smiled even bigger.

You gotta love a man with this particular plan.

I think I might.

Chapter Fourteen

A. Wellborn's fingers laced with mine while we walked to his apartment. Even though I liked his touch, I could barely contain all my jumpy thoughts and nervy emotions. I stood by as he opened the front door, and with a hand set to my waist, he ushered me inside.

Lucky attacked us. I scooped him up and cradled him to my chest, brushing my nose against the top of his in an Eskimo kiss. "Hey, kee-cat. You're sooo soft."

A. Wellborn had fulfilled his fatherly duties by responsibly caring for Lucky. His fur felt not only softer, but cleaner from the frequent brushings. I carried him to the couch to play, keeping an eye on A. Wellborn who climbed the loft stairs and disappeared in the bedroom.

Upon his return, I noticed he'd pulled off his coat and tie. The sleeves of his shirt were rolled to the elbow, exposing the man hair covering his wrists. The top shirt button had been unfastened. *Lordy*, I swallowed deeply. He looked so sexy like throw-him-on-the-ground-and-roll-around-like-heathens sexy.

He crossed to the media center and turned on his iPod stuck in a sound dock. A Chris Botti song, one of my favorites, filled the room with its sexy jazzy sound. Arousal instantly covered my body from head-to-toe. Feeling self-conscious, I pressed my nose in the cat's fur to cover my translucent imaginings.

A. Wellborn stood by the music player all the while silently observing me.

Totally aware, I hoped he thought terrific things about me like the ones I had about him. After a while, he made his way to the sofa and casually sat next to me, setting his arm on top of the sofa cushion.

How does he do that? How can he act so calm, cool, and collected? I felt ready to pop like a balloon, and he seemed so at ease.

"Hey, bud," he said to Lucky and removed him from my lap.

After a bit of t-l-c, A. Wellborn released our pal to the floor. Scooting closer, he placed his arm around my shoulders and squeezed. His other fingers trailed in slow gradual stages from my neck, along my chest to rest between my breasts, and further along to my waist.

He said, "Now, I can tell you how wonderful you look in the dress."

My senses jumped a notch higher. Deep inside, I understood what he'd offered. And I wanted what was coming.

I sensed a flush covering my cheeks as I stared at my hands resting in my lap. First, he'd said he liked me in the dress. Later, I looked stunning. And now, *now,* I looked wonderful, the very words a girl hoped to hear. Nothing would ever sound better. Score one for little black dresses everywhere.

He took my smile as one to proceed with his unspoken intentions. His hand moved caressingly along my arm, to my wrist. Lifting my hand, he kissed my palm tenderly.

Biting my lower lip, I suppressed an immense cry.

His finger turned my head with firm gentleness

toward him.

I lifted my gaze slowly to find lust and desire lighting his.

He shifted closer and placed light kisses near the corners of my eyes and pressed more along my temple. He paused and drew back for a moment as he stared.

With warm awareness, I noted he looked at me like I was a beauty contestant.

His mouth dropped to mine and dragged against my lips. His tongue pushed gently, yet firmly, to tangle with mine. My hands circled his shoulders and brought our kiss deeper. Our breathing came faster. Through an inhale, my sigh slipped out.

After a few soft, teasing moments, he broke off, and ever-so-caringly, he eased me back into the couch cushions.

Overwhelming feelings of possession obsessed me. I had to have more of him. Grasping his hair, I pulled him to my mouth as his body slipped on top of me. Our tongues touched and swiped. A pulsing hunger, a needy throb, grew inside my girl parts. A. Wellborn's right hand passed across my breasts; my nipples tightened to hard knots. I broke away when my back arched in the age-old sexual response.

"Ah," I murmured. Our hips wriggled closer. His mouth fastened on mine. Eventually, I managed to break the kiss, panting. His lips followed my slanted neck—from my ear, to my throat, and lower to the upper curve of my breasts. They desperately desired his mouth on them.

After more shifting and pressing of our bodies, we became fully aware of male and female parts connecting. He was hard, and I was wet.

My dress had crept up my thighs as my body moved around. He nudged aside the little black dress' strap to expose a shoulder. His other hand rested on my knee. But it didn't stay still for long. He slid it under the hem and up the outside of my thigh to finger underneath the elastic of my underwear.

The thudding sensation I experienced grew stronger and stronger, like a bubble close to popping. I cried, "OhmyGod."

He murmured into my ear, "I've waited a long time for you, ever since I can remember."

Pausing, I wasn't sure what he meant by "waited a long time" and "ever since I can remember." But the phrases sounded terribly romantic, something like Cinderella would hear from her Prince. Aware he rested lightly above me, I gazed at his striking face painted with longing. My fingers caressed his cheek.

He bent, his lips nibbling my throat again. His right hand moved and stroked the length of my arm. "Hattie, let's go upstairs."

His voice wrapped around me like a favorite blanket my grandmother had made. I didn't need persuading. I knew he'd planned this rendezvous. And to be totally honest, I'd planned for my own special evening with him. The undeniable sexual attraction mounting between us had convinced me it would only be a matter of time before we ended up in bed. If we were at my place, the outcome would have been the same.

He wanted me.

I wanted him.

Pretty simple.

Standing, A. Wellborn extended his hand and

helped me rise. Hand in hand, we climbed the stairs, not speaking, just letting a shared synergy link us. At the top, I looked his way, and without saying a word, sensed he understood. *More.* In that moment, I knew how much he valued me. And he would comply with thought and tenderness.

His bedroom appeared neat, typical of his fashion. A corner of the gray-and-navy plaid comforter had been thrown back to reveal white sheets. I gave a small, pleased smile as I observed his meticulous effort. A bedside lamp had been dimmed low and the seductive sounds of jazz trumpet floated up into the loft.

His mouth touched the back of my neck, leaving gentle kisses which trailed to my shoulder. I stepped out of my heels. They'd done a good job.

With intentional care, he slowly unzipped the little black dress. A push sent it with a silky swish to pool on the floor.

Suddenly, timid inner feelings—*should I? shouldn't I?*—overcame me.

Little-by-little, he turned me to face him. He gasped. "I like pink."

I liked pink, too.

Sexy undies were way too flamboyant for someone as conservative as me. I kinda liked the idea of days-of-the-week panties, thinking they would be easy to track. However, a special occasion dress deserved special occasion underwear. Jenny had an advantage in knowing the right sales people at Tuckers. She'd presented me a pink lacy bra and matching itty bitty panties for my birthday last year.

When I put on the lacy underthings, I knew exactly what I was doing.

I needed to thank Jenny later.

However, the admiration of the bra seemed short lived as A. Wellborn's arms reached around my back. I closed my eyes, dropping my forehead to his shoulder and sensed him unsnapping the clasp. When my body straightened, I felt the tickle as the bra disloyally dropped to my wrist. A slight flip of my hand and it landed on the floor.

"Beautiful," he said in a low sexy voice as his gaze scoured my body.

Again, my breasts ached for his mouth. My fingers fumbled the buttons of his starched white shirt. After tossing the garment aside, he enveloped me and pulled me closer for more. My hands took in the warmth radiating from his skin, the moisture on his back, the intimacy of his big body. *God help me.* No feeling was better than the sensation of my man on my naked skin. "What a man."

He laughed softly. "Thanks."

Oops. "I can't believe I said that."

"Not something I hear every day. I can't believe you're in my arms."

Neither could I and never wanted the moment to end. Our gazes focused on each other as he guided me to the bed and pressed me into its comfort.

He shifted to stretch out next to my side and urged my head to rest on his shoulder. His hand smoothed across my waist.

My hands played across his hard chest lightly covered with crisp, dark hair. Our kisses resumed the intimate exploration of each other.

Taking all my moaning and groaning as an encouraging sign to continue, he rose to his hip, and his mouth located my right nipple, fastened on, and sucked, pulling it taut.

"OhmyGod!" He must have taken my cry as a *yes* and moved to the left one. In my delight, I called, "Don't stop."

Thankfully, he excelled in following directions.

In due course, I opened my eyes to watch his face. I traced a hand the length of his neck and flowed down the span of his arm, stopping to tug slightly on the arm hair. I continued to explore his body, moving to his stomach and then under the pant's belt, under the undies' elastic, my fingers tangling in the fluff covering his belly.

He dropped his head.

His groan almost sounded like he was being tortured. "You like?" I asked with a teasing smile, hoping the question sounded seductive.

"Ah...yes."

So going lower, I repeated the move, and he moaned again. Obviously, he liked what I was doing to him a lot and generously repeated the same moves on me.

"Me...too." I pushed my heels into the mattress. As the tension inside me ratcheted, my body swung from one hip to the other. Our touching deepened even further. The shimmery emotion escalated, and our kisses became wet, sloppy, hungry, fiery.

His manhands slid the length of my back and under the lacy, pink panties where he lightly grasped my hips, drawing us closer.

A thick maleness pressed against my femaleness. *Oh my. He's ready.* He touched a sensitive spot, and suddenly, I transformed into the most beautiful, wonderful, sexually charged woman on earth.

Sensing the moment, he pushed off my underwear, gradually, deliberately, slowly. With his fingers, he resumed exploring the spot between my legs. A gush wetted his hand. Embracing the passionate sex goddess within me, once again, my back arched in response. Stars appeared.

"Now," I commanded and whipped off his belt. His pants were next. Lastly, went the cute whitey-tighties.

His body was firm and strong, yet his skin smooth, covered with hair which caused teasing sensations when brushing against my breasts. His arms wrapped around me, sharing the heat of intimacy.

Nothing felt quite like a stripped man. Never had my favorite chocolate-covered peanut candy been this satisfying.

Naked to naked, male part to female part, we kissed, oohed and awed, gasped and clawed our way to the point we needed the final, but most important, element—the condom.

He rolled one on and returned to settle between my splayed thighs. We were so involved in exploring each other, that at first, I didn't feel a soft slap on the top of my head. After another and another and a fourth, I rotated my head from side-to-side. *Why is he hitting me? Is this some kind of sex game?*

The annoying pats persisted, and ultimately, claimed my interest. My eyes fluttered open to determine why A. Wellborn hit my head. Instead, I found him giving lots of undivided lapping attention to my breasts. Watching him, I arced my body. "OhmyGod."

He murmured, "Good?"

"Y-yes," I said, closing my eyes to take it all in.

Another slap.

What the hell? Who multi-tasks during lovemaking?

Looking again, I found his hands weren't on my head. They were tweaking the tips. *What the hell is going on? What's slapping my head?*

Now, with my concentration quite diverted, I tilted my gaze toward the headboard. I bowed my back even farther for another look, and there, high on the pillow, sat Lucky. Lucky, the rat cat culprit, with suspended paw as he prepared for another whack.

"Stop it." I flapped a hand in a small shoo-shoo motion, hoping to provoke the cat to go away and no more coitus interruptus.

No go. "Pupppppupppppupppppppppupppp," went Lucky's purr instead.

"Stop," I called again.

A. Wellborn paused, resting his face on my shoulder. He inhaled deep heavy breaths. "I-don't-want-to-stop."

"Me, neither." Another slap. My arms flailed and swatted around my head like I chased a herd of mosquitoes. "Stop it," I ordered. "Not you..." meaning A. Wellborn. "The cat."

My body rotated ever-so-slightly to the left, and then the right which joggled A. Wellborn's position on top of me. My hand connected with a furry rump. "Stop. It."

The headline news was the cat jumped off the bed. The blah news was our lovemaking drew to an unscheduled pit stop when I heard a buzzing noise. My gaze flitted around the room, searching for the poorly timed sound which could only come from a phone, and it wasn't my ringtone. My phone was tucked in my handbag which I'd left downstairs.

He said, "Oh, hell."

Our rendezvous positively screeched to a halt.

He rolled off me, swinging his legs over the side of the bed. After grabbing his cell phone and glancing at the screen, he snapped it open. "Wellborn."

Who is more important than me? Sitting up, I tucked the sheet around me. My forehead rested on my bent knees as I collected the unsatisfied throbs quaking throughout my body. I underwent the ol' *three is a crowd* experience. A. Wellborn, the cat, and whoever called his cellphone were way too many disruptions.

"'scuse me," I said, tugging the sheet from under him. Regretfully, resignedly, and a little pissed, I collected my scattered clothing from the floor and skimmed to the bathroom, quietly shutting the door behind me. With a blotchy face and a fully aroused body, I tried with shaky hands to tidy my person. After rinsing a washcloth in cool water, I pressed it to my neck and arms.

"You stupid ass, you wanted this," I berated myself. "No harm done. Now go back to his room and grab him." But I couldn't do it. My embarrassment held me back.

Black smudges were wiped away with a tissue. After which, I finger-combed my hair, then stopped, knowing nothing would help bed head. *Does it matter anyway?* Somehow, I managed to put on my bra and dress, but not my underwear. With frantic moves, I scrambled around the bathroom floor for the dropped undies with no luck. Going commando was so not me.

"Where are my panties?" I searched again for the missing lingerie, but couldn't locate them. With a final glance in the mirror and followed by a half-ass shrug, I surrendered.

I peered around the bathroom door to find A. Wellborn gone. Tiptoeing through the empty room, I picked up my shoes, sat on the edge of the bed, and put them on. I searched under his bed, through the sheets and comforter for my lost underwear. No luck.

At the loft's landing, I looked over the railing and found him in the living area, staring out the apartment's front picture window. He'd dressed, the shirt tail hanging out in a rumpled suggestive way, causing me to crave him even more. The music had been turned off. Ill at ease with what had transpired, I descended.

"I hate to say this," he said without looking. "I need to take you home."

Maybe hopefully, regretfully? Maybe, he sounded, *oh, I don't know*, dejected? "Is something wrong?"

He turned, his gaze meeting mine. "The station called. I have to go in."

"Why? It's so late."

"It's the big case I'm working on. Can't explain. Gotta go."

I stared at the perfectly polished hardwood floor. I already had feelings of confusion; now I could add self-doubt. "Oh."

"Look, only my mom, sister, and the office have my cell number."

"And me."

"And you." Stepping closer, he pressed an errant strand of hair into place. "I wouldn't go unless it's very important. Are you okay?"

Hearing the tenderness in his voice, I nodded. Maybe everything between A. Wellborn and me had moved too fast. Too much wine and the almost wild, almost sex had left me with bewildered flashes tornadoing in my head. I collected the rest of my belongings and met him at the door.

He gathered me in his arms, pressing his face into the hairline at my temple. "I'm sorry, Hattie. I can't say it enough. I've dreamed of this night." Abruptly, he released me to open the apartment door.

Damn. Damn. Damn.

While driving me home, he broke the awkward span hovering over us, by asking, "You mentioned something about a large proportion of stolen parts claims being a particular SUV?"

Still in a confused stupor with what hadn't taken place, I blinked while his question leached into my brain. When his query finally resonated, I drawled, "That's right. I told you, I made a list to show Lester on Monday."

Again, his cell phone rang, and he snapped it open. "Okay. I said *okay.* I'm dropping off something, and I'll be there"—he consulted his watch—"in approximately thirty minutes. Yeah, right." He snapped shut the phone.

Indignation straightened my spine. The *something being dropped off* appeared to be me, and I didn't like the way the phrase sounded, like—I put a finger to my lower lip—extra luggage.

After A. Wellborn escorted me to my door, he smacked his lips against my forehead. "I'll call," and then he ran back to the truck.

What the hell had happened?

Chapter Fifteen

The day after the party, I wandered around the apartment waiting for a phone call from A. Wellborn. Would he call me? Should I call him? If he did, then what?

This was the stupid dating game part.

I hated this game.

His call never came.

Jenny and I talked about the engagement party and our respective after parties. Hers sounded way more fulfilling, considering how she floated around on cloud nine. When Sunday afternoon passed, neither of us held much hope for me. I found myself on the well-known emotional roller coaster, and as a consequence, an emotional overeater. Translation: chocolate consumption hit an all-time record.

Jenny felt compelled to eat chocolate as well. Good pals do sympathy eating. Tossing back another handful the colorful peanut candies, she observed, "He must be over his masochist phase."

Like that observation made me feel better.

On the way to work Monday morning, I prepared for my meeting with Lester. I had some concern about Opal and her thinking I'd meddled by doing something not required, and possibly, I'd broken an unspoken and undocumented B. R. A. guideline. An angry Opal could be a dangerous Opal.

I reviewed some more and came back to Buy Rite Employee Guideline #3: Show initiative. *Oh hell*, since the report was already done, I might as well go for broke and give it to Lester. After all, I was only the temporary. The worse that could happen was termination and rejoining the ranks of those searching for employment—again.

I watched Lester sequestered behind his desk, reviewing settlement checks against estimates. When I'd asked, he said he liked to do a "check and balance thing" on occasion, sorta like an internal audit. After I knocked on the doorframe and waved a little finger *hi*, I spotted him beckon me in.

Cough, cough. Outrageously thick cigarette smoke hung heavy in the air. A desire to flap the door back and forth to clear the room seized me, but I didn't.

Lester pointed to a once yellow vinyl armchair, now tinged gray with smoke, located in front of his early dental desk.

I sat on the edge to avoid contaminating my clothing. "On Saturday," I began, "I did the data entry left unfinished when the computer crashed on Friday. Opal spoke to you about it and obtained a key for me to use."

Lester nodded.

"While working, I suddenly realized... I can't explain... I had an odd feeling. It's like this: I entered a lot of Jeep claims."

"We discussed this the other day," he said, leaning back in his chair. "Some models of cars are stolen more than others. Sometimes, we have a rash of claims on a particular make because of its popularity."

"I understand. However, the number of claims is

increasing, even whole ones are stolen. Gone. Whatever. The whole thing bothers me." I waved my hands around for emphasis.

"Bothers you? In what way?"

I heard curiosity in his words and continued, "Like I said, I had a funny feeling. This is probably because I have a car with stolen parts. A couple of weeks have passed, and I'm still waiting for my settlement check."

He took a thoughtful hit off his cigarillo. "The ol' check is in the mail.'"

As an offensive cloud wafted around me, I held my breath and discreetly fanned the air with the papers I held. A cough threatened to erupt. "Must be. Anyway, the thought stuck with me. I checked the program to see if a special report might be generated, and sure enough, found one I could use."

"So, let's review here. You ran a special program to generate a report, one which detailed all the Jeeps which were stolen or Jeeps which had stolen parts."

"Yes."

"Over what time frame are we talking here?"

"The last three months, but you could run it longer."

He strummed his fingers on his desk. "What did you find?"

"I found more than fifty models were missing parts or had been stolen."

"None were involved in any accidents?"

"Only one."

"Only one." Lester leaned back in his arm chair. His brows scrunched together and his fat lips pursed. He flicked his cigarette in an ashtray.

God, if only he'd stop smoking. And instantly, I

knew I could never be employed with Buy Rite for the long term. "I found some more claims in Opal's inbox and processed those, too. As of now, the report is up-to-date."

"Please leave me a copy, and I'll look it over." He sat taller while he straightened his reading pile. Picking up his stinky stick, he tapped ash into the ashtray and then dismissed me with a wave. "Thank you for your attention to your work."

"Sure." I put the report in his in-box. As I walked to the door, I remembered what we'd talked about before and turned back. "Excuse me, Lester, I'm curious about something else."

"What, Hattie?"

"What did Buy Rite's internal squad say when you called them?"

"Internal squad?"

"The other day you said you would call them about looking for an unusual number of Jeep claims."

He smacked his hand on his desktop hard. I jolted. "I knew I had forgotten something. Must have had a senior moment. I haven't called the Internal squad yet. I'm definitely putting this on this reminder pad." He scribbled something on the yellow ledger next to his phone. "How's your court case going?"

"Fine, I guess. We meet later this week, hopefully to conclude."

"Well, good luck, and thank you for the reminder."

"You're welcome." Hurriedly, I exited Lester's office, coughing and waving my hands to clear away the smoke. In my haste, I almost ran into Opal who dallied outside his office. She had probably smashed her ear against his door so she could listen in on our entire conversation.

Precisely at noon, when I staffed her desk to answer the phones, the outer office door opened. A. Wellborn entered as silently as an exotic feline stalking his prey. *Interesting,* I widened my eyes, displaying my disbelief. First, because I hadn't heard from him, and second, because I hadn't anticipated him showing at Buy Rite. "What are you doing here?"

His gaze flicked around the office. "I need to talk to you."

He seemed different. I couldn't put my finger on it. Edgy. Dark. His tone sounded somewhat… preoccupied. "Oh? What about?"

"Stuff."

"I haven't a clue as to what 'stuff' is."

While pacing the floor in front of my desk, he brushed his fingers through his hair. Frustration took over his eyes when he stood squarely in front of me, legs spread, hands on hips. "Hattie, quit fooling around. We need to talk about your job at Buy Rite."

My left eye squinted, giving him the *You Did Me Wrong After Almost Wild, Almost Sex* eyeball. "My job? Why the big interest in my job? You know everything there is to know because I've told you everything there is to know. It's just a plain-o, no big deal job."

"I can't explain and"—he darted his look around the office again—"won't explain here."

I arranged the items in Opal's pencil jar, careful to avoid being punctured by her letter opener. "I need more specifics than that."

"The report."

"The report? Why would you care about the report?" I reshuffled the papers on Opal's desk into neat stacks. "I told you I was giving it to Lester."

"You gave the report to Lester?"

I patted a manila folder into place then looked up to meet his gaze. "Yes."

"The same report you told me about on Saturday?"

"Didn't you hear what I said? I gave it to him first thing this morning."

"What did Lester say?"

"Thank you."

"Smart aleck."

I made a *whatever* face which involved rolling my eyes and crossing my arms across my chest.

"Did he call the internal squad?"

"Not yet. He said he'd forgotten and thanked me for the reminder." All this interest in the stupid report messed with my brain. I planted my hands on the edge of Opal's desk. "What's really going on here?"

"We need to talk," he said.

Obviously, he was evading my question. I leaned across the desk and papers. "What about? Oh, *I* know." My finger went to my heart, and I plastered a firm look on him. I hoped he felt bad because I certainly did. "How about we talk about Saturday night and the phone call I didn't get on Sunday?"

"Sorry. I've been"—he searched the ceiling for the appropriate word—"uh, busy."

"What a news flash. Everyone's busy."

"I told you I had to go to work when the office phoned," he said, and paced a three-foot path and returned.

"Well, why don't you just explain something so little ol' ignorant me will understand better what came up?"

"When do you go to lunch?"

"I go to lunch, let's see," I consulted my watch, "in precisely fifteen minutes when Opal returns in precisely fifteen minutes. Are you asking me to lunch?"

"Yeah. Sorta." He swiped a hand through his hair again, his irritation showed in his jerky, abrupt movements. "How about I meet you outside?"

A. Wellborn seemed preoccupied with something and his "something" had piqued my curiosity. Not every day Mr. Hunky Detective *sorta* asked me to lunch. He'd quizzed me hard about the report, Buy Rite, and Lester. Maybe over some food he would relax and tell me what all the questions were about.

"Okay, out front, by the main doors in fifteen minutes. But the wait may be more like twenty as I can't leave until Opal returns and the elevator—"

"I get it." He departed as silently as he'd entered.

I watched the door shut behind him.

How long can fifteen minutes take?

In this case, it seemed to be forever.

****

Thankfully, Ms. Exact-on-Time-from-Lunch returned early. "I saw the cutest guy standing outside the building entrance, pacing about while waiting for someone." Opal sighed, her eyes tilted with a wistful look. "Wish a boy waited for me."

The temptation to say in "your wildest dreams" almost popped from my lips. Instead, I said, "I think you might be referring to my lunch date."

"The tall, dark, handsome man who kept staring at his watch?"

"That's him."

"Is he the same detective you told me about, the

one who wrote the ticket?"

"Yep, you just missed him. He popped by a few minutes ago. He seemed agitated."

"Better hurry along," she ordered.

I made my quick exit. While waiting for the elevator to come, I tapped my right foot. Talking about Saturday night and him not calling me back felt uncomfortable. Sorta like high school feelings. We had a grown-up relationship which needed to be sorted in grown-up way.

After pushing through the revolving door, I scanned my gaze from left to right to locate him and did. Whether dressed casual, formal—or even better, naked—easy on the eyes best depicted A. Wellborn. Resting his shoulders against the exterior wall, he waited, tension clearly showing in his crisscrossed arms. His glance took me in as I made my way over to him.

"Hey." His remark had been stated in an off-handed style, like a guy would to his football buddies.

"Hey," I replied in my lame jock voice.

"You look nice."

I did. Today, I'd revisited the late sixties in a short red dress without sleeves, banded in white around the neck and armholes. On my feet were matching shoes with a white pinstripe, and I carried a handbag woven like thick, white lattice work. "Thanks. You do, too."

He wore khakis, a white shirt tucked inside, a navy blazer, black belt and shoes. I wondered when paired side by side, if we resembled Barbie and Ken dolls.

"I'll drive," he said. Companionably, we walked to his truck where he helped me inside. He moved to close the door.

I said, "Opal saw you standing out here."

He made a soft snort. "I thought I heard a funny swish-swish sound."

"Ha."

He drove to the nearest fast food restaurant. It looked crowded and sounded loud with little kids running in and out of the gym area. I fell back on my favorite remedy, a large diet drink, to assist me through our conversation, and the restaurant's newest offering, chicken Caesar salad. We sat in red, molded plastic chairs near the kiddy section, the only available seats. He looked out-of-place as his size dominated the smaller-sized chair. Not my usual kind of setting but it didn't matter. Being with him was more important.

He chomped on a bite of burger while I tore into the salad dressing packet and squeezed every drop on the chicken and lettuce. After a couple of bites, he wiped his hands on a napkin and began his apologizing up front. His hand slid across the table. With a couple of fingers, he stroked my left hand. "Regarding Saturday, I'm sorry about Lucky and the phone call. Sorry how they interfered. What we shared was indescribable. I want you to know I had a hard time taking you home. I missed you. I can't stop thinking about what might have happened. I want to finish what we'd started."

My heart stopped with a hard thump. Funny, how his confession resembled mine. "I missed you, too. I didn't sleep well."

"Me, neither."

Our fingers laced, squeezing, absorbing each other's admissions. Our gazes fixed, and I saw care and concern for me in his.

The noise level increased, and gradually, awareness of our surroundings brought us to the present. Our hands released, and automatically, we resumed eating. I shoved my fork around the salad and speared a soggy crouton.

He said, "I have another problem, though, and it means I won't be around."

"Why?"

He bent closer, nearly touching his fries with his chest. "For your ears only, I'm working on a hush-hush case."

This sounded interesting. Not wanting to miss any of the good dirt, I scooted my chair nearer to the table. My boobs almost rested on the table top.

"I have to tell you something." He inhaled. "The case I've been working on is investigating the death of June Short, formerly an employee of Buy Rite Automobile Insurance. The police believe she was murdered."

Murder. My eyes went large and wide. I stopped chewing to lean back in the plastic kiddy chair. "No way. No freaking way. I don't believe it."

"Believe it."

"It can't be true. You're lying."

A. Wellborn laid on me a *Don't Be Stupid* look. His head tilted aside as one brow lifted.

No, not with that face, he wasn't lying. The white plastic fork I held plopped into the lettuce as my taste for food vanished. "How? Who?"

"The only thing I can say is her death was very nasty."

"Oh my." My hand circled my throat. "Lester and Opal haven't said a thing."

"Right now, they don't know about the investigation."

"How could they not know?"

"'Cause we're good?" He shook his head. "Sorry. They think her death has been ruled a suicide."

I took in this new information. June Short had been murdered. June Short worked at Buy Rite. A. Wellborn was investigating June's murder. This seemed surreal, like the Salvadore Dali painting with the wilted pocket watches. "Do you have any suspects?"

"We're interested in a couple of people."

"Who?"

Sighing, he eased back in his chair. "Honestly, Hattie, I can't tell you anymore."

I bit my lower lip. "But I work at Buy Rite."

"I know." His hand scrubbed his forehead. "This is just a big, fuckin' coincidence. What I need from you is the Jeep report to see if something's there, something which could connect us to the killer, a possible link."

He could have any and everything he wanted if it solved June's murder. "Sure."

I'd made two copies and removed mine from my handbag, passing it to A. Wellborn.

Interested, he thumbed through the pages, stopping sporadically to do a speed reading scan.

I waited with silent screaming tolerance for him to let fall a crumb or even better, a tidbit. Instead, I occasionally heard a *hmm*. He handed back the report.

"Keep it. I can always print another."

"Thanks." Carefully, he folded the report and tucked it in his inner jacket pocket. "This is intriguing."

"It'll help?"

"It'll help." He gave a brisk nod.

"You think June knew something about stolen cars?"

"Anything's possible. Gotta go." He stood, ready, his body twitching and itching to take off. He wanted to take this new information and resume his investigation. Unable to confess how scared I felt, all I could do was stare.

I really needed hold yous.

I really needed more time.

We looked at each other, unsure what should happen next. Finally, my silly girl attitude took over, and I gathered my handbag and box of lettuce, trailing him to the truck. He drove me to Buy Rite's building.

While parked at the entryway, he bent across the console and kissed my forehead, resting against me for a moment.

I closed my eyes, never wanting the sensation of closeness to end. However, nothing does last forever, and we drew apart.

"I'll call," he said. "I promise." His gaze connected with my questioning one. "I don't think you need to worry about anything."

As the whole scenario dawned on me that this was for real, I shifted my gaze to the building and back. My pulse jumped a notch. Completely mystified, I pretended to have courage when I said, "Sure." The word came out like a mouse squeak.

I climbed out of the truck and watched him wave and drive away. Waiting fifteen minutes before going to eat lunch with A. Wellborn had been hard to tolerate.

Going back to Buy Rite's office afterwards was the hardest thing I'd ever done.

Chapter Sixteen

Not worry?
Wrong. I was way too worried.
What is going on here? June Short, a former employee of Buy Rite Automobile Insurance who, according to A. Wellborn, had been "nastily murdered."

None of this pleased me, not at all.

Nobody deserved to die like she had. By using the Jeep report in his investigation, he hoped to find a possible link to connect her death and the murderer. My thoughts returned to the sweet picture of June and Mike, her dog.

Nobody.

And undoubtedly, the most important thing—*I* was temping in June's place.

As I approached Buy Rite's office, the jumping beans in my stomach, the ones which accompanied tension and full of trepidation, shifted into high gear. My pulse accelerated with each step moving me closer to the door. I so didn't want to go inside, but had to. Pushing it open, I took a few steps and glanced around. Through the glass sidelight next to Lester's door, I watched Opal and Lester reviewing paperwork.

I considered *Opal? Lester? What are they really doing?* What if one of them had murdered June? Or even worse—my eyes rounded with this thought—they both had done it.

When they noticed me looking toward them, they separated, breaking the conversation. To cover my ass, I quickly went to my desk and stowed my handbag in an empty desk drawer. I set my hands to the keys and pretended to resume typing.

A. Wellborn's eye-opening revelation possessed my mind. I hadn't been around any mysterious deaths before. Learning about June's murder felt outrageously out-of-this-world shocking. My thoughts kept returning to the time I'd boxed up her belongings and the dog photo. Neither Lester nor Opal had ever uttered an explanation about her demise. When I started the temp job, they'd said she had passed, and her family had held a nice memorial service.

Obviously, there appeared to be more to the sordid story.

Frightened and scared inhabited my body, so much so, I couldn't think of anything else *but* June. Somehow, I managed to make it through the day, but I did a crappy job at best. My main goal was for five o'clock to arrive. And when it did, I raced for my car. I couldn't drive home quickly enough.

****

The next couple of days passed pretty much the same as always. Claims kept coming in, but no more Jeep ones.

So much for my theory.

One day, my work slowed to almost boredom. My time at Buy Rite appeared to be up. Perhaps, I'd disappointed Opal somehow. Who knew? She didn't say and I didn't ask. After hearing what had happened to June, I didn't like working at B. R. A. anyway. I didn't like Lester and Opal. I didn't like data entry at all. I would never be what Opal wanted, and I didn't want to be.

Over a phone call, I consulted with Kellar for her expert opinion on whether or not I should stay at Buy Rite.

"Do you have another job lined up?" she asked.

"No. I should call Trixie."

"There you go."

Kellar seemed full of level-headed advice.

A. Wellborn had phoned once to say *hey* which qualified as hearing from him. We held a short conversation, talking about Lucky and his work load, family, but nothing about June's murder.

Jenny had put in her two cents worth. "Don't worry. It's a good sign he keeps coming back for more."

Easy for her to say.

****

The following Wednesday, I drove downtown for my court date and parked in the garage. I walked to the municipal building and went over to the elevator which took me to the courtroom floor.

The roly-poly bailiff greeted me with familiarity. Was being recognized by a bailiff ideal? Mom would pass out if she knew. For the third time, I took a seat. This time, the proceedings seemed more comfortable.

Meanwhile, Judge Miller studied the papers gripped in his fat fingers and glanced briefly when I took a seat on what I now called *my* bench. I inspected the court room and, like the previous times, observed nothing had changed. Detective Wellborn had yet to appear which caused me to wonder what the hell game he played this time. He'd told me he would be here. I re-gripped my tote. I really wanted this issue to conclude today.

The bailiff called my name. As I approached Judge Miller, the squeak of the court room door opening captured everyone's attention. We all turned toward the sound and, surprise, surprise, Detective Wellborn entered. *Finally*—my body eased with relief—*we can get this show on the road.*

I gave him a second glance. My man continued to look like a top model in clothes, not to say he didn't without them. With that thought, I sensed a blush race from my face to the tips of my ears. Today, he wore a white shirt with blue pinstripes tucked in charcoal wool slacks and a navy blazer, black shoes, and black belt. A maroon tie with tiny gold dots complimented the outfit.

"Detective Wellborn?" Judge Miller asked.

"Yes, Sir."

"Have a seat."

"Yes, Sir."

Judge Miller beckoned for me to come forward.

I took tentative steps, passing through the wooden gate in the banister.

"Okay, Ms. Cooks, please continue."

"Thank you, Sir." I released a deep breath. "A few weeks ago, I was stopped by Detective Wellborn"—I pointed a neatly manicured index finger in his direction—"for a taillight out on my car. The problem with the citation was the box had been checked 'taillight out,' but what we really discovered was the entire bumper including the taillights were stolen."

"How unfortunate. You didn't notice the car parts were stolen before then?"

"No, Sir."

"And your contention is the taillight wasn't out because you didn't even have a taillight to be out?"

The judge appeared to be sympathetic to my plight. "Yes, Sir. On the prior Sunday, I'd helped my dad change the oil. Afterwards, I washed my vehicle. At that time, the bumper and the taillights were on the car. A couple of days later, Detective Wellborn pulled me over. We believe the parts had been stolen sometime after Sunday evening." I handed a photo to Judge Miller. "I took this photo with my cell phone and it shows the missing parts."

"I see. And you informed your insurance company of your loss?"

"Yes, Sir." I passed him another piece of paper. "This is a copy of the estimate from the claims adjuster—"

"Thank you."

"And a copy of my driving record."

"Thank you again." Judge Miller stacked my papers in a tidy pile. Afterwards, he rested his forearms on the desktop. "Okay, Ms. Cooks, anything else? If not, have a seat and we shall hear from Detective Wellborn."

I paused at the gate which Detective Wellborn politely held for me to pass through. My head dipped, giving my own small acknowledgement to his slight smile.

"Detective, let's hear your side of the story," said Judge Miller.

"Yes, Sir."

He consulted his citation book and relayed to Judge Miller about pulling me over and pointing out the missing car parts. He said I was quite distressed and had given him the same information I'd given the Judge about when the parts were last seen on the Jeep. He said he pulled me over specifically because my parts were missing which looked suspicious, not to mention dangerous. If need be, he could obtain a copy of the recording from the squad car's camera.

I raised my brow, knowing my eyes bugged like a frog's. *He has a recording of what had happened? Fantastic. Yeah, let's go back to that horrible day and let everyone see my mascara-blackened face and sweaty arm pits.*

On the other hand—my eyes narrowed—they could also see the parts missing off my car. All this time, he'd possessed the truth and played with me.

Judge Miller reclined in his chair and contemplated us. "No tape is necessary. I understand where you are coming from. Ms. Cooks, have the taillight and the bumper been replaced?"

I jumped to my feet. "No, Sir, not yet. According to my insurance company, the check is in the mail."

"Standard operating procedure," said Judge Miller. "I'm ruling in favor of Ms. Cooks, Detective. Technically, she should've been informed about the missing taillights and bumper and given a verbal warning, not a citation. Therefore, no fine." The studious look he fixed on us read something like *I know you two aren't telling me everything.* "Let's keep it in mind, shall we?"

"Yes, Sir," A. Wellborn and I said in unison.

"Case dismissed." Judge Miller smiled, winked, and slammed his gavel.

Woohoo! I grinned, batting away the desire to do a happy dance. I didn't have to pay the outrageous fine, and Mom would be ecstatic, knowing her beloved daughter wasn't destined for jailbait.

A. Wellborn grasped my elbow and propelled me with expediency through the courtroom into the hallway. Furious, I yanked my arm from his clasp and turned on him, indignation bursting from every pore.

He chuckled.

"This isn't funny, Allan."

He laughed again.

I stomped my foot. "Stop it! It isn't funny. I wouldn't have been in this predicament, wouldn't have wasted all this time from work, wouldn't have wasted the taxpayer's money if you hadn't written me a phony citation."

He sobered, pressing his lips into a tight line. "Oh, come on, Hattie. I did you a really big favor. You wouldn't have known about the stolen parts for a while. You should thank me for pointing it out."

"E-ven-tu-ally," I said, each syllable emphasized. "I would have seen the problem." Clomping over to the elevator, I pushed the call button.

He followed me. "Okay, *eventually* you would have seen your taillights and bumper were missing. But you wouldn't have seen me either."

"And seeing you is great because…?" I set my hands on my hips while contemplating his circulatory thinking. We stepped in the elevator car, and I stabbed the button labeled for the lobby. "I'm getting vibes you're feeling proud of how you arranged everything, aren't you?"

He rubbed a finger across the cleft in his chin. The alluring twinkle danced in his eyes. "I think everything is going just fine."

The elevator dinged, the doors opened, and I exited with quick steps.

At the courthouse entrance, he caught up with me. He circled his hands around my upper arms to pull me to his chest. "I've missed you," he said in a low arousing voice. His arms slipped around my waist, pushing his maleness to my femaleness.

A womanly heat encompassed me. *God, how I craved him.* I stared at the third from the collar shirt button. "Yeah, well you said you would be busy."

"I am. Day after day, I get up early and go home late. The same thing the next day and the next. Pretty boring in my book. I hardly have any time to sleep."

Needless to say, I had little sympathy for him. "So, your life is boring, and you aren't getting much sleep. Too bad. Maybe I should play a whiny tune on my teeny weenie violin."

"I'm thinking I need to take a break from work."

"You're in charge of your own destiny."

"I have a great idea."

"I bet you do." Look what his last brilliant one brought me. My forehead rested on his shoulder. *I never want to leave him.*

"Your perfume smells like the one you wore the other night. It's driving me crazy. Did you splash some on just for me?" He snuggled his face into my hair. "How about we check on Lucky?"

Ordinarily, I would have appreciated this kind of suggestion, especially considering the almost wild, almost sex. Appalled, I slammed my hands against his chest and pushed him away. I punched his bicep. "You aren't taking care of Lucky?"

"Ow! You slug hard for a girl." He rubbed his arm.

"I could file police brutality charges against you."

"Don't change the subject! I could take care of him."

A mischievous grin glinted in his eyes. "Not that kind of lucky."

I caught the joke. "You're a-a pill."

"Yep, my mom says the exact same thing." His psychic capabilities were eerie. He hugged me tighter.

Horrified, I made a half-ass attempt to twist and turn from his grasp. "We're in a courthouse. There's no hanky-panky here."

"I'm not aware of any rules about prohibiting kissing a pretty girl in the courthouse hallway."

"Really?" I stopped wiggling and regarded him in disbelief, crooking my head and squinting my eyes. "Exactly how do you know?"

"I just know."

"Sounds as if you've tried to make out with other girls in the court house before."

"Nice probing technique. However, there has been no one else. Maybe if you'd shut up, you'll be the first."

"Well, what are you waiting for?" I raised my head and closed my eyes to receive his kiss. When his huff blew across my cheek, I knew he'd lowered his face toward mine. A few moments passed.

Nothing. Nothing-nothing-nothing. My brows twitched.

Once again, A. Wellborn's cell phone went buzz, buzz. My eyes flew open. *Unbelievable*. This cannot be happening again. I took two steps backwards and sighed. "Not again. No way."

"Shit. I'm getting tired of interruptions." He pulled the phone from his pants' pocket. "Wellborn."

Me, too. My dedication to his job was way beyond the call of his duty. I walked toward the wall in frustration. With my shoulders propped against it, I overlapped my arms. I didn't understand why he couldn't make the caller wait. Instead, he had to be the conscientious, Mr. Always Perfect Policeman, ever prompt and efficient, ever loyal to his job, putting it above all else.

Even me.

This is horrible. His extreme dedication interfered too much in our relationship, and I didn't like it.

With a glance, he caught my hostile posture. His eyes gaze flitted to me and back to the floor a few times. "I'm just about finished here and can be there"—he checked his watch—"in fifteen minutes." He snapped shut the phone and looked my way. "Gotta go."

Girls didn't use the *gotta go* line. I'd heard this expression too often and had been left exasperated each time. I continued to stand apart with my arms crossed, foot tapping. Once again, I assigned him a quizzical look. With a lifting crease in my forehead, I said lightly, "Gotta go?"

"You're mad."

"Where on earth did you get that idea?"

"Hell." He scrubbed his hand over his face. "Cut to the chase, Hattie."

Did he sound a little irritated? *Excellent.* "I haven't an inkling what you're talking about, Allan."

"Nuh uh, don't go all girly on me. I don't have the time. I have to go."

"So…go."

Hands went to his hips. Impatience clung to his

227

words. "What. Is. It?"

"Nothin'," I said, utilizing my best southern girl drawl.

A. Wellborn shook his head, an age-old man-signal of disbelief.

I wondered if the great detective could figure this out. I flung my arms from my side. Lengthening my spine, I tried this line. "Okay, fine. If I didn't know any better, I might be thinking you have another woman."

"Ha. I'm not dating anyone else. Only you."

He-he-he. He didn't get it. "You're always saying gotta go and racing off. What is a girl supposed to think?"

He wrapped his hands on my wrists tightly, and wiggled me a little. "Get this: You are the only woman in my life, and I barely have time for you."

That so-called wonderful statement is supposed to make me feel better? Not. I rolled my eyes, but in a fake way. The good news was my attempt worked. Guys could be so dumb when understanding the female species. Truly, he'd had no chance. The most unwelcome news was guys didn't come running at the drop of a hat anymore.

"Hattie, I—I can't do this now. Please understand."

He sounded as if he was begging. I gave it one more college try, hanging my head low to imitate being overcome with reluctant sadness. "I understand, but it's tiresome and frustrating and sometimes, I feel... unwanted." *He-he-he. Acting, my second career.*

"I'm sorry, sweetie. Soon, this whole case will be finished and we can—"

"I understand," I interrupted and bestowed a charming smile on him. "You've got to go."

He buzzed my mouth and took off for the front doors.

Slowly, I followed, my fingers resting on my lips to absorb the kiss he'd deposited. Had the great detective figured out my game? I didn't think so. At least I knew where I stood. He'd called me *sweetie* and said I "was the only woman" which sounded superior.

I tilted my head. I was right. A. Wellborn did have a rocking view from behind.

****

The Funsisters loved to celebrate anything and everything. This time over dinner, we honored Maggie and Kellar's birthdays. How many dildos and resuscitation kits could a girl receive?

Jenny and I hosted the special occasion at our place and contributed the birthday cake and wine. I savored the scrumptious white cake with lemon curd sandwiched between layers, topped with a delicious fondant and decorations. The Funsisters helped with the meal by bringing different types of salad or bread.

The Funsisters also brought gifts other than the sexual-oriented ones. Since handbags were my favorite accessory, I gave straw clutches embellished with embroidered flowers which I found at Tuckers end-of-summer sale. I applauded myself for taking advantage of another opportunity to keep my pro-shopper skills up to speed. I doubted the others could match my expertise.

Jenny and I placed our dishes on the kitchen counter which Trixie arranged in an artistic, pleasing manner. When all of the Funsisters had arrived, we uncorked the chilled Chardonnay. We began by singing "Happy Birthday" to Maggie and Kellar. The ringing of our glasses in the toast sounded joyful. We filled our plates from the variety of salads and slices of the whole-grain bread.

We seated ourselves on the sofa in the living room, on the floor, or in what chairs were available. Lots of lively chatter passed back and forth, catching us up with our lives, clothes, and other interesting tidbits.

"Mmm, yummy bread."

"I want this chicken salad recipe."

A few of us had filled our plates with seconds when Jenny revealed, "Hattie had almost wild, almost sex with Allan."

How dare she! I dropped back in my chair and set the back of my hand to my brow. I gave her the *I can't believe you said that* look which she blew off.

"They were interrupted by his cat..."

Jenny had crossed the line. I would have to kill her. It was justified. I continued to give her the *not again* look which still didn't faze her.

"...and his phone buzzed which brought the whole rendezvous to a screeching halt."

Meanwhile, the other Funsisters imitated meerkats. Sitting upright in full attention, eyes perpetually rounded, they stared. Arms poised, holding a fork which hung suspended in mid-air. On cue, faces turned in my direction, and simultaneously, they swiveled back to Jenny.

Older, wiser, and more self-assured since Jenny did this to me at the last book club meeting, I continued with the *not again* look, crossed my arms, and shook my head. *No way. Nuh uh. Not this time.* I was not playing along. They would have to find someone else to pick on. I, for instance, was well aware Trixie was dating weatherman Jon Bob of WSFO and things looked especially promising. My gaze focused on each sister for a moment. When they didn't comment, I let her rip, "How's Mr. Weatherman, Trixie? Hot things happening under the covers?"

My diversion worked for a nanosecond.

The Funsisters gasped in horror. Normally, sweet Trixie was off limits, too nice to partake in this kind of heart stripping.

"Oh, sweetie," I said, "I hope I didn't embarrass you."

"Don't apologize. Jon Bob's fine, and things are progressing very nicely. I'm happy to report we've rounded third base, and I'm thinking a home run is coming, possibly, later tonight."

My diversion did work after all.

Dumbfounded, the Funsisters' mouths dropped like large-mouth bass as they stared at her instead of me, not believing the words coming from her mouth. Trixie certainly didn't sound sweet and innocent, but more like she was about to practice Meatloaf's "Paradise by the Dashboard Lights." Maybe, just maybe, she possessed more of a wild side than we were aware. Unquestionably, the Funsisters would have to play this game more often.

My thoughts switched to the dark side of the Funsisters' lives we could explore.

"But Hattie, I'm interested in almost wild, almost sex," Trixie said, lobbing from left field. "I'm not familiar with the term. It's my understanding either you do, or you don't. So, how does one have almost wild, almost sex?"

Damn her. She'd turned the tables on me. My body

morphed into a Popsicle. With a naughty twinkle in her eyes, she ducked her chin in a coy move and shrugged. The Funsisters' attention had volleyed back to my side.

Maggie caught Trixie's ball. "Yeah, I want to know, too. Please explain."

My gaze roved around the room as I searched for an ally. "Well, uh..."

Smarmy grins were plastered on the Funsisters' faces. No matter how embarrassing, they went after every freakin' intimate detail and wouldn't let go until they wriggled it out. Even though I wanted to keep my feelings, my relationship with A. Wellborn private, as if telling anyone would curse it, I would have to tell... No, confess... No, give up the "whole truth, and nothing but the truth, so help me God."

I glanced at each of them, trying to find the spot within to draw on for courage. But no help could be found. Blowing a breath, I dropped my chin in resignation.

Trixie rubbed her hand over my shoulders, providing comfort. "Oh, just tell us. We don't want to embarrass you. We love you and want to share."

True, we did love each other. But I knew the real truth. The Funsisters lived vicariously through each other's love lives.

What the hell, I could always die from embarrassment. Of course, I'd never heard of anyone dying from embarrassment. Slowly, I began to divulge the details, "I invited him to the big engagement party, the one for the guy at Tuckers, the guy who used to be my boss?"

The Funsisters nodded.

"I didn't think he would come, and at the last

minute, he showed. Seems he did leave a message, but I didn't receive it due to a jumbled voice mail." I swallowed. "He looked so nice in his suit, I almost passed out."

Happily, I recollected how nice he'd looked in the suit, and more importantly, how very arousing he'd looked in the suit, and even better, how extraordinary he'd looked in no suit at all.

The other Funsisters who'd attended the party nodded.

"I could see how you would. He's migh-tee fine," Kellar said.

Maggie said with sarcasm, "Any man would look good to you right now."

"Isn't that the truth?"

"Quiet!" I yelled. After Maggie and Kellar settled down, I continued, "He said he liked my little black dress—"

"This part is so romantic," Jenny interrupted, her chin propped on her palm.

"He also said I was stunning and wonderful in the little black dress." I clasped my hands and this time with a dreamy look in my eyes said, "We danced. He smelled fresh like pine cleanser. He kissed my hair." Instinctively, I touched my hand to the sweet spot above my right ear. "We wanted to be together more."

"Oh my. I might have an orgasm," said Trixie.

Wow. Who knew?

"Me, first," said Maggie.

"Shush," said the rest of the Funsisters.

"After the party, he drove me to his apartment instead of mine. He said he thought my apartment would be quote—crowded—unquote."

My eyebrows rose as I looked in Jenny's direction. She had a little secret. Her cheeks turned rosy, knowing I could divulge the whole enchilada. She shook a negative.

"I felt intoxicated on something—"

"Allan," a Funsister supplied.

"His arm slid around my shoulders. And we..." I hesitated before the final confession.

"Don't stop now!" Maggie said.

"Immediately, we hit third base." I smothered the last phrase in my hand, hoping they would miss it. But not a chance. I was naïve to think they would, and as proof, Trixie held up three fingers.

Now everyone knew how she got the nickname Cesspool. Her mind went straight to the sex gutter. Maybe she read way too many romance novels.

I glanced at Maggie who waved her hands, urging me to continue. "He suggested we move upstairs to his loft. He unzipped the little black dress, kissed my neck, and—"

"Harriette Lee Cooks," Jenny warned.

I rolled my eyes to the heavens. "He said he liked pink."

"Pink? Why pink?" asked Maggie, momentarily taken back.

"Oh-oh-oh, I know, I know." Jenny's hand shot in the air while she did a seated jump up and down. "Hattie wore the pink lacey bra and panty set I gave her for her birthday."

"Oooh," chorused the Funsisters.

Maggie nodded. "A delicious choice, but personally, I like the sheer baby blue one you gave Trixie for her birthday."

"This isn't about me." Trixie shook her head. "Go on."

Kellar passed Maggie a five dollar bill which Maggie stuck in her cleavage.

"What's with the money?" I asked.

The co-conspirators giggled. "Oh, this?" Maggie pulled the fiver from her bosom and dangled it. "We have a side bet."

"You have a side bet on what?" *Uh oh.* I got it. "On when I'm getting lucky?"

"You're a very interesting game," she said.

I twitched the corner of my mouth. Another reason to feel dumbfounded. My own best girlfriends, my Funsisters, had gambled on my sex life.

"It has to be the pink lacey panties and bra set. This kind of stuff really turns on guys, especially the pink part," Jenny said.

Sidetracked, the Funsisters argued the merits of pink lacey versus black lacey versus crotch-less, et cetera. Their conversation moved to nighties with cutouts in strategic places, which was followed with a heated debate on the characteristics of different kinds of condoms.

I felt so not with it. So green. So ignorant. I had only seen crotch-less on mannequins in store windows and in racy magazines. Did real live human beings actually purchase, much less, wear this stuff?

And I knew nothing about banana-flavored condoms, only ribbed ones.

After a long while, the lurid talk subsided. Since nothing disastrous had happened thus far, I said in a loud voice, "Well, do you want to hear the rest or not?"

The girls settled and their attention focused on me

once again.

"We made it to the bed, stripped naked."

"Yeah," they chorused.

I considered the ceiling while overlooking their outburst. "And as we became involved with using the condom"—I drew a deep breath and said rapidly—"Lucky hit my head several times which distracted me... Meanwhile, Allan's cell phone buzzed and he had to take a call and I felt funky, out of place, unsure...you know what I mean...I raced to the bathroom to get dressed, and he brought me home, so he could go to the office." I stopped to gulp another breath. "The End."

Maggie and Kellar engaged in a small tug of war over the fiver.

"I almost forgot. I can't find my pink panties," I said.

Eyebrows raised, the Funsisters looked at each other.

"I don't get it," Trixie said.

"It means I had to go home—"

"What?" Trixie yelled.

"Commando." *Whew.* Now they knew everything.

A refrain of great big gasps and an OhmyGod followed.

"So, where do you think the undies are?" Trixie asked.

I shrugged pitifully. "I don't know. Not by the bed."

The Funsister Greek chorus chimed a refrain which sounded sorta like a Dr. Seuss rhyme. "Maybe they're under the bed. Maybe they're in the sheets. Maybe he picked them up. Maybe the cat hid them. Maybe they're in the bathroom…"

The Funsisters had thought of all the scenarios I'd considered. "I don't know. They have to be at his apartment. I didn't like the idea of poking around."

"You've seen him since?" Tracey asked.

"Well, yes. Very briefly. We had lunch. We talked about my work and the Jeep claims. And we met at the courthouse for the citation." I remembered his comment at the court house. "He did say there is no other woman, and he barely had time for me." I explained how I used my womanly tactics to trick A. Wellborn into admitting his feelings.

The Funsisters applauded my covert effort.

"Good move. Proud of you," Maggie said.

"So, he does like you," Trixie said.

The Funsisters broke into discussion groups on whether or not A. Wellborn liked me, and whether or not I would see him, and whether or not I'd ever get lucky. Giving up, I sipped from my glass. Numb with alcohol, I'd forget the whole mess.

They had better settle soon or I would rip open the birthday presents.

****

I liked electronic machines to work like they were supposed to. So on Friday, when computer problems cropped up again, I groaned audibly. Data entry sucked, and the thought of coming in to work on a Saturday sucked, too. I preferred to spend my weekend occupied elsewhere.

When I reported the problems to Opal, I led her back to my desk and she watched me take a stab at making the computer operate. I pointed to the blank monitor. "See? Nothing."

The fashion police should arrest Opal. She wore a

lime-and-lemon plaid pantsuit in her favored bullet-proof fabric with a matching, silky shirt underneath the jacket. Her big butt resembled a stadium blanket.

"I do," she said. "I think we should make a service call and let the technicians unravel the problem. Do you have any other ideas about what should be done?"

I found it hard to believe Opal, of all people, had asked for my opinion. Of course, I wanted to say *trash the damn thing*—but that was my anger talking. However, I'd already considered this problem, and even though Opal could help me, perhaps an hour or two on a Saturday wouldn't hurt. Wham bam, I could knock out the work quickly.

"Perhaps, you should call the technicians. And I'll come in on Saturday."

Opal passed me the key. "Keep me informed if anything is required."

I didn't anticipate any problems. "Sure."

****

On Saturday, I rose early and went for my run. I'd downloaded an audio book, one by my favorite mystery author, Dick Francis, into my iPod.

I ran, but the sight wasn't pretty. After half a mile, I slowed to a walk and barely finished moving. Downright disgraceful. This time I couldn't blame treats. My chocolate deposit ran at an all-time low. I would have to finish the audio in the car.

Back home, I showered and did the minimum in war paint and hairdo. I slipped into jeans and a stretchy t-shirt decorated with a summery, Paris café scene. And because I was the handbag queen, I selected a tote embellished with the same picture, purchased at an excellent price at an outlet store.

I drove to Buy Rite's office and parked under the only tree in the lot near the building's entrance, just like the prior time. I opened the office door with Opal's key. At the main switch, I turned on every light and illuminated the entire office. Silly me took a quick look around. Of course, no one was there, and in my gut, I didn't expect anyone to be. But the spooky, watchy feeling overtook again. Considering June's death, I had to be especially convinced for my piece of mind and toured the premises a second time. As far as I knew, her murder hadn't been solved, and I still didn't know if someone at the office could be the murderer.

Sitting at my desk, I turned on the CPU, hearing it doing the start up thing. The monitor blinked to life. *Hallelujah, Praise the Lord!* I clicked on the claims program. After organizing my pile of paperwork, I inputted all the data entry easily. With some time to kill, I decided to catch up on filing. I alphabetized the appraisal copies which went quickly.

A glance at my watch read told me I could do more work. I eyed Opal's inbox which held a few unopened envelopes. *No time like the present*, I thought while fingering them. I could get ahead, the ol' *show the initiative* plan. Using her letter opener, I sliced through the envelopes, being careful not to slash myself again on her weapon.

I sorted the few claims I needed. I took the appraisals as well and made copies. After that, I matched the copies with the respective files. Matching was easy to do with the files in alpha order, but just to be sure, I checked every piece of paperwork as I worked.

#50003: Camp, Henry, date, 2003 Black Jeep

Cherokee stolen. Appraisal: $1,000. Settlement Check: $925.00.

How funny. The numbers didn't match. *Aren't they supposed to be the same?* Again, I looked at the settlement number on the check and verified it against the appraisal amount. The check had been cut short by seventy-five dollars. My brow pleated like an accordion as I looked at the papers again.

I set the check aside to deal with later. Since this problem appeared to be beyond my skill set, I decided to review it with Opal and Lester on Monday. I continued to work my way through the files, and all in all, I found three more in which the settlement numbers did not match the appraisal amounts.

"Geez." How could the check be different from the claim? Opal had informed me the two should be equal. I shook my head at the obvious error, not getting how this worked. When the customers discovered the differences, they would be ringing the phones incessantly. Definitely not happy campers.

After making copies of the checks, I labeled a separate folder, put these papers in it, and stored the folder in my desk to review with Lester & Opal. Another implementation of Buy Rite Employee Guideline #3.

I straightened my desk, nice and neat. After turning off the computer, I grabbed my handbag and then speed-walked to the door to flip the lights. *Goofy girl.* Nothing had happened after all and nothing to worry about.

****

In the parking lot, a different story revealed itself: My left rear tire had a puncture in the sidewall. The tire wasn't the new one I'd purchased to replace the damaged one. When I bought the new one, I instructed the service guy to put it on the front and to rotate the used one to the back.

"Crap." I squatted to take a closer look. Flatter than the western Kansas prairie. Remembering the difficulty with the tight lug nuts from last time, I parked my carcass in the little bit of shade under the lone tree and phoned Dad. Unfortunately for me, Mom answered.

"Hey, Mom." I hoped by using an uplifting tone she wouldn't garner anything from my voice. And if she did, I hoped to deflect her from the inevitable little talk.

"Hattie? Is something wrong? Where are you? I can tell from my caller ID you're calling from your cell phone." Mom lowered her voice, "Don't tell me. You're in the hospital—"

I hung my head. "Mom—"

"I'm on my way—"

"Mom, I'm not at the hospital." With extreme reluctance, I apprised her of my predicament.

"What's going on with you and tires? Tires don't grow on trees, you know." Her statement diverted my attention to envision multiple tire swings hanging from tree branches. "You need to be more careful. Are you driving through construction sites and picking up nails?"

Mom could be right; this could happen. Mentally, I plotted my route from my apartment to Buy Rite's office. *No. No. No.* As far as I knew, I hadn't driven through any construction sites, but that didn't leave out stuff tossed onto the streets with reckless abandon.

"I don't think so. Besides, these cuts are in the

sidewall and look like a puncture, not a random nail or screw in the tread. Usually, regular flats are easily fixed with a plug or a patch."

"A cut, you say? I don't like the sounds of that. Tires are expensive, and I'm worried because you don't have a permanent job and don't have enough savings. You should report the incident to the property management company. Or maybe the police. Call Allan Wellborn."

"Yes, Mom."

"You need to be more careful."

The truth was her daughters could never be careful enough. "Yes, Mom."

"Let me get your father," she said abruptly.

Mom trotted off to find Dad. After I'd explained my problem, I heard him sigh. "I'm on my way." Dad put Mom back on the phone.

I could picture her in the background, waving her hands for him to turn over the handset. I wouldn't label Mom a nag. No matter what age I would be, she would always be my mom and didn't let go easily. I half-listened as I sat on the curb, doodling with a stick in the gutter dirt while she delivered one more piece of information.

"...ran into Shirley Wellborn at the grocery store yesterday."

Whoa. Her tidbit brought me to attention. "You ran into Mrs. Wellborn? Where?"

"If you would listen," Mom chastised. "I said, I ran into Shirley Wellborn, you know, Allan and Sarah Anne's mother, at the grocery store yesterday. Over sweet potatoes, she told me you've had a few dates with Allan. How come I didn't know about this? I would like to know these things before my friends tell me, especially when my own daughter is involved."

I didn't have a chance to say anything. Which was normal.

She continued her scolding, "Allan's such a nice boy. Were you nice in return? Are you minding your manners?"

Will anything in my life be mine? Now, every time I would see her, she would ask about A. Wellborn. "Yes, Mom."

"So, what did you and Allan do?" She went on and on, extolling his virtues and pontificating on what "a nice boy he is" and whenever she saw him at the grocery store, service station, et cetera, he always spoke to her and helped her with her bags or pumping gas.

Her *nice* made me want to gag.

She rolled out more of the *How to Treat Men* little talk, and like I'd told the Funsisters, I could repeat it verbatim. She meant well, but after the forty-eighth millionth time, she sounded way beyond tiresome. After a while, I tuned her out and picked up my stick to continue the dirt doodling. My stick figures were outstanding. "Yes, Mom," I confessed randomly when she drew a breath, "We ate pizza a couple of times. We went to a party. The End."

I left out the parts about throwing him out, slamming the door in his face, our court dates, and *yeah, sure*, I thought sarcastically, I really wanted to tell Mom about the time A. Wellborn and I had almost wild, almost sex. *Ick*. Nobody talked about sex with their parents.

"Hattie, just remember being nice is a desirable quality. Do the right thing."

Nice. Mom needed a new word. A. Wellborn was nice. I was supposed to be nice. After years of being a "nice girl," I wanted to break this habit. I liked *dangerous* and *sassy* and *daring.*

"Hattie." Her voice pierced through my musing. "Did you hear me?"

Who couldn't? "Yes, Mom." I saw Dad had parked his car by mine, ready for daughter rescue. "Gotta go." I punched the off button to silence her and walked over to meet him.

He gave me a hug. Crouching by the punctured tire, he rubbed his finger over the cut. "Do you have any enemies?" he said in jest, glancing around. "This cut looks exactly like the other one. What do you think?"

"You're right. It's like the other one." I ran my finger across the tire to examine the damage further. I was no expert in flat tires, although I appeared to be on the fast track to becoming one. However, two punctured tires in the same parking lot in the same parking place seemed too coincidental. We stared at each other while I asked the question crossing both our minds, "Could someone do this intentionally?"

Dad tilted his head. "It's very odd you've had two tires punctured while parked in this particular space. I was joking earlier when I made the remark about any enemies. Seriously, have you made someone angry?"

I considered this. I hadn't been really angry, except with A. Wellborn, and he'd managed to redeem himself. The Funsisters' jesting had upset me for a little while, but I was over that. Besides, they wouldn't do this.

Is someone angry with me? I hadn't a clue. "I don't

think so. If so, I don't know who."

He removed the tools stowed under the passenger seat to jack the car. Companionably, we changed the tire and stored the damaged one on the front seat. "Guess I'd be making a trip to the tire store. Again."

"Hattie, watch out." Dad wiped his hands on a cloth. "Don't you need money to buy the replacement tire?"

Since becoming gainfully employed, I'd put aside some greenbacks. Granted, I wanted to use it to escape from Buy Rite and to continue my quest for the impossible dream job. I sighed with regret. My sparse savings would be enough to fund the tire. I pecked his cheek. "No, Dad, I'll use my savings. More chocolate chip cookies?"

"Great minds, etc," he said. "The others went real fast."

"Mom?" We knew she'd sneak a few.

"A good guess." He hung his head and studied his shoes before asking, "Date tonight?"

I shook my head. "Not tonight."

He scratched his temple. "You could come over and have dinner with your mother and me."

Right now, boring sounded more exciting than dinner with Mom and Dad. He really was sweet, but after Mom's lecture on tires and A. Wellborn, I just wanted to be alone. She had *little talk* momentum going and would pop in her other lecture tapes, which would not make for a fun evening. I would take a pass, but I didn't want to hurt Dad's feelings.

"Thanks for the offer, but I think I'll hang at my place, do the piles of laundry, and pump up the résumé."

Dad nodded. He probably understood more about Mom and her little talks than we knew. Many a time, he'd heard her dispensing them and had retreated to his recliner with the evening paper. With a wave, he drove off.

Chapter Seventeen

Another week passed. A. Wellborn phoned while I was involved with ironing.

All this time alone gave me plenty of opportunity to ponder things, like almost wild, almost sex. I really wanted to finish what we'd started after the engagement party. My thoughts shifted to the almost kiss in the court house. I really wanted to finish what we'd almost started.

Hell, I wanted to finish something with him.

A. Wellborn asked about work.

I said it was the "same-o, same-o," and offhandedly, I mentioned the check discrepancies I'd found.

"Tell me about it," he said.

"Aren't you tired of Buy Rite stories?"

"Anything you do interests me."

Whatever. I had a hard time believing Buy Rite would ever be interesting to anyone. Removing a blouse from a hangar, I described the computer crash and entering the new data. I told of finding the appraisals and the settlement checks with discrepancies on Opal's desk, and how I'd gone ahead and filed those away after making copies.

What I had done seemed ordinary, routine, and efficient. I told him about the special folder I'd made which contained the information. After laying the shirt collar open, I adjusted the temperature on the iron to delicate.

"That's it?" he asked.

I made a few swipes across the collar. "I guess so. Like I said, I haven't found any problems since. Maybe the computer glitch cleared up."

"So, the discrepancies aren't normal?"

"I don't think so. Perhaps someone's computer program messed up, and thank goodness, I found the mistakes."

"I would like to see the checks to better understand what you're describing."

I straightened a sleeve on the ironing board, matching the seams. I passed the iron over the length of the sleeve. "Hmm... What about after work?"

"Can't."

I heard pages flipping while he answered. Guess he was multi-tasking. That sorta felt...annoying.

"This case has me tied up. I know. How about you fax me the stuff?"

"Just a sec. I need something to write with." Setting down the phone and iron, I ran to my desk and grabbed paper and a pen. "Shoot."

And A. Wellborn rattled off the fax number. "Are you okay otherwise?"

I guessed from that remark he still cared. I decided to go for broke and admit the truth. I set pen and pad on the bed. "A little lonely."

"Me, too."

This sounded encouraging. I perked up. I went to my bed and flopped down, watching the ceiling fan turn. "I do know one other thing, but it's not exactly about B.R.A."

"Tell me about it."

I twirled a strand of hair round my finger. "After I finished last Saturday, I found my Jeep had another flat tire. For the second time, I called Dad for daughter rescue. I owe him a lot of cookies."

"I would have come."

The twirling stopped. For a teensy sec, I'd contemplated calling A. Wellborn, but felt more comfortable asking Dad. I shifted the phone to my other ear. "I know you would have and thanks for the offer. Dad thinks it's his duty to rescue his darling daughters."

"I remember, Harry's harem."

"Yes. And Dad likes chocolate chip cookies. He complained Mom doesn't make them since she began dieting."

"I like chocolate chip cookies, too—Hint, hint."

"Poor baby. Hold on." I returned to my ironing, checked the water level, and added some. After smoothing the other blouse sleeve, I picked up the iron. "I'm back."

"What are you doing?"

"Ironing."

"You like to?"

"It's a Cooks' graduation requirement."

"I see. I can't do daughter rescue, but I can do friend rescue," he said. "Honest, I won't mind."

"It's a deal. Next time, I'll call you." I shifted the shirt to the other sleeve. "Dad said this puncture looked like the other one."

"Tell me about it."

I held the iron in mid-air while considering this particular phrase he'd used. He'd said it many times. I reached back, and *yeah*, he'd said it about the files, the report, the appraisals, and my job. And now, he'd made this same remark about my tires. I found it hard to believe punctured tires were interesting. "You say 'tell me about it' a lot."

"Sorry. Bad cop habit."

"It's okay, I just noticed. Anyway, Dad said the cut looked the same as the first one. Both tires had been stabbed in the sidewall."

"Describe the cuts."

"About a half inch in width, maybe smaller than, say, the width of a dinner knife. Right in the sidewall, three inches above the rim. You know, on the smooth part that looks super when Armor-alled." I shook out the blouse and opened it across the board to run the iron the length of the back. *Five more to go.*

"Why would someone cut tires? Tires aren't cheap." He cleared his throat. "I don't know how to put this without upsetting you."

"Lay it on me."

"Do you need some help, you know, with buying new ones?"

Shocking. Label me officially embarrassed. Mom, Dad, and now, A. Wellborn all knew about my financial difficulties. I shouldn't complain about them asking. They had the best intentions.

Setting down the iron, I draped the wrinkle-free blouse over a hangar. "No, thank you, I have a little money banked. I suppose it's why I haven't left B.R.A. yet. I keep bringing home the almighty bacon. You're sweet to offer." My hand smoothed another blouse collar across the ironing board.

I heard a *huh*. All guys wanted to be called sweet.

"Dad's concerned my tires have been ruined in the

same parking space in the same parking lot at about the same time. He wanted to know if I've made somebody angry."

"And have you?"

"I told him no. I didn't say, well, maybe you."

"Frustrated is a better word and sexually frustrated is an even a better one."

So A. Wellborn thought about the almost wild, almost sex, too. I smiled happily, then I stuck out my tongue at the receiver. I repositioned a sleeve to ready for a pressing. "Gee, I hate to hear that."

"Anything else?"

"Dad asked me to be careful. Ouch." I shook my burned finger.

"You okay?"

"Just a slight burn."

"Ironing sounds...dangerous."

"Sometimes, even I am a klutz. Where were we?"

"Talking about the parking lot. It wouldn't hurt to check with the property management company for the security records for the Saturdays when your tires were damaged. Did you report anything to security?"

"No, I hadn't got around to it. Mom asked the same thing. I'd assumed the first time was a random act."

"Two times are more than random. You need to be careful."

"Yes, Sir. Anything new concerning June's murder?" I asked, still nosy about my predecessor.

"You know I can't talk about on-going investigations."

After setting down the iron, I paced the bedroom, the phone smashed against my ear. "Oh, come on. I work at Buy Rite, and you're investigating the murder of a former employee. Aren't you concerned, knowing I work at the office where someone had been murdered?"

"Of course I am. I told you the other day to be careful."

Last Saturday's visit to the office had felt weird with the lights off and me all alone. And now, with another tire ruined, my concern had heightened. Chills raced up my arm. "You don't have to yell."

"I'm sorry, I didn't mean to," he said. "It's just this stuff is scary, and you're too close to the situation. A former employee of Buy Rite was murdered, and the murderer is still on the loose. Don't forget that, Hattie."

God, I wanted to wring his neck and squeeze out better answers. "I don't see how I could forget 'cause I think about it every freakin' day I go to work. What I don't get is why you can't tell me more about what's going on?"

"I tell you what I can."

"Like that's good enough."

"Tough."

Unbelievable. This conversation had flipped to the dark side. My grip tightened on my phone. "'Tough'?"

"You heard me. I have my job to do. I can't talk about any aspect of any on-going case. I'm not bending any rules," he said.

This part wasn't sounding good, not at all. *I wish he wasn't so hard core.* I bit my lower lip before venturing to say, "Not even for me, for my safety."

"You don't play fair."

"Fine." My blown-out breath ruffled my hair. "I know where I stand. I hope you can handle my possible murder."

"Not funny."

"Didn't mean to be."

"You could always quit."

"Sure I could, and as the saying goes: money grows on trees."

"Dammit, Hattie, let's be serious," he said. "Watch your back and be careful. Listen to the number one cop rule: If it feels bad, it is."

Great. Another rule. Little irritations pricked my spine. "Fine."

"You know the part about frustrating?"

I wondered about this question. With unease, I said, "Yeah..."

"Add annoying." A. Wellborn hung up.

What? I stared at the phone, so not believing what I'd heard. I wasn't annoying. Only a man from his perspective would state that. I wouldn't have said annoying. I would have said...persistent. A good word not used often.

I didn't want to argue about June and Buy Rite. I would rather argue about a movie or a restaurant selection or a sex position. However, devotion to his work was an admirable quality. Let's face it, if I was too close to danger, he wouldn't let me go there.

I returned to my wrinkled clothing. *Men.*

****

On my Monday morning commute, I stopped at the red traffic lights and reviewed the appraisals and settlement check discrepancies. I continued on and parked my car in a different spot than the one under the problematic tree. I exited and made my way to the building with the folder stuck under my arm.

At the office, while Lester and Opal communed over a morning coffee fix, I fiddled around my desk, adjusting the stapler, pencil jar, and sticky pads just so. When the coast seemed clear, I faxed the discrepancy copies to A. Wellborn like I'd said I would.

I waited for Opal to leave Lester's office which she did. I carried the folder tight against my chest and knocked on his door.

He signaled for me to enter.

"Eh-eh," I coughed and took the chair in front of his desk. *Hel-loo cancer.* I so didn't love the idea of risking life and limb for a crappy job. "Morning, Lester. I had to come in on Saturday to finish the work I couldn't complete on Friday when the system crashed."

"Opal told me about it," he said. "Thanks for your dedication."

Even though Lester had a grotesque habit, he always said nice things. "Yes, well, I finished the data entry, and since I had plenty of time, I checked Opal's desk for settlement claim checks to be copied and filed in the client's respective folder."

His brow shot up. "Oh?"

"As I filed the claim checks, I found the settlement checks didn't match the appraisals. I'm wondering how this could happen?" I opened the folder and handed it to Lester. "Could something be wrong with the machine which prints the checks? Or could someone be entering the wrong amount?"

As he examined the information, Lester adjusted his glasses. "Yes, this is an interesting error. I'll have to investigate further."

"Has this happened before?"

"Mmm, I don't recollect any, but my memory isn't always perfect."

"Occasionally, I receive phone calls when I answer

the phone at lunchtime, and sometimes, the customers have complained about checks, particularly the sport utility vehicle customers. I collect the pertinent information and pass it on to Opal. I think some of those discrepancies are directly related to these complaints." I waved my hand toward the documents.

Closing the file, Lester leaned back in his chair, and studied me thoughtfully. "Thanks, Hattie, for a job well done. I'll call the Home Office, and we'll uncover what's going on. Obviously, something isn't right."

"You're welcome," I said and stood, taking my leave.

Opal passed me in the doorway to Lester's office as I exited. Surprisingly, her ear hadn't been plastered to his office door to eavesdrop on our conversation. *Cough-cough.* I hurried to the corridor for a gulp of fresh air.

The rest of the day, I accomplished more of the grunt work. I checked the files and found no more matching problems between the estimates and the settlement checks. Guess I'd had a computer fluke after all.

****

The week passed quietly. So quiet, I had very little data entry to do—which seemed odd. I asked Opal what was up with that.

She shrugged while looking over her glasses' rim. "Maybe it's a slow period. Maybe a hold up with the adjusters. Or sometimes, we don't have any claims until we have rain. Rain and ice are great for business. Lots of crashes."

She sounded happy? I said, "No kidding."

"Yes, the body shops love inclement weather. We

Vicki Batman

call them a Big Money day. I'll check." She turned away, pressing the phone to her ear.

Her way of dismissing me. I used the down time to straighten files and dust. Yuck.

****

Later in the evening, A. Wellborn phoned, saying he'd received the fax with the settlement check discrepancies and reviewed the information.

I sat on my bed, hunched over my toes as I applied a second coat of nail polish to my freshly manicured nails.

"Tell me again what you're thinking about this," he said.

"I found the settlement checks and the appraisal amounts don't match. They're supposed to be identical."

"So, why aren't they?"

"Don't know. I asked Lester, and he said sometimes mistakes occur."

"Most of the discrepancies are for Jeeps which were stolen or parts which were stolen."

"I noticed that, too."

As I shook the bottle of Beautifully Pink, I shifted to adjust my right foot just so. "When I cover the phones at noon, the customers' complaints seem to be confined to the Jeep owners."

"Interesting. Did Lester ever call Buy Rite's internal squad?"

"No, at least not as of Monday. I asked Opal, and she said she didn't know either, said she would follow up, and thanked me for the reminder." Quiet on his end. I concentrated to make each nail perfect. "Why are you asking me these questions? What does the fax have to

256

do with June's death?"

"I didn't say it does."

I stopped painting and sat upright, staring at the wall as if I was staring at him. "You know, I'm sick of the bullshit. I've asked about this stuff before and all I get is your macho policeman line." I changed my voice to a superior manly tone, mimicking his, "'I can't talk about on-going investigations.' "

"Hattie, we've been through this before. If we can't talk like adults, I'm hanging up."

Hanging up? Talk like adults? Are we six years old? This whole line got my back up. "Fine. But somehow, the newspaper seems to know more. An article appeared in *The Sommerville Express*."

"I didn't say a thing to the paper. Any information came from higher up the food chain."

"You were interviewed for the article."

"Well..."

Does he actually think I'll tell the world what he's up to? "Come. On. I work at Buy Rite, and I need to know if I'm in danger."

"I told you to be careful. Are you? Are you carrying pepper spray, watching for strangers, and parking in lighted lots?"

How funny. I'd just stashed a new canister of pepper spray in my hand bag yesterday. "Yes."

"Why don't you quit? Your friend'll help you find a new job."

"I-I..." I was flummoxed. Truthfully, I still wasn't motivated enough to quit. Incoming cash made my life so much easier. Anyway, I had serious doubts about Opal and Lester as killers. They seemed too ordinary. "I'm not a quitter."

"Suit yourself. Gotta go."

I let the phone slip from my left hand and focused on the one remaining toe to paint. If A. Wellborn really cared, surely he would be more concerned about me. And maybe he was. Maybe he just didn't know what to say. I needed to think about everything.

I twisted shut the bottle and wiggled my painted toes. Beautifully Pink.

****

On Friday, the computer crashed. Irritated, I pushed my chair away from my desk and went to Opal's desk. "Opal, the computer is driving me crazy.

She pressed her glasses into place. "Oh, how so, Hattie?"

"It's gone down, a-gain." I huffed a breath in exasperation. "I'll come in on Saturday, but for the last time. The computer needs to be fixed, no if, ands, or buts. Or Buy Rite should buy a new one. I am not donating any more of my Saturdays to the freakin' computer."

She bobbed her head. "You're right. The computer needs a thorough check-up. If that doesn't help, we should invest in a newer model. Yours is the one I used before I got the one I'm working on. I told the Home Office to send two, but they only sent one. I'll make the call." She retrieved the spare key from her desk drawer. "Thank you for giving up your time and keeping us on schedule. After Saturday, you will have made up all the time you missed with your court dates."

I was shocked and amazed she'd agreed with me on anything. I took the key. "I had the same idea."

"Humpf." She didn't move, acting reluctant to release me. "By the way, how's your detective?"

"Technically, he isn't *my* detective." My mouth curved into a bit of a smile as my cheeks went red and hot. "He's fine, tho' lately, I haven't seen a lot of him. He said he's working on a murder case."

"Really? How interesting." She relaxed back in her chair. "Crime in Sommerville seems to be up."

"I guess. From what I read in the paper it is. Stolen cars and murder." Murder made me think of June. "Opal, can I ask you something?"

"Of course."

"How did June die?"

"The only thing I know is the police found her dead at home, an apparent suicide."

"Oh." Opal's story about June's suicide coincided with A. Wellborn's.

"Yes, Lester and I were-are"—she turned her head aside to conceal her spilling tears—"grief stricken."

I moved closer and patted her sleeve. Her bullet-proof polyester jacket felt thick and had to be hot. "I can only imagine. June worked here a long time didn't she? I know she felt like family to you."

Opal reached for her tissue box on the credenza. Removing one, she tented it and dabbed the corner of her eyes in a delicate fashion. "She'd been with Buy Rite for three years. We were a happy little family. June had always talked about staying with us until she retired. I never thought something like this would have happened. Never."

June had retired, just not of her own doing. I picked up a pencil, rolling it through my fingers. "By the way, Opal, did Lester tell you about the folder I made, containing information regarding appraisals and the settlement check amounts not matching?"

Her brow narrowed. "No, he hasn't shown me anything."

"I also told him about some phone calls I'd received at lunchtime. The insureds were complaining about checks, and how I'd passed the information to you."

With a short sniff, Opal went back to her prim-and-proper self. After tossing the tissue in her wastebasket, she shuffled her mail into a neat pile. "I clearly remember those messages, Hattie, and I've handled them. As usual, you're your efficient self. I'll consult with Lester regarding the check discrepancies, and we'll handle the matter through the proper channels. I'll correct any errors. Buy Rite and Lester's reputations could be affected by mistakes of this magnitude."

I lingered by her desk a moment more. "Opal?"

She slapped down her letter opener on her desk "What-is-it-now, Hattie?"

Yikes. "Did Lester contact Buy Rite's internal squad today about all the unusual SUV claims?"

"I don't know. Thanks for reminding me to check with him and thanks for working on Saturday."

Obviously, she wanted me to leave her alone. Before turning away, I said, "You're welcome."

****

Another Saturday and another guilt run. Chocolate consumption ran at an all-time high. I'd purchased the one pounder of chocolate covered peanut candies on sale at a big box store, two for three dollars, and felt compelled to use my money wisely by stockpiling when they were such a good value. After all, as a pro-shopper extraordinaire, I had a reputation to maintain.

But along with guilt consumption came guilt runs.

Determined to finish a two-miler one of these days, I repeated my mantra, "No more chocolate. No more chocolate." But I knew me. This approach wouldn't stick. I loved chocolate way too much to give it up.

After my run, I took a refreshing shower. Jenny popped in my room to ask what I'd planned for the day. I told her about Buy Rite's piece of junk, freakin' computer, and my plan to catch up. She bounced on my bed while I styled my hair in the bathroom.

"Hey," she said in a loud voice to be heard over the hairdryer. "Are you interested in doing something for dinner, and if not, something else?"

Silencing the dryer, I heard the mattress spring up and down. "Sure." I gave my hair a quick comb and spritzed it three times with hard-to-hold hairspray. "Anytime. Anyplace. Don't you have a date?"

She stopped the bed bouncing. "Not tonight. He's out of town. A bachelor party in Cancun."

Dressed in my fuchsia capris and white tee, I checked the mirror one last time. "How about I call you after I wrap things up?"

"That's a plan."

I picked up my tote bag, a knock-off of a top designer's. "But be warned, I haven't had meat-for-the-week in a long time, and I'm thinking steak. A big juicy, nine-ounce fillet mignon at Yahooooo! Ranch. Onion strings are calling me."

Jenny laughed. "I can deal with it."

****

My piss-poor attitude transferred to hating every minute of the drive I made to Buy Rite. Seated at outdoor restaurants, happy people enjoyed the fresh air and eating good food. Probably the last time before the wet, fall weather set in. Through the open car window, I heard laughter and the chinking of china and silver.

Passing the independent theater, I glanced at the marquee to see if the features looked worthwhile. "Play it Again, Sam" and "Casablanca" were showing, back-to-back—an excellent pairing.

I really needed to talk to Trixie about another job.

Pulling in the parking lot, I thought about the pros and cons of parking my carbaby in the spot under the lone tree. If I'd parked somewhere else, maybe I wouldn't have had the punctured tires? I considered moving to a different spot because the corner parking space could've been the source of my bad luck.

My alter ego, perched on my shoulder, said, "But the lonesome tree provides the only bit of shade."

What the hell. Since I was fully armed, and mostly dangerous with pepper spray, I slotted my car in the spot anyway. With summer almost over, I wouldn't have to worry about soaring temperatures for much longer. The stores had begun to feature the fall clothing lines, and I had an itch to splurge on a seasonal change.

After opening the office door, I flipped the light switch, and did my quick swat team reconnaissance around the workplace. But no bugger bears jumped out to scare the crap outta me. Deep in my gut, I knew nothing would anyway. In all likelihood, I sensed a lack of familiarity when I worked on a Saturday. After snapping on more lights, I made my way to my desk and turned on the computer.

Nothing happened. I clicked, pushed buttons, and in anger, slapped the top of the monitor and the desktop to make the thing operate. Nothing at all.

Damn. Damn. Damn. I checked the cords plugged

into the surge protector. Na da. I followed the thick rope to the wall outlet where I tested the plug. Everything fitted nice and tight. I stomped my foot in irritation, hands on hips. I hated when this happened. Machines were intended to facilitate our work, not make it more difficult.

What the hell is wrong? God. Aggravated didn't begin to describe how I felt.

Crawling on my hands and knees, I rechecked the plugs at the back of the processing unit. At the sound of the office door closing, I peeked over the desk top and spotted...Opal?

Why is Opal at the office on a Saturday?

Startled by her unexpected appearance, I jolted and bumped the side of my head against the side of the desk. My fingers rubbed the sore spot. She'd said nothing on Friday about coming in today.

Uh oh. I bet Miss Plump-and-Proper wanted to check on me. She thought I fiddly-farted around when she wasn't present to supervise.

I studied Opal. I don't know why she seemed so, so scary. Her pompous tone of voice reminded me of Mrs. Phillips, my fourth-grade teacher which, now that I thought about it, was scary, especially at Halloween when she spit plastic roaches into her palm.

Office politics were the pits. On one hand, I could have a dysfunctional childhood issue in dealing with adults. Or maybe I have a confrontational issue. I didn't want to rock the boat ever. Nevertheless, she had come and needed to be dealt with.

"Howdy, Opal." I stood, brushing carpet lint from my knees. "Nice to see you."

"Hello, Hattie."

Opal and I were having our usual social skill issues, meaning she had few. I tried sucking up. I flashed an impressive, almost brilliantly, freshly-brushed, dazzling smile. Leaning forward, I rested my hands on my desk. "What a nice surprise. Are you behind on work, too? I mean, you're always so efficient, I wouldn't have ever thought you'd have to play catch up."

Plopping in my chair, I waved my hand toward the equipment. "I still can't get the damn computer to turn on. I've checked all of the plugs, all of the outlets, et cetera. Do you know what to do? Did you remember to call the service technicians? Are they coming today?"

Opal's lack of response led me to assume she must be really angry. I took in her appearance as she made her way to her desk. She needed to evolve. Today, polyester jeans in the University of Texas burnt orange covered her legs and matched a flowered blouse, cut western shirt style. Surely, she could pull together a more pleasing ensemble.

She dragged her chair away from her desk with deliberate care and placed her handbag in the seat. Her fingers played with the perfectly arranged pens and pencils. She extracted her favorite letter opener.

From the corner of my eye, I caught her observing my poor attempts to activate the computer. The blade of the letter opener slapped against the palm of her hand and somehow, she managed to do it without cutting herself.

"No," she said, "I don't have to play catch up. You might as well stop playing with the computer. I didn't call the service technicians."

My fingers halted their scrambling across the

keyboard. Opal didn't seem to be herself at all. I frowned, trying to figure out why she hadn't called the repair company. As I blinked a couple of times, I sensed confusion encompass me. "I don't understand. Why didn't you call? On Friday, we'd agreed you would contact the technicians."

"I know what the problem is." Slap-slap sounded the letter opener as the blade hit her hand. She pushed her big butt away from her desk and swished her way to mine.

"Can you fix it? What do we need to do?" I asked. "I'm so illiterate when it comes to computers. I wish I knew better how to repair them. The best I could do was, like I told you, check the cords and the outlets. I've pushed all kinds of buttons. I even cursed and slapped the stupid thing. Sorry."

"I'll explain." Opal walked toward me, with an eye on the computer. Unexpectedly, she swung her arm, and the letter opener carved my bicep.

"Ow!" Blood poured from the cut, causing tears to stream from my eyes. Automatically, my other hand closed over the painful wound, squeezing like a tourniquet to staunch the bleeding.

She stepped back to admire her cutwork.

I stared at her, not believing what she'd done. I moved the hand clasped over my arm and took a quick peek. The cut looked big, about three inches in length, and deep, requiring stitches and throbbing with pain. I scooted away from my desk and backed toward the copier. I had to get out of here.

Opal caught the look I shifted to the door and shuffled with surprisingly quick steps to block me.

"What do you think you're doing, Opal?" I

screamed. *God, the pain.* Little drops of blood seeped from under my grip. "You cut my arm, and it hurts and I'm bleeding. I'm going to the emergency room. I bet I'll need stitches and a tetanus shot. I know I'm not number one on your hit parade, but you didn't have to cut me. Now, get outta my way."

Slap-slap went the letter opener.

Again, she advanced with a look in her eye which definitely was not prim nor proper. Her face looked menacing, evil danced in her eyes. Her grip tightened on the opener as she pointed it in my direction. I swore I saw a drop of my blood on the tip drip to the floor.

"You've caused problems from the moment you came to Buy Rite."

I danced away from her. I surely didn't want another hack job. Cutting a look to the door, I worried at what she would possibly try next. "Me?"

"You."

"I don't think so. I did everything you said to do." I brushed tears from my cheeks on my lifted shoulder. Red rivers trickled down my arm. The smell was unpleasant. Queasy, my stomach seized.

"No, you didn't."

"Yes, I did."

"I've never met such a stupid girl," she said.

She would not make me feel weak. Would not. I stood fast and firm. "I did! I know I did. I did the copying, the filing, and the data entry. I answered the phone," I said more to myself as my voice trailed off.

"You did. But you did more."

"What's wrong with doing more? Your Guideline #3 said: Show initiative. So I did. I put together a few reports on a couple of problems."

Tears flooded my eyes which in turn, causing my mascara to dissolve. The sludge burned and obstructed my view.

Like a flash of lightning, she struck at me again.

I noticed in the nick of time and flinched to one side. "Stop it, Opal. Stop hurting me," I said. "I thought we were friends."

"Friends?" She pushed her glasses into place. "I could never be friends with someone like you."

Bloody beads plopped to the floor, leaving splotches on the new oatmeal carpet. I peered at her through my watery eyes. "This is not in my job description."

"You think you're so funny."

"I don't. I am quitting. You can find some other temporary."

"You aren't going anywhere."

Her laugh carried a wicked tone and frightened me. I had to get out of here. I didn't think my legs could support me much longer. *Allan?* "Yes, I am."

"No, you aren't. I won't let you." And again, she jabbed at me with the sharp opener.

I dodged to my left. Now, I was truly scared. She looked deranged and sounded insane. Her perfectly coiffed page-boy stuck out wildly at the crown. Her eyes had narrowed with intent to kill. *How does she get her energy? Why is she angry?*

Perhaps if I kept her talking, I could convince her not to hurt me. Or maybe, I would slow her down and get away. I took small rearward movements across the room with quick side-to-side glances to uncover a way to escape. I staggered and reeled through the office, trying to put something in her way to stop her. My backside hit her desk chair, and I circled around it.

I heard the slap-slap of the opener striking her palm as she followed my progress and felt her threat. If only I could knock her to the ground. I said, "Let me go to the hospital, Opal. I'll say I cut myself on a fence. They'll believe me. I don't know what you've done, but whatever it is, I won't tell."

"I told you, Hattie, you won't be leaving Buy Rite."

And now! I grabbed her desk chair and flung it in her direction. My hope and prayer was the chair would knock her down like a bowling pin, and I could run. The chair tripped, flipped, and rolled her way in a clumsy effort.

And missed.

Damn. Desperation inundated me.

Opal moved faster than I gave her credit. She smiled at my failure. Now, she stood closer than ever. Her eyes burned with delirium, reflecting more rage. "Your little stunt didn't work well, did it? I told you, you won't be leaving Buy Rite."

Eventually, she had me backed against Lester's office door. She struck again, this time nicking my neck. More tears poured. God, I hurt terribly. All the icky bloody stuff made my stomach roil again. My head went woozy and I had a tricky time thinking straight because of the vortex circling through my brain. My body tightened. Crisscrossing my arms, I placed hands on all my cuts. "Opal, why are you doing this? Why are you so angry with me?"

"Why?"

I nodded.

"Because you found the checks."

I felt clueless in America. "What checks?"

"The settlement checks. How dense can someone be?" Squinting, she leaned forward. "Do I have to spell it out to you?"

I nodded.

"You noticed the amount was different from the appraisal, pointed out the discrepancy to Lester in your reports, and told me about it the other day. Just like June."

"June? I don't understand. June is dead." And then, I knew.

I could see from the gleam flaming in Opal's eyes she knew I knew. My skin went cold.

"Yes, June Short, our former employee, had figured out everything. *Everything.* She discovered the check discrepancies and caught Lester writing new ones. She confronted him, saying he skimmed off the settlement claim checks. She called Buy Rite's internal fraud squad.

"I overheard her accusations. Lester would've been exposed, ruining him. He would've been thrown in jail, and I couldn't let something disgraceful happen to him. For more than thirty years, Lester has been an upstanding man, a pillar in the insurance community. He would be...humiliated. June had to be stopped."

For a moment, Opal ended her tirade. Her eyes glazed over with her bizarre obsession.

I said what was obvious, "You love him." She didn't reply. She had to love him. What else would explain why she'd done these terrible things?

"I had to stop her. Lester did this for his family. You've seen his fat, slovenly body. His constant chain-smoking. Last week, he was diagnosed with stage-four throat cancer. Only a matter of time before he dies, and he knows the end is near. He wanted to leave his family with a secure future. With this plan, he could. Buy Rite would never know. They would never investigate him. Or maybe he would be dead, and they'd leave him alone.

"But June didn't care. After work, I'd asked her to stay late and help me fix a claims mess I'd fabricated. I offered her a ride home when she missed her bus. She invited me in for margaritas. I watched her cut and squeeze limes. All the time my head was racing. I acted fast and seized my letter opener. I forced her wrists to the counter. The opener is sharp, very sharp. I scored her wrists with fast slices. The cuts were deep and the blood poured out. She opened her mouth and..." Opal swallowed hard, "she slumped to the floor. I-I watched her lying on the floor, unable to do anything, the blood p-pooling beside her, all life draining away."

Gradually, her voice grew weaker as the story unfolded. "I couldn't move. I had-had no idea. She slipped to the floor and died. I didn't know, didn't know about all the blood...so fast. I just wanted her to stop. To leave Lester alone."

She wept openly, the tears flowing freely with her remembrance. With the back of her hand, she swiped them aside. "I cleaned up the limes and drink stuff, wiping down the bottles for prints. After I dipped her paring knife in her blood, I dropped it by her hand. The next day, Lester was concerned. June never missed work; so I pretended to call her at home. I knew she wouldn't answer. After a while, he made me notify the police who got the property manager to open her apartment. They assumed she'd committed suicide from the slit wrists and her single, solitary lifestyle with only a dog for company." She shook her head. "Lester never knew, never knew."

Opal seemed to be visiting la-la land, providing me a small window to edge my feet toward the door. But at my slight movement, I saw her blink and focus again, pointing the letter opener at me. "*And you*. You're dating a detective, and according to the paper, the same one who came around Buy Rite, sniffing for information."

My head went from side to side. I would invent any fabrication to save my skin. "He doesn't know anything."

"I doubt it. You're so much in love, you probably told him everything."

My mind raced around what I could have said to him, but concentration eluded me.

She pushed her face toward mine. "Haven't you figured this out?"

I must be stupid because all I could think of was how horrible I hurt and how I wanted to get away. "I haven't figured anything out."

"You bimbo. I never wanted to hire you, but Lester did. With June gone, he said I needed help because I'd fallen behind. You..." She stabbed the opener at me.

My reflex turned on, and I jerked back.

"You come in here with your fancy clothes, your cute figure, and hair, exuding your young attitude of ready-to-take-on-the-world. How naïve, how stupid, how sickening."

Horrified, I stared at her. Opal was batty.

"Lester is skimming money off the claims, particularly the Jeep claims. You discovered the discrepancy and made a report. You threatened to tell the police and the internal squad, just like June. I had to stop you. I tried to scare you away with the punctured tires, but you kept coming back just like a homeless dog begging for a last supper."

She pushed her chubby body forward. She shoved her hand to my cheek to hold me in place.

I squirmed a bit, but couldn't move much. I heard the draw of her breath as she lifted the arm which held the sharp opener. Instinctively, I raised my hands high, fingers curled in a claw formation for protection. I thrust one punch, rapidly followed with two more. My foot kicked out.

I missed.

With a loud explosion of wood, the office door burst open. I saw A. Wellborn drop to his left side and roll behind Opal's desk.

He zoomed in on her with his gun, his aim steady and true. "Police! Opal, drop the knife and back away from Hattie."

Over her shoulder, she turned her gaze on him for a nanosecond. The smile she gave him was malicious. Just as fast, she returned her attention to me. "Your man of the hour has arrived."

"It's all over," he said, his gaze finding mine, then refocused on her. His hands tightened on the gun. "We know everything. I'm warning you. Drop the knife and back away. Let Hattie go. Now." Standing slowly with his legs spread, he looked in control and sounded every bit a policeman. Briefly, he dipped his head to his right.

I understood his signal and bobbed my head just a tiny bit.

Unexpectedly, he lifted his hands in a surrender

posture. His thumb pressed the gun to his palm, a sign of backing off. "Look, Opal. You don't really want to do this. Put down the weapon. And let's be done."

Her nasty smiled deepened.

He took a step forward. "You don't want to get hurt. You don't want to hurt Hattie. Let her go."

She favored me with the vile look, just like the possessed one she'd bestowed on me earlier. Eyes flat, an evil curl to her mouth. She leaned ever-so-slightly toward me. Her breath blew across my face when she said, "Bimbo."

Her hand holding the letter opener rose.

Repositioning his body, he took aim.

As the letter opener drove down, I jerked from her reach and crashed on my side, landing on my hip.

A. Wellborn shot to kill. The bullet slammed into her head. The impact flung her body backwards. Blood and gray matter exploded from her head, staining the carpet. The letter opener dropped to the floor. Later on in my mind's rerun, this scene had cop show written over it.

A. Wellborn stole a quick glance my way and then checked on Opal's dead, dead body.

Scared shitless, I sat up and scooted far, far away. I couldn't stop weeping and shaking, first with fear, and second, with relief.

I didn't know gunshots were so loud.

I didn't know there would be so much blood.

I didn't know there would be brains.

I didn't know anything.

Maybe I really was a bimbo. Maybe more stuff was in the big world than what I knew.

Satisfied Opal wouldn't be going anywhere, A.

Wellborn rushed to me, communicating into a radio and requesting an ambulance. He yanked me to my feet. His arms wrapped me close, and he held me tighter than tight.

I continued to sob and sob with great release.

He tied his hanky over the cut on my arm.

My blood.

Opal's blood.

Her brains.

I took in the distinctive metallic scent of blood. My head began to swim. Pinpricks dotted my vision.

A. Wellborn pulled me firmly into his body. "Are you okay?"

The room went round and round. "She was trying to k-kill me."

He rocked me back and forth. "I know."

"I'm bl-bleeding."

"You'll be okay. A few stitches and good as new."

My words slurred. "Opal...said...June found out... Lester...skimmed checks. Said...I wouldn't...leave...Buy Rite." My legs felt like rubber. The room faded to black. The whole situation overtook me, and I collapsed to the floor, taking A. Wellborn with me. "I...hate...Buy Rite."

"I know," he said.

Turned out, he really did know.

Chapter Eighteen

The police responded to A. Wellborn's call. They took one look at the god-awful mess and notified the paramedics and the crime scene investigators. The coroner took Opal's body away while the ambulance rushed me to the hospital.

Opal had sliced my arm and my neck with her sharp letter opener which meant significant blood loss. Right before I'd passed out, I remembered seeing stars and feeling thirsty. The trauma of the overpowering episode could be why as well.

Later, Jenny told me while the emergency crew had loaded me in the ambulance, A. Wellborn phoned and filled her in on what had transpired. She had called my parents and all our friends who rushed to the hospital. She said Mom paced the hallways and wrung her hands, and Dad looked like he wanted to cry.

The hospital staff took first-rate care of me. They gave me stitches and a tetanus shot because Mom didn't remember my last inoculation. Otherwise, I checked out okay. A nurse sponged my outfit to a passable clean while I waited. A big bandage covered my arm and a smaller one had been placed on my neck with my hair mostly hiding it.

Later in the evening, Jenny took me to the apartment with instructions to stay quiet and rest for several days. The hospital provided pain pills and antibiotics. Mom wanted me to go home with her, but I knew she would overdo with her hovering concern.

Mom wasn't who I wanted anyway.

Jenny and I were a little confused about what went on behind the scenes. She said she didn't know much. From our other discussions about working at Buy Rite, she'd wondered if Lester could have been June's murderer because of the check scam I'd uncovered.

"Why did A. Wellborn turn up at the office?" I asked.

"He phoned not long after you left. We talked, and he disconnected the moment he heard you were working there." She stroked my hair.

Guess I blew the cops' number one rule: Not careful enough.

I asked, "Where is he right now?"

"Wrapping up?" She shrugged. "He said he would stop by the apartment later and explain everything."

Allan? I need you. A lot.

At home, I shuffled my way to the bathroom. Jenny had offered to prepare a bath, but I turned her down. I wanted to be alone for a while to reflect. I sat on the vanity chair, not moving. Just sat. And thought.

And finally…wept.

After my watery barrage had subsided, I cleaned myself with a soapy wash cloth. I rubbed my face close to dirt free and brushed my teeth. With slight difficulty, I pulled on my favorite pair of pink pajamas. A barrette clipped my hair on back of my head. The bit of clean up exhausted me and hurt my injured arm, despite the anesthetic numbing the area. I slipped on my crimson-framed glasses and ignored my reflection.

I inched to the couch. After propping myself on the

comfortable pillows Jenny provided, I relaxed my body into the softness.

Jenny sat nearby in the club chair with our cell phones placed on the coffee table so she could answer the multitude of calls.

Thank God for my friend.

The shooting incident, the subsequent discovery of June's murder, and the stolen car thefts made the six o'clock news. Afterward, Mom and Dad called. The Funsisters called. Seemed like everyone I knew called, demanding more gruesome details than the news had reported. Jenny was too exhausted to answer and turned off the phones. The whole apartment went dead quiet.

I sucked soda through a straw. The painkillers I popped took effect, and I fell asleep. My dreams were funny. Feeling dopey sucked.

A. Wellborn stopped by our apartment around ten. In my comatose state, I didn't hear the front door open at his soft knock. Jenny told me later A. Wellborn and she had talked quietly for a moment. He insisted on seeing me.

My body flinched at the light touch of his finger stroking my hair. Opening my eyes, I found him sitting on the coffee table by my side.

Soothingly, he stroked his hand on my arm, caressing me in a comforting manner.

Unbounded love for him more than filled my heart.

He said, "I didn't mean to disturb you. I'm sure you need to rest."

My mouth felt clogged, like cotton balls had invaded. I fluttered my fingers at my soda, and he passed it to me. After a sip, I said, "It's okay. G-glad you came."

He handed me a familiar paper bag with my name scribbled in black marker, fastened with a Get Well balloon shaped like a flower pot. I looked at him and couldn't generate any words. Too tired to care about the restorative and curative powers of chocolate, I let the gift bag slip onto the cushion by my side. The balloon came undone and floated above me, playfully bouncing against the ceiling.

Please love me, Allan.

"How are you feeling?"

"Tired. Funny." Removing my glasses, I rubbed the corners of my eyes. I shoved them back on and studied him. His face, creased and gray with the heaviness of exhaustion, looked as ghastly as mine. "You don't look so good, either."

"It's been a long day. I need a shower. Sleep."

Knowing the feeling all too well, I nodded. I'd give anything if he'd hold me all night.

"The funny's from the pain pills. It'll fade soon." He pointed to my arm. "Big bandage."

"Yeah." But I didn't want to talk about owies. I really wanted more hold-yous.

"Your arm bled a lot. You have stitches?"

Remembering, I suddenly teared.

He took my hand. "It's okay, sweetheart. It's all over." His thumb rubbed a circle pattern over my palm. "I guess you might be wondering why I showed up at Buy Rite today."

I'd wondered. Little did I know, the true nightmare had just begun. Adjusting my glasses again, I said, "Jenny told you I was at the office. You came because of June Short's murder."

"Yes. And other reasons."

What does that mean? Opal had tossed the same remarks at me. Somehow, somewhere, I was not able to piece together the entire puzzle 'cause I'd missed critical information. With the way my head worked, I doubted I could figure it out. "O-other reasons?"

Releasing my hand, he stood and walked toward the front window. Fatigue slowed his steps and slumped his shoulders. His hand mussed his dark brown hair as he gazed out the window. Both hands fell to his hips. He nodded to himself as if needing confirmation, and turned. "By telling me what was going on."

The painkillers caused focusing issues. I sat straighter to better comprehend exactly what he'd said. I stared, trying to take everything in. What exactly did he mean by "telling him what was going on?"

I remembered the silly conversations A. Wellborn and I'd had about my job, including Lester and Opal, the missing car parts, and the stolen automobiles, and the computer breakdowns.

Then...*click*.

After peeling away the pebbly outer skin from the proverbial orange, I discovered the truth. I had indeed told him what was going on, thereby providing him everything, absolutely everything he needed to solve the case.

I'd given him the report which contained the information on stolen claims with Buy Rite.

I'd given him copies of the settlement check discrepancies.

And Detective Allan C. Wellborn figured out the whole enchilada, tying together Lester's scam of stealing money off the settlement checks and subsequently, June's murder to cover up his enterprise.

I considered this information. "You knew Opal killed June Short, and Lester stole money from the settlement checks."

He didn't answer for a while. "Yes."

"Opal confessed everything to me."

No comment, merely a sharp glance in my direction.

"I gave you the files which noted the claim checks' discrepancies and the appraisal estimates."

"Yes."

While something unsettling began to churn in my tummy, I said evenly, "I gave you the report which contained the information on stolen Jeeps."

"Yes."

"Both of those reports were the key to the skimming operation."

I waited, but no answer came. My heart missed a beat. "I think you used me."

Nothing.

Empowered with the truth, I sat up and pointed my finger accusingly in his direction. "Yes, you did. You used me."

"Sorta."

My uncharacteristic shouting caused Jenny to open her bedroom door. Her stare went from me to him before she asked, "Hattie, is everything okay?"

I ignored her. Outraged, the fire of anger increased within me. My pulse accelerated. "Sorta!?"

The ache in my head exploded. Pressing hard, I kneaded tight circles on my temples. A. Wellborn's revelation injured me almost as much as the wounds Opal had inflicted. My arm and neck throbbed. Tears dribbled down my face. I wasn't aware I possessed so many tears. "Whadayamean *sorta*? How do you *sorta* use somebody? Either you do or you don't. No 'sorta' in it." I took a deep breath.

"No way you could have solved June's death without the information I gave you." Roughly, I brushed the drops away. "You better tell me everything, and I don't want any of your upright, uptight policeman crap."

"It wasn't deliberate. More...coincidental." He jammed his fists in his pants' front pockets.

I rolled my hand to speed him along.

"The police were conducting a major investigation into a stolen parts ring. We patrolled Sommerville and searched for cars which had parts stolen off them. I pulled you over because you had missing," he made a pitiful laugh, "taillights and bumper."

"In other words, you lied."

"No."

"You lied to me when you said you were doing a buddy a favor."

"No. Yes. No. It was a cover."

I went dead calm and said with a sarcasm Mom would have chastised me for, "Oh, I feel so much better."

His hands hit his hips again. "In another case, we had a woman, June Short, whom we'd found murdered in her apartment. Her wrists had been cut, which at first, led us to believe she'd committed suicide. But forensic evidence proved someone else did it. The cuts didn't match the paring knife found by her body.

"As you know, June was an older woman who lived alone with her dog, just doing her job as a longtime employee of Buy Rite Automobile Insurance where, coincidentally, you worked. She, too, did claims data entry."

He itemized the facts on his fingers. "When we went to dinner, you told me about the woman's death and your temping job at Buy Rite. You told me about Lester and Opal. You told me about the unusual number of SUV claims. You gave me a copy of the special report you ran. You told me about the customers calling about the checks. You gave me copies of the mismatched appraisals and settlement checks. You told me you asked Lester about Buy Rite's internal fraud squad. With all of this information, and what we discovered in our own investigation, everything pieced together."

"Thanks for putting me in the picture," I said.

Nothing.

"Why did you come to the office today?"

He sighed. "After the second puncture, I was worried. Something didn't feel right. Sure, those things can happen. Everything seemed correlated. Why would both of your tires be damaged in Buy Rite's parking lot on a Saturday?"

He lifted his shoulder. "It bothered me. Like I said I would, I obtained a report from the property management's security service. Every Saturday you worked at Buy Rite, Opal's plate had been written down as well. The security officer said someone matching her description walked toward your car and bent by the tire.

"I had a nagging hunch and called your cell. You didn't answer. I called Jenny. She said you were at the office working. When I arrived, I located Opal's sedan in the lot." He shook his finger at me. "I warned you

Buy Rite could be dangerous. I suggested you quit."

Narrowing my eyes, I said with new-found viciousness, "Don't think your so-called damn advice covers your ass."

His body drew back. His eyes widened. "I drove so fast. I was so scared. If anything had happen—"

"It did."

Nothing.

"Opal said I was naïve. Very. But I'd never felt like such a dummy…until now." Pushing my finger his way, I said, "You used me."

No comment.

"Allan, you used me," I cried. My voice grew hoarse. "I feel betrayed. You could've told me all of this. I asked you to tell me, but you were too concerned with doing the right thing."

"I—"

"I trusted you." My heart sank, knowing the primary building block for a heart to heart relationship was trust, but one he hadn't honored with me.

"I didn't use you. Not really. This is a big coincidence. We—I," he said, with a shake of his head, "the police don't discuss on-going investigations. I didn't deliberately send you to Buy Rite to uncover information. You taking a job with them was totally unplanned." He paced several feet and then turned.

"Maybe I underestimated the amount of danger. Without a doubt, I underestimated Opal. I thought Lester might have had something to do with June's murder. Because nothing pointed to her, I had no idea little chubby, bad-dressing Opal who swished, swished when she walked could be June's killer or she'd try to kill you. She seemed harmless. I didn't know she was the one who punctured your tires. The paperwork pointed to Lester and as a result, the possibility he'd murdered June Short.

His hand cupped the back of his neck for a moment. Then he flung it off and said, "Opal's letter opener linked her to the crime. Crime scene investigators found your blood and June's on it. And tonight, after we searched Opal's car, forensics determined a letter opener found in her glove box and identical to the one she used in the office had been used to puncture your tires. We had nothing, ab-so-lute-ly nothing on Opal."

Our conversation was not going well. Not at all.

"We did pick up Lester to question him about the checks and cars. Turns out, Opal was our missing piece. You said she acted so prim and proper. You said she seemed so helpful."

"Some great detective you are. Aren't you perfect? That's what everyone believes, but you aren't really, are you?"

He made no effort to refute my comment.

My hands coursed over my overlapped arms, but it wasn't that soothing. "And you were around me just so I could help you figure things out."

He raised his hand. "No."

"Yeah, well, I'm sorry, too," I interrupted. "You're a big mistake. Because of your underestimation, and your extreme dedication to your j-job, you nearly got me k-killed."

His hand rubbed a fast swipe across his face. "Oh, God, Hattie, I'm so sorry. To some degree, my hands were tied."

But this apology wasn't enough.

"Quit using such a pathetic excuse," I said, strength and anger expressed in my voice. "Imagine how I feel right now, knowing you wanted to be with me for any information I could give you."

"I never said that. It's not true." He shook his head. "This was my first big case, and it affected you inadvertently."

His words held conviction, but the tone wasn't comforting. "That's not what I'm hearing. I thought I meant more to you than what you're saying."

"You do! I want to be with you. Ever since I can remember, I've wanted to be with you." His mouth softened.

Abruptly, our heated exchange halted. *Had he said what I thought he had?* I stared. I'd had enough. My voice rose to a decibel I didn't know I possessed. "You used me, Allan. You let me go there. Opal was crazy. She tried to k-kill me." I coughed, choking on tears. My hands covered my face as I endeavored to conceal the misery consuming my heart. "How could you? How could you let me go?" I shook a finger his way. "I never-never, ever-ever want to see you again.

A. Wellborn stood by the coffee table with his head bent, being a guy who didn't know what to do with a sobbing female. He took a step closer. "Hattie, I don't want to go. I want to be with you."

Tears pooled in my eyes. I shook my head.

"Please let me stay. I want to take care of you."

"I don't want you." I struggled to my feet and pushed myself past him, dragging my sore and aching body to the door. This time, vengeance was mine. I flung open the door. *Ow!* My hands clinched my head to capture the pain from the headache. "Get. Out."

Jenny took a step in my direction. "Hattie."

He moved reluctantly, slowly to the door. "Hattie, you're hurt and upset. You don't mean this."

"I mean this: Get out. Now," I shouted and shoved his body across the threshold.

I slammed the door shut behind him. My body scraped the hallway walls as I ran to my bedroom. I lay face down on my bed where I sobbed through the whole event again.

Jenny came in and sat beside me, lightly massaging my back. Her teardrop landed on my arm.

Opal attacked me. Opal was shot.

Opal attacked me. Opal was shot.

A. Wellborn knew. He used me. He didn't tell me anything.

I meant nothing to him. I meant nothing to him.

Opal attacked me. Opal was shot.

Opal attacked me. Opal was shot.

I meant nothing to him. I meant nothing to him. I meant...

The day's events and the pain pills took hold. Weary beyond belief, I fell asleep.

All along, he knew.

Chapter Nineteen

While my arm and neck healed, I took time off from job searching. I sat around the apartment reading romance novels, which created unsatisfying female urges, and watched way too much television. With all the *M*A*S*H* reruns, I relived the Korean War.

Eventually, my wounds mended, and the stitches were removed. I ate dinner with Mom and Dad. I ate a lot of chocolate. So much in fact, I considered— briefly—not liking it any more. All of my clothes were ironed and so were Jenny's, who expressed her appreciation.

I didn't feel like talking with anyone.

For several reasons, I decided not to share my parting with A. Wellborn. I didn't want everyone to know how he'd betrayed me. How he wasn't so perfect, after all. I certainly didn't want Mom to know as I had concerns about how her longtime relationship with Shirley Wellborn would be affected. I didn't want to hurt his sister, even though I knew, for my sake, she would disown him.

Parting was our business. What we did was separate from them. And if I didn't talk about him, maybe the whole episode would fade away. Maybe, someday, I'd even forget he existed.

I didn't want to answer questions from my friends, from my family, from anyone, but more importantly,

287

from myself.

****

Jenny and I attended book club at Maggie's apartment. After reading a hilarious murder mystery, we should have been in stitches. Instead, the Funsisters acted more subdued. I knew why. They understood my fragile state. They held back laughing and teasing, not wanting to upset me by accidentally talking about murder and death.

I consumed a great deal of mimosa, and as a result, sprawled in an unladylike fashion on the sofa. With Trixie and Maggie's help, I managed to weave my way to the car so Jenny could drive us home. Outdoors, the fresh air perked me up. I looked at my friends with renewed affection and gushed, "You're so great."

Trixie and Maggie smiled. "We know."

"No, I mean it. I really, really," I hiccupped, then smacked my lips, "mean it. You're sooo great. I loovve you."

I broke from their grasp and waltzed like a drunken sailor around the parking lot, eluding hands. "I love the Funsisters. I love Mom and Dad. Wheee!"

A thought sidetracked me. My ballet imitation halted. I frowned. "I almost loved Allan."

Champagne—the great revealer of truth.

Trixie and Maggie shared a look I didn't comprehend. I hiccupped. "But he hurt..." I sulked, "...me."

My funsisters shoved me in the passenger seat of Jenny's car and strapped the seat belt across my body, mostly to hold me upright. I waved bye-bye to them. As the car jolted forward, my forehead smashed against the window.

****

A. Wellborn didn't come back into my life. When I'd felt better, I met another detective who interviewed me for what seemed like hours about Buy Rite, Lester, and Opal. And cars, settlement checks, and claims. And murder.

The interview process and the stress of reliving the unbelievable nightmare drained my body. My head throbbed so much, I seriously considered going back on the pain pills. The detective reassured me he wouldn't have to come back.

He didn't, but the nightmares and headache did.

As did the heartache.

The coverage in *The Sommerville Express* reported Lester Johnson's arrest within hours of Opal's death. He confessed to the settlement check scam. He told the police he engineered the swindle because he wanted more retirement money in the bank for his no-good son to inherit.

Lester suspected Opal killed June, but didn't know for certain why. He didn't ask, and she didn't tell. He told the police he thought of Opal as a "guardian angel," attentively attending his needs which allowed the scam to perpetuate. The police thought her motive protective, like a mother hen hovering over her baby chick. Or an obsessed lover.

Really, Lester was a big turkey.

The investigative story told how Lester specifically had requested the parts or cars stolen belong to Jeeps. With Jeeps being a highly desirable car, he thought no one would think anything about the model being targeted when a few other SUVs were thrown into the pot. A connection had been uncovered between the guys stealing the parts and him.

Detective Allan Wellborn with the Sommerville PD was interviewed, as well. He said a gang had been directed to steal the parts. A shady associate collected the pieces and sent them overseas. This enabled the crooks to make money off the parts, and Lester to set up the scam.

The customer would make a claim with Buy Rite for a stolen car or parts. The claims adjuster would write the estimate for repair value. The paperwork was turned over to Lester for processing the checks. Lester wrote the customer's checks for a lesser amount. Once a month, he wrote a check for the difference to himself which he deposited to another account. When Buy Rite customers had complained about the difference, Lester explained cheaper parts or labor were available for the customer to utilize.

The Express followed with a story about Buy Rite letting Lester operate on his own terms and didn't do any backup audit to spot potential problems. Buy Rite felt Lester's reputation impeccable, and no internal investigation had been required.

Now, a new guy had been installed at Buy Rite, and everything was being examined with a fine-tooth comb.

The police thoroughly searched Lester's home and business office. They questioned his family. And audited his accounts, but no trace of the money could be found.

What a big, fat mess. Forensic auditors would have a nightmare figuring this one out. And what a difficult time for the insurers. Who knew when they would, if ever, get any of their money back?

At last, I received a claims check from Buy Rite for the missing taillights and bumper. I suppose Lester received his final share as the check hadn't been written for the proper amount. After what had taken place, I didn't care to know.

Once I'd replaced the parts, my carbaby looked brand spanking new. I wanted to disconnect from anything to do with Buy Rite and moved my insurance to another company. Maybe with time, I would forget the tie my car had with a murder.

Mom called morning, noon, and night. She pestered me with wanting to know how I fared, lecturing me on proper health care, fretting about whether or not I ate properly, took my vitamins, and slept enough. One morning, she shared a piece of news, "Did you read the obituaries in the Metro section in today's paper?"

"No." Thinking, how I wished she would go away.

"Lester Johnson died."

Her words caught my attention. "Really."

Mom read the story and funeral arrangements aloud.

Out on bail, big, fat, chain-smoking, Lester Johnson died of a heart attack while showering. *What a surprise.* His wife found him flopped on the tile floor, water cascading around his body. The overflow seeped into the hallway, soaking the carpet.

In my opinion, his obese size, cigarette consumption, and guilt over what he'd done were what did him in. Services would be held at The Sommerville Friendship Church. "Good riddance," I said, which sounded callous. "I don't really care, considering what he did, and the murder he'd condoned."

"Hattie!" Mom said. "You shouldn't speak ill of the dead."

"Mother, his cohort nearly killed me."

"I know, my darling, I know. Just be…nice."

"I think I'll go to the funeral," I heard myself say.

"Probably not the best idea. After what happened, why would you want to be anywhere near those people?" she asked.

"I suppose I'm kinda curious."

The truth? Curious to know who allied themselves with crooks. Maybe I'd find some closure. And…just curious.

"I'm not thrilled with the idea of you going."

Big surprise. "I'll be fine, Mother. I'll carry the pepper spray you gave me."

"Good. I knew the keychain size would come in handy. By the way, how's Allan?" Mom asked, changing to her favorite subject. "Have you seen him lately?"

"No, Mom, not lately." *And never would again, either.* I fingered my lower lip and then lied, "He's probably very busy with wrapping everything up."

Well, maybe it wasn't totally a fib.

"Behave yourself and be careful."

Mom always parted with a mom-ism. Clicking end call, I let loose a long, relieved sigh and dropped the phone by my side. I would be careful. What if Lester's family came after me? Once in a lifetime had been enough.

Justice hadn't been served, in my opinion. Opal was dead. Lester was dead. June Short was dead. Someone really needed to pay for June's death, but how did one point fingers when all the bad guys were dead?

****

A couple of days later, I went to Lester's funeral. I sat on the back row of the Sommerville Friendship Church, tucked discreetly into a corner, far away from the other mourners. The sanctuary had plenty of carved, wooden pews, but only the one in the front held people.

I wasn't too shocked.

Maybe a few family members were present, but I didn't know them to recognize any. Even after seeing Lester's son's picture, I couldn't identify him.

Ordinarily, a funeral for a person with Lester's status in the insurance industry would have brought forth lots of colleagues. I thought a few participants came because of a small sense of family or because of curiosity like me. I also thought most people stayed away because of shame, the whole guilt-by-association thingy.

The flower arrangements were limited to two items: a large spray of flaming orange gladiolas slightly wilted and tied with a matching ribbon, which lay on the oversized coffin. And a sickly yellow-green potted plant, probably over-watered, placed at the foot of the pulpit.

Let's be nice and blame the heat.

While waiting for the service to begin, I glanced around the sanctuary. "Oh dear," I murmured barely aloud when I spotted someone I knew.

A. Wellborn stood off to the side, leaning somewhat inconspicuously against a column. He must have arrived earlier than me. My heart pounded harder. My teeth bit into my lower lip. I felt so not ready for this, and yet, wondered if Lester's funeral could be a kind of closure for him, too.

While the service progressed, I observed him. Golly, he looked handsome, good enough to eat. He'd dressed in a charcoal suit, bright white shirt, and a navy striped tie. Proper funeral attending attire.

I crossed my legs at my ankles, and my hands lay folded in my lap. A longing ache grew deep in my stomach. I resisted the urge to call out and say something...anything. Almost desperately, I wanted to. But I didn't.

After the service ended, he turned to leave and spotted me. Pausing at the opposite end of my pew, he stared, his gaze locking with mine. We both acted as if we wanted to make a move, like teenagers mooning over heartache. Neither of us knew where—or how—to begin.

So he left.

He'd taken me at my word to stay away. And he took my heart with him.

Another door in my life closed.

****

Several weeks later, Trixie placed me in a new job. She told me I needed something undemanding. "Someplace where you can put your life together."

But I heard *safe* in her unspoken words.

I began working as a sales clerk at Buttons & Bows Stationary Company. Located in the mall not far from my apartment, the beautiful little store sold a variety of greeting and note cards, letterhead, invitations based on vintage styles, and provided custom printing. The owners were keen to hire me because of my extensive retail background.

Gradually, my life improved, and I truly enjoyed working at the stationary store. I would receive a significant commission on top of my regular salary for placing a large order of wedding invitations and other related items. For the first time in a long time, an overwhelming euphoria consumed me. On my lunch break, I called Jenny to relay my news. "Hey girl, you want to help me celebrate?"

"Sure. What do you have in mind?"

I heard a distinct perkiness in her voice. "How about we do dinner?"

"I'm dying of hunger. What sounds good?"

"Since I haven't been out to dine in a long while, I'm thinking Mama's and Pappa's Italian Bistro. I'm craving lasagna, wine, and lots of giggly girl laughs."

"Mmm, I like it and you know how much I love Italian food. You want me to text the Funsisters?"

We hadn't had a good girlfriend time in a long while. And I missed it. "Sure."

"I'll tell them to meet us at six-thirty at the restaurant, and we'll celebrate in style."

"Thanks. See you then."

It dawned on me why Jenny had sounded chipper: I was at last coming out of my despondency. I'd lost my *life is an adventure, go and live* philosophy and had passed through the days, not getting too excited, not committing myself too much.

A psychologist would say I'd had a depression problem, which is common with victims of violent crimes. Somewhere, I'd read or heard time healed all wounds. After a couple of months, my physical and emotional wounds had faded, and I'd found myself again.

Mamma and Pappa's Italian Bistro was the perfect restaurant for a celebration or a cozy twosome. The interior walls had been stenciled with a faux stone motif. Antique window frames and silk vines with scarlet and yellow climbing flowers provided a corny ambiance. Votive lights placed in sparkling glass holders sat in the center of the starched table cloths and lent an air of intimacy. Garlic and yeasty bread permeated the air.

Jenny had made a reservation for our party. Like she'd promised, she rounded up all the Funsisters—Maggie, Trixie, and Kellar. Excitement gathered in the air as we chatted and circled the table. I felt elated with my news, and they expressed interest in hearing everything about my first big commissioned sale at Buttons and Bows Stationary.

We ordered our entrees and two bottles of cold Pinot Grigio. After decanting the wine, the waiter poured a glass for each of us. Together, we raised a toast with Maggie saying, "To good news!" We merrily shouted "to Good News" back and touched our glasses in salute.

As I lowered my glass, I spied a couple seated across the room, gazing deeply into each other's eyes. With a wistful look, I watched them for a bit. They appeared to be in love. Maybe I had nostalgic feelings, wanting what they had. I wanted to be a part of a loving relationship.

I didn't mean to be snoopy and stared again. Due to the candlelight, I had to squint harder to focus. My body went still as I recognized someone familiar. A. Wellborn. A. Wellborn with a date, a small, beautiful blonde.

It can't be—can it?

Close to two months had passed after I'd ordered

him out of my life. I hadn't spotted him around town at all, except at Lester's funeral. At the grocery store over tomatoes, The Mothers Always Know Network had reported he was deep into a new case and traveled with it.

He had taken me at my word to stay away and maybe it was for the best.

The truth was, perhaps, I was almost certain I'd fallen in love with him. The all-consuming kind of love which would have deepened into love everlasting. A true Happy Ever After, just like in the romance books I'd read when recuperating.

As I watched in secret, I felt my stomach clinch. A. Wellborn and friend seemed to genuinely enjoy each other's company. Her head drew close while they talked as lovers do. Her hand rested on his and crept up his forearm. With a light touch, his finger stroked her long hair from temple to ear.

Oh God. He'd touched my hair the very same way. I looked away and swallowed. The empty ache returned. I squished my eyes tight to quell the growing waterworks before looking his way again.

The Funsisters' chatter fell into the background. I tilted my head slightly while I studied the girl who looked different from me, similar to high school cheerleaders, the same ones I'd always envied. Her blonde locks had been styled into Texas big hair. She wore a tropical print sundress with tiny straps and high heels. Picture perfect.

When I noticed A. Wellborn's glance went around the restaurant, I quickly cut my gaze away. However, my body was possessed, and I turned back. Our stares locked. Tears formed, and I tried, tried hard to suppress them. But nothing worked. The old familiar anguish had set in, and crying seemed to be the only way to rid myself of the pain.

I pressed my napkin to my eyes and stood. Motioning toward my face, I said brightly to the Funsisters, "Excuse me. Contact trouble. I'll straighten this out in the girl's room."

Instead of going to the restroom, I detoured out the exit. Closing my eyes, I inhaled deep breaths to shed the tension which had ratcheted within me. After a few drips, I let my body relax. I opened my eyes and located a Victorian-styled bench parked in front of two retail shops.

The sky had darkened. My eyes shut again as my head tipped backwards, letting the gentle breeze blow on my face. I sensed fall in the air.

I ought to be doing better than this. Like a balloon stuck with a pin, totally deflated, all energy and life evaporated from my soul.

Apparently, A. Wellborn had moved on.

I should move on, as well.

A few minutes later, Jenny and Maggie passed through the restaurant doors and turned in my direction. I patted places on the bench on either side of me. As they sat, Jenny handed me a to-go box containing my uneaten lasagna and my handbag. "Hi.

"We were concerned when you took so long in the ladies room," she said, breaking the silence hanging over us. "I figured it out when I saw Allan and his, uh, friend."

"Jenny told us, and we decided to give you some space," Maggie said.

My head rested against Jenny's shoulder. I loved

my Funsisters. "Hmmm. Fall's coming." Deflated.

Jenny, Maggie, and I sat on the bench and watched A. Wellborn and his date leave.

He had indeed moved on.

So should I.

Chapter Twenty

So much for celebrating. I flopped across Grammie's old iron bed, staring at the ceiling fan going round and round. Ordinarily, time spent in my room seemed enjoyable, especially so when putting on 'jamas and climbing under the bedcovers to read or watch television.

Not today.

Deep inside, I knew this true blue feeling was unlike *moi*. I hadn't been really, really happy for a long time. Like a windup toy, I clicked through the motions of life while wrapped in despondency.

I assessed my life and thus far found:

- *I'd recovered from my physical injuries.*
- *I'd recovered from Detective Wellborn's sorta using me.*
- *I hadn't recovered from my feelings for Allan Wellborn.*

Tonight revealed a turning point. Sick and tired of being this way, I wanted the old, fun me back. Stuff happened for a reason, and sometimes, we don't know why at that particular time.

But stuff can be changed.

I wanted A. Wellborn. I still loved him. Once, I'd felt angry, but I wasn't any more. Now, we needed to talk and reason our problems out.

I *could* do something about change.

Making a decision, I formed a loose plan. While muttering supportive words to myself and with my key fob in hand, I found Jenny stretched long on the khaki sofa, getting a head start on our next book club selection. I jingled my keys.

"Going out?" she asked.

"I need to talk to A. Wellborn."

"Really? Interesting, especially considering tonight's encounter." She lifted her brow in her questioning way. "Do you want me to ride along?"

Her bit of moral support raised my spirits. I grinned. "Nope, I'm a big girl. I need to do this myself." I moved to the door and twisted the knob.

"He'd be a fool not to love you."

"I know." I glanced over my shoulder and made a weak grin.

"At that party, you both wore your emotions on your sleeves. It was a beautiful thing to see love blossom."

Surprising. I'd had no idea we were that obvious. "Thanks."

My first steps forward.

On the drive to his apartment, I rehearsed my speech. Frankly, I had never confronted anyone, particularly a man, and certainly not in this fashion. Being shy and too easily embarrassed held me back. But if anything had taught me how to get over it, tonight's dinner had.

Nothing positive could ever be accomplished in embarrassment or shyness.

At his apartment, I sat in the Jeep and watched his door. He was home. Through the window, the bluish light of his television flickered. And my gaze found his

4-Runner parked nearby, a confirmation. I exited and slowly made my way to his apartment. I massaged my hands while I stood on his threshold for a time. Pressing my ear to his door, I—thankfully—didn't hear any female voices, then rapped.

After a small pause, A. Wellborn answered.

Yep, he looked surprised. And confused.

He cocked his head sideways and narrowed his eyes. With an outstretched arm, he propped open the door. Old faded jeans covered his long legs. His ratty *Accountants Rule* t-shirt stretched over his broad chest. And astonishingly, he held black plastic-framed glasses, similar to the ones from high school, in his other hand.

The memorable shimmery feeling fluttered deep inside me. The heartache returned. Overwhelmed, tears formed in my eyes. *Damn. I didn't want to cry.* I turned my head aside, my fingers pressed the bridge of my nose and squeezed.

Lucky shot out the door and wrapped his supple body around my legs. I caught him and cradled his body close, burying my nose in his soft fur. After a quick love, I handed him back to his dad.

A. Wellborn dropped him in the apartment and shut the door, preventing another escape. He shoved on his glasses. "Hey."

Golly. Somehow, somewhere A. Wellborn ceased to be geeky even when wearing glasses. My gaze turned bashfully to the ground at my feet. "Hey."

"You look well."

"I'm fine."

"Something wrong?"

"No, for once nothing's wrong."

A brief moment passed. "Hattie, what's going on?"

Oh, how I wanted to throw myself in his arms, to sense his body taking in mine, his breath stirring my hair. To meld his essence, body and soul, with me. To make love. To know everything I'd gone through the past few weeks were worth it.

Determined to see my clumsy endeavor through, I drew a deep breath. "I had to come, to clear up something weighing on my mind. Since the investigation, I haven't been happy for a long time. Too much happened. But after seeing you at the restaurant tonight, I figured a few things out."

"Hattie—"

Like a traffic attendant, I stuck out my hand, then rubbed the scar on my arm. "I've recovered from my physical injuries."

His feet shifted.

"I recovered from being sorta used in the investigation."

His gaze cut away.

"But I haven't recovered from you."

I guess A. Wellborn hadn't heard many heart-to-heart confessions before mine since he looked extremely uncomfortable. He moved from a semi-relaxed position to one of arms crossed, legs braced. His mouth twisted as he watched me.

Time for the really big show.

"I'm just an ordinary kind of girl. I want a job I like. I want to have fun with my friends and my family. And maybe, some day, have a fantastic life with the right guy..."

He took a step forward. "You aren't ordinary—"

I waved my hands to stop him. Now was not the time to hear what he had to say. "Let me finish." I

303

glanced at my feet. "I know how I really feel." I looked him in the face, noticing the chocolate-colored eyes and the crinkles around them. And maybe some hope for us. "I miss you."

As if he found my words painful to hear, he turned his gaze to the ground. Dropping my hands to rest on my thighs, I made a quick rub. I might as well go all the way. "I've been very unhappy and don't like feeling like that. That's not me. So, the more I thought about my life, the more I decided I wasn't really in control. I've been carried along like a silly little twig floating in a river. I don't want to…float...anymore."

Watching me intently, A. Wellborn curled his hands into light fists, then relaxed.

Please, God. I rested my hand on my chest, took in a breath, and said, "In order for me to feel whole, I decided to come and bare all. This isn't easy. I've never done this before."

I'd rehearsed. If I was a big girl and if I truly wanted what my heart truly desired, I had to continue. Gathering my courage, I looked at his lovely face, the one belonging to the man I adored with my heart, with my soul. His stance softened. *Please.* Taking another breath, I mustered every ounce of bravery I possessed and said, "Choose me."

A word about the author...

Like some of her characters, award-winning author Vicki Batman has worked a wide variety of jobs, including lifeguard, ride attendant at an amusement park, and hardware store, department store, book store, and antique store clerk; administrative assistant in an international real estate firm; and a general "do-anything gal" at a financial services firm—the list is endless.

Writing for several years, she has completed three manuscripts, written essays, and sold many short stories to a variety of publishers including The Wild Rose Press, Inc.

She is a member of RWA and several writing groups and chapters. In 2004, she joined DARA and has served in many capacities, including 2009 President. DARA awarded her the Robin Teer Memorial Service Award in 2010.

Most days begin with her hands set to the keyboard and thinking "What if?"

Visit her at:

http://vickibatman.blogspot.com